BLACKWATERS

A KATE REID NOVEL
BOOK 4

ROBIN MAHLE

HARP HOUSE PUBLISHING, LLC.

Published by HARP House Publishing
December, 2015 (1st edition)

1

The **hollow slab** of wood that was Braydon's bedroom door felt cold on his skin as he pressed his ear against it. Muffled voices sounded in the distance and then he heard the front door close. It wasn't until the smooth purr of a car engine rumbling to life could be heard that he breathed a sigh of relief. Stepping out into the hall, he looked left, then right, confirming that his parents had cleared out of the house for work. "Connor." His voice easily carried down the short and narrow hallway. "They're gone!" Braydon, the eldest of the Rucker boys, had coerced his younger brother Connor to ditch school this day in favor of dropping a line into the calm waters of the river.

At fourteen, Braydon considered himself a highly skilled fisherman and took the task of ensuring his brother, two years younger, would turn out to be the same. Since their mother remarried, the boys were the only Ruckers in the household. She took on their stepfather's name of Sykes. It wasn't often the boys got to see their dad. He lived farther south, near Tampa. It was about a three-hour drive, depending on traffic, and because their mother worked such odd hours at the distribution center, Braydon counted himself lucky to see his dad once a month.

McLeary was about as small-town as you could get in northern Florida. In fact, it was only a few miles from the Florida-Georgia border near the Saint Marys River that formed the boundary between the states in this particular area. And Braydon had a great little spot near the popular cove of this river in which to hook his spotted sea trout. "You ready to go or what?" he asked Connor who had just emerged from his tiny bedroom.

The younger and, much to his dismay, shorter boy, pushed the hair from his face. "Yeah, I'm ready. What happens when the school calls Mom?"

"I'm gonna send her a text in a few minutes saying you weren't feeling good all of a sudden and I was gonna stay home with you."

"Me?" Connor's incredulity appeared in the form of widened eyes and a hand thrust upon his chest.

"That's right—you. I can't be the one who's sick 'cause she'll still get a call about you." Braydon took the boy by his scrawny shoulders. "Don't worry. She's not gonna leave work and check. Now come on. Fish won't be biting once it heats up and we got a ways to ride."

Braydon was always the one to take charge and today was no exception. He led the way to the small shed out back to get the fishing gear and bikes. Trampling through the overgrown lawn that was littered with rusted machine parts, he made it to the side of the house and inserted the key to open the padlock on the shed. Movement in the grass caught his attention and he jumped back until he realized it was only coming from a scarlet king snake. Other, more menacing cold-blooded reptiles like coral snakes were often found in this part of Florida. Although similar in appearance, a bite from a coral snake would make a visit to the hospital entirely necessary. That was not part of Braydon's plans.

The boys put what gear they could inside their backpacks, along with plenty of water and some snacks to tide them over. It was a six-mile ride to the cove and they would work up an appetite for sure. Locking up the house, Braydon hopped on his bike and waited for Connor to do the same. It was 6:30 in the morning and the rising sun was heating the air, making it good and sticky on this late fall day.

The aged manufactured home, painted a shade of mustard yellow that bore a resemblance to baby shit, was starting to shrink in the distance as the boys rode along the blacktop. *Freedom*, Braydon thought. No one telling him what to do—not his teachers, not his mom, or the stepfather with the oversized beer belly and loud booming voice. All he wanted to do was fish, just like he used to do with his dad. Connor was probably too young to remember all the times the three of them went out for a day's fishing on the Hillsborough River. Braydon smiled and began to pedal faster. "Come on, now. Keep up." He looked back at his weighed-down brother as he struggled to pick up speed.

They were starting to tire out, but Braydon could see the entrance about a quarter-mile ahead. Without all the gear, they probably would have made it in twenty minutes or so; instead, it had been nearly thirty-five. No matter. It was still early enough to get to his spot and drop a line.

"Wait up, Bray!" Connor noticed his brother getting a second wind as they approached, clearly excited to get down to the business of fishing.

"This is it." Braydon laid down his bike with care. It was his only mode of transportation since his mother was generally too busy to take him anywhere, so he treated it with kid gloves. "Looks like no one's even here." He placed his hands on his hips and surveyed the calm waters. The cove was mainly popular with teenagers and twenty-somethings. Its white, sandy beach was perfect for hosting bonfire parties on a clear summer's night.

The Saint Marys River was born out of the Okefenokee Swamp that lies primarily in the southernmost part of Georgia but straddles the two states. It flows from there farther south and then east to dump into the Atlantic. The cove was tucked along the part of the river that dipped south.

"Let's start heading this way." Braydon pointed his finger east and the boys started walking along the banks. Connor was never more than five feet behind his brother.

Braydon stopped after walking about fifty yards. The spot where fallen tree limbs scattered the grounds, shallow sand bars were just visible in the water and tall shady trees hovered. "Right here." He dropped his gear and nodded at Connor to do the same.

They perched atop a fallen bald cypress tree that had burned in the wildfire back in 2007. Its thick stump offered better stability and leverage for fishing than sitting on the ground.

"You hungry?" Braydon unzipped the outer pocket of his backpack that contained a few granola bars and pulled one out. Not his favorite, but his mom rarely let them eat candy bars.

"Yeah, sure." Connor ripped open the wrapper and shoved the bar into his mouth. His bobber dipped beneath the water's surface just for a moment. With a mouth full of food, Connor tried to speak. "Did you see that?" He gripped his pole with both hands and waited with eyes peeled for any further evidence that a fish was nibbling on the line. Moments passed, but nothing. No more bobbing, no more tugging.

"I bet it got your bait," Braydon said. "Better reel it in."

A sound in the near distance followed by a rush of wind caught the boys' attention. It was the flapping wings of an osprey as it came in for a landing. Although it was a good twenty feet away, the giant bird of prey made his presence known. Notorious

4

for having keen vision and ripping its meal straight from the river, the bird landed and began to peck at the waters.

"Must be a snake caught up in that branch." Braydon's stare took in the enormity of the bird. Its yellow eyes flicked for just a moment in his direction, then back to its prey. He knew it was an osprey because of its white head, almost like an eagle.

Connor jumped when the bird whipped its wings out, seemingly to pull the snake out of the water, only it wasn't budging. "Holy cow! Did you see the size of those wings?"

"Those are some big birds," Braydon replied. At two feet tall and a wingspan of nearly six feet, that was no lie.

"You sure he's not trying to go after some gator?" Connor still peered at the bird.

"Nah, you kidding? Ain't no way that bird would be messing around with a gator. Besides, we'd see the gator's tail or something. No, that bird's after something small. Gotta be a snake, maybe a trapped fish. I don't know."

"Well, let's go see." Connor quickly reeled in his line and set his pole down in front of him.

"All right, all right. We get much closer and it'll just flap on away, but we'll go see what he's after if you want." Braydon laid down his pole, the line still in the water, but feeling confident he wouldn't be getting any bites, especially with the commotion that bird was starting to make. "Damn thing's gonna scare the fish anyway. Best to shoo him on out of here."

The boys stood up and Braydon started walking toward the animal kingdom show up ahead. They were already on the outskirts of the cove and, the deeper they walked, the less shoreline they had. In fact, it was turning downright swampy up ahead, but Braydon had been here plenty of times. He knew how to handle himself and keep his brother safe. They continued along the tapered path, balancing one foot in front of the other.

The osprey whipped its head toward them and began to make a dreadful sound—a high-pitched whistle, like a kettle boiling on a stove. It flapped its vast wings again as they drew nearer.

Braydon held out his arm to stop Connor in his tracks. "Wait." But it was too late. The bird must have felt threatened by their proximity, now only a few feet away, and took flight. "Come on; let's see what it was after."

They made their way over the rock outcrops and tall grasses to the downed log that was half in and half out of the water against the shoreline. Braydon stood on a boulder and peered over the log to see what was trapped. A rush of panic bolted through his body and he began to lose his footing on the moss-covered stone. His arms flailed as he tried to regain his balance, but when he looked at Connor, they both knew what was about to happen.

Braydon plunged into the shallow waters right next to the very thing that sent him off-balance in the first place. "Holy shit!" He scrambled to get away from it and back onto the shore.

"Grab my hand!" Connor yelled until he saw what his brother had seen. The boy screamed almost as high-pitched as the bird had. "Get out, Bray! Get out of the water!"

Braydon looked again at the hand that was stuck between two branches just at the water's surface. Below, an attached arm led down into the darkness of the river, but Braydon didn't need to see anymore to know what lay beneath in the depths. It was all he could do not to scream like his little brother. Finally, he pulled himself up and onto the shore, kicking his feet to get him out of the water as quickly as he could. "What the hell was that?" He returned to his feet, trembling, but not from the water's temperature. It must've been in the low seventies. No, he was trembling because he'd never seen a dead body in real life before, even if it was just a hand—a horrible, bloated, purple hand.

"We gotta call the police, Bray." Connor wiped the tears that had pooled in his eyes as he watched his brother thrashing in the water.

"Calm down, Connor. It's all right now. I'm okay." These were just words to soothe the younger boy. Braydon was anything but okay. He didn't know what to do. No one else was out there. They were alone. He had his phone but instantly recalled that it had been in his jeans pocket when he went into the water. "Son of a bitch." His mother would have slapped his butt if she heard him say that. Of course, she never hurt him. He was too big now and stood taller than she did, but it was the principle. She would've tried to inflict at least a little sting through his thick jeans, just to prove the point.

None of that mattered right now. There was a dead body in the water and Braydon's phone was wrecked. "We'll have to ride to the sheriff's office. It's closer than going back home."

Connor looked into the water again. "Who do you think that is, Bray?"

"Turn around now. You don't need to be seeing that kind of stuff."

"Well, neither do you." Connor was right about that.

"Let's just get the hell out of here." Braydon took his brother's hand and led him out on the treacherous path, back to their fishing spot. Connor began to pick up their belongings. "Forget it. We gotta go now."

The boys reached their bikes and headed straight for the Baker County Sheriff's office.

Agent Dwight Jameson was a man of thick stature, square-shaped, and hair to match. He approached Kate's desk and reached out for her shoulders, placing his ham hands gently upon her.

She glanced up at him, half-knowing why he was there.

"They're ready for you." His voice conveyed a softer side of him that was reserved for fateful times such as this.

Kate rolled her chair away from her desk and took in a deep breath. The past six weeks had indeed been arduous. As if being a brand new FBI agent wasn't enough of a challenge, her future was still up in the air too. Although the time for resolution had arrived.

"You lead." She followed Dwight to ASAC Campbell's office and began to recall the conversation she'd had with Agent Nick Scarborough this morning. They both knew that word was going to come down today and he tried to prepare her, forgoing the fact that his own fate remained to be seen. He'd been on administrative leave since the day she graduated from Quantico.

So now the time had come. Dwight held Campbell's office door open and he waited for her to walk inside. He'd been there that night with Scarborough but hadn't seen what happened. Everyone else had his back, except for Agent Hughes. Well, no one could fault Hughes, not really. He was doing his job, but then so was Scarborough.

"Agent Reid." Campbell offered a handshake. "Please, have a seat."

Kate lowered herself onto the chair across from Campbell and next to Dwight Jameson. Behind her boss stood a man she knew to be the Assistant Director of the Academy. He was in charge of the field office assignments.

"Agent Reid, you are aware of the purpose of this meeting?" Campbell asked.

"Yes, sir." She glanced sideways at Dwight, who remained stone-faced.

"The Assistant Director and I have determined that because of your familiarity and the comradery you've developed with the other agents here at the Washington Field Office, and the fact that you desire to continue working in BAU with Agent Jameson, it has been decided that you will continue your work here in our office."

Kate tried to hide her satisfaction, which was taking shape by way of a smile.

"However, as your mentor is otherwise unavailable now and will be for an indefinite period of time, Agent Jameson will continue to guide you as required during your two-year probationary period. I'm sure this has been a most unsettling time for you, Agent Reid. However, given the unusual circumstances of your arrival here, we had to be sure this would be the right fit for you, with or without SSA Scarborough."

Unusual circumstances. Could Campbell have been any more transparent with his choice of words? Kate was grateful for the decision, but it was clear he wasn't sold on her abilities. Either that or he just didn't like the attention that often came her way via the media or otherwise. She was anything but an attention-seeker, and she figured she was going to have to earn her position and not just accept it as fact because Nick Scarborough pulled every string he could to get her here.

And now Dwight was going to be her assigned mentor, at least, in the interim. That was okay, she supposed. Nick was facing some serious charges from the Bureau and she'd hardly been able to talk to him, mostly because he was on leave and she couldn't discuss any cases with him. So, the occasional drink at the bar or dinner with him and his girlfriend, Georgia, was about all she ever got to see of Nick in the past month and a half.

"Thank you, sir. I am grateful to be staying here at WFO. I don't think you know just how much. This is home for me and I hope one day you'll see that I've earned my spot here."

"Agent Reid, it was never a question of that." He trailed off, seemingly unsure of how to continue, which was answer enough. "You are dismissed. I'd like to speak with Agent Jameson for a moment."

Dwight nodded to her as if giving her permission to leave. She knew they were about to discuss the happenings at the raid and the ensuing allegations against Nick. Allegations that Kate could still scarcely believe would ever have been considered. Nick told her exactly what happened that night. There was no way in hell he killed that man without cause. She would have pulled the trigger herself just knowing what the son of a bitch was doing to those girls. Still, Nick had been on the right side of the law and she was certain that would come to light eventually. Or she would make damn sure that it would.

THE BOYS ARRIVED at the sheriff's office in record time. Without their gear and given their present state of mind, it was easy for them to move fast. Braydon jumped off his bike and let it fall to the sidewalk just out front of the building's entrance. Connor was steps behind. He pushed through the glass door, still damp from the fall into the water, but no longer dripping.

The woman behind the front desk wore a uniform. Hair pulled back tightly and heavy-set, she rose quickly at the sight of what she seemed to recognize as two frightened kids. "Can I help you boys?"

Almost on cue, Connor started up the waterworks. Not intentionally, of course. It just happened. He was a scared twelve-year-old boy.

"It's okay," Braydon reassured him before returning his attention to the female deputy. "Ma'am, we found something in the river, down past the cove." He could hardly bring himself to say what it was. As if the mere mention of a dead body would somehow make it haunt him.

"What did you find, son?"

Braydon was a pretty tough kid, but this was too much for him. His eyes reddened as he tried desperately to hold it together, but soon his bottom lip began to quiver. For a boy who stood nearly six feet at only fourteen, the incident had reduced him from the man he was trying to be to the boy he was. "It was a hand."

"I'm sorry? Did you say a hand?" The woman's brow narrowed and the lines in her forehead turned severe.

"Yes, ma'am. A hand and I'm pretty sure it was attached to a body, but I just couldn't see. I fell in and..." His words dropped off. Controlling his emotions was a skill he no longer possessed and his eyes spilled over with tears.

"For Pete's sake." She walked around the desk and took Braydon by his shoulders. "Come sit down. You too, young man," she said to Connor. "Now, I need you to calm down. Relax and take a deep breath. Can you do that for me?"

Braydon nodded and took Connor's hand as he sat down next to him.

"Okay, then. Where were you?"

"At the cove. We were fishing," Braydon replied.

"Yeah, just fishing," Connor agreed.

"And you saw a hand? Are you sure it was a hand?"

Braydon was growing impatient at her condescension. "I'm sure. I fell into the water and I—I was up close to it. I saw an arm—but nothing else. Water was too murky."

The deputy pursed her lips and began to nod. "I see. Okay, can you boys just sit here for one minute? I need to get Deputy Burgess to come talk to you." She hoisted herself up and shuffled into the hallway, the sound of her polyester uniform rustling wildly with her hurried steps.

Connor waited for the woman to disappear beyond the corridor. "Are we gonna get in trouble for skipping school?"

Braydon rolled his eyes and cast a disapproving glance. "I think they've got bigger problems than us missing a day of school."

Connor nodded. "Sure, you're right." A brief pause followed as he seemed to consider an additional point of concern. "Mom's gonna be pissed."

2

M idday on a Thursday would normally find Supervisory Special Agent Nick Scarborough buried in paperwork on his desk or traveling on a plane somewhere to investigate something. But not today and not for the past several weeks. This afternoon would find Nick perched on his favorite barstool, staring at the television above, and well on his way to a soothing state of inebriation. The last of his bourbon burning his throat, he looked at the barman. "Can I get another, please?" His weary brown eyes matched his tired expression as he stared at the man, waiting for him to do what he'd asked.

Nick was well aware of his weakness for the drink but was generally able to keep it contained, mostly due to his preoccupation with a case of one kind or another. Without work, it was the best way for him to kill time—and he had a lot of it right now. Except that today he'd had a meeting with the guys in the Inspection Division—internal affairs for the FBI. The so-called "shooting incident review team" had a few more questions for Nick to answer. Although he'd recounted the events so goddamn many times, the idea that he still hadn't conveyed enough for them gave him a bad feeling. That was partly the reason he was here now.

"Here you go." The bartender placed the drink in front of Nick. Double Jack and Coke. "Maybe you might want to slow down after this one."

Nick's eyes were fixed on the drink, but he shot a quick look up at the kid who was serving him. The young man was probably right, but he didn't care too much for being called out. "Yeah, thanks." He picked up the drink and brought it to his lips, his eyes never leaving the kid. He poured in a large mouthful and swallowed it down. A grimace formed on his already lined face making him look years beyond his actual age of thirty-eight. It took a minute for the fire in his throat to pass.

The bartender just looked at him, thin-lipped, and walked away.

Nick was being an ass and he knew it. He shook his head and when he closed his eyes, he saw the man again, holding the girl with a gun pressed against her cheek. *Let her go,* he'd said to him. But the man seemed to understand that he was either going to prison or going to die and it appeared as though he would prefer the latter. The rest of the team was fighting their own battles. Taking down the suspects, trying to protect the victims in the process, and no one else was there. It was Nick and the son of a bitch who was holding one of the victims hostage, under cover of thick trees and off the road where they'd staged the raid.

Yelling and gunshots were all that could be heard in the distance and Nick was forced to do what he felt was right. *Put the gun down and let her go.* He stepped closer to the suspect. *You hear that? All your buddies are going down, my friend. You can go with them or you can drop your weapon. I swear I'll put you down if you hurt her.*

In a split second, it happened. The suspect pushed the girl

down and began to lower his weapon. That should have been the end of it, but it wasn't. She fell to the ground and struck her head on a large rock. Nick glanced down at her. So did the suspect. The man's eyes widened, believing he'd just shoved her to her death. He began to raise his weapon again. At least, Nick thought he was.

The weapon fired a single round and the suspect dropped. The entire incident couldn't have lasted longer than a minute and Nick pulled the trigger believing his own life was in danger. He rushed to the girl. She was alive.

"Nick?"

The call of his name brought him back to the present. He turned to confirm to whom the voice belonged, already knowing her identity. "How you doing, Kate?" He patted the seat next to him. "Sit down."

She would know he'd had too much to drink, and there was no point in trying to convince her otherwise. He had no excuses to make and besides that, with Kate, excuses were unnecessary.

"I'm glad they're letting you stay put," Nick began. "No matter what shit storm I'm facing, they had no right to throw you into the mix, threatening to move you. It wasn't right and I'm glad they finally saw that."

"I'm pretty sure Dwight had a lot to say on the matter too." Kate looked at Nick's half-empty glass. "Anyway, they said he'll be my mentor, at least until you return."

"Good." Nick waved over the bartender again. "You want something to drink?"

"Blue Moon. Thanks."

"You heard the lady," Nick replied, but not before considering ordering another for himself. In the end, he decided against it, for the moment.

"How'd your meeting go?" she asked, nodding to the barman who'd just set down her beer.

"They're still drafting the narrative to send to the big boys for review. I won't know anything for a while."

"For God's sake, how long can they drag this out for?" Kate tossed back a frothy swig.

"As long as they want, I guess. Just red tape bullshit. They all know I complied with Bureau policy. It's Hughes' testimony that's causing this to be dragged out. He didn't show up until the man was already down. He doesn't know what the hell happened out there." Nick could feel his pulse rise and the heat crawl up the back of his neck. He cocked his head in each direction to loosen the muscles that were starting to tense. Another sip of his drink to keep the edges softened should help.

"I'm sorry, Nick. I know I've said this a hundred times before, but I wish I had been there. Maybe I could've—I don't know."

Her tone seemed to bring him some peace and he reached out for her. "There's nothing you could've done. In fact, if you'd been there... hell, I don't know either." He turned away and rattled the melting ice around the empty glass. "Can I get another over here?"

Kate and the kid behind the bar, who hardly looked old enough to serve alcohol, exchanged a glance. Nick wasn't blind. He knew what they were thinking and maybe they were right. He could feel himself sliding down that slippery slope. He'd been on this path a few times before over the years and, in this job, who the hell could blame him? But he'd always been able to reel it in. It felt different this time like he might be sliding too far.

"You know what? Never mind. I'll just take the bill, please." He looked at Kate. "Unless you want another beer?"

"No. I'm good, thanks. Have you eaten today?" Her eyes scanned his body as though he'd suddenly appeared too thin for his own good. "I didn't have a chance to grab anything yet." She pressed the button on her phone to check the time. "Feel up for a late lunch?"

Nick smiled and dropped some cash on the bar. "Sure."

THE COVE HAD BEEN CORDONED OFF—SHUT down to any and all visitors. Patrol cars with flashing lights were parked at the entrance. Deputies stationed on the beach. To the boys, it looked like something out of a movie. But when Braydon saw his mother step out of her old blue Toyota Sentra, the look on her face suggested that this was anything but a movie and that he was in some kind of serious trouble. Deputy Burgess insisted he had to call her because they were minors or something like that. He figured the deputy was right to do so, but it was going to mean problems when they got home later.

"Oh my God, sweetheart." She ran toward Braydon, her face softening at the sight of his trepidation.

He found himself inside a great big hug from his too-skinny mother. She was a smoker, although never inside the house. Braydon was old enough to notice that she hardly ate and was approaching a three-pack-a-day habit. "I'm okay, Mom. I promise."

She gently held him at arm's length. "Where's your brother?"

Just as the words left her mouth, Connor emerged from inside one of the patrol cars. The weather had heated up, thickening the air, and the boy needed a place to cool down. "Momma!" He ran toward her and flung his arms around her waist.

"Oh, baby, are you okay?"

"Somebody died, Momma." Connor looked up at her with eyes that had seen too much for their age.

"I know, baby. I'm so sorry you two had to see something so awful. Where's the sheriff? I need to see him."

Braydon looked down along the path where they'd left their fishing gear. "It's Deputy Burgess. I had to show him where it was

—the body. I think he's still down there." He pointed in the direction of the gruesome discovery.

"Now you boys stay right here. I'm going to go find him."

Deputy Michael Burgess stood with his arms folded against his broad chest while the dive team began to carefully bring the body to the shoreline. At first glance, he believed they'd have no trouble bringing it up to the surface once they pulled the branch away, but it was caught on something else, and rather than risk damaging the body and, more importantly, destroying physical evidence, Burgess thought it better to bring in the divers and employ a more meticulous approach. He was glad to have made that call.

"Deputy Burgess?" The boys' mother carefully navigated through the other officers and rugged terrain. "I'm Jenny Sykes, Braydon and Connor's mother."

"Ma'am, you shouldn't be over here." Burgess began walking toward the woman who appeared to be in her late thirties, but the obvious odor of cigarettes that lingered on her clothing could have meant that her habit made her features appear more aged. "Let's go over here and talk for a minute." He led her to a safer spot, away from the scene. "I'm sorry to have had to pull you away from your job, but your boys... I'm sure they told you what happened?"

"Yes, sir, they did. Are they in any trouble?"

"No, ma'am, of course not. I know they were skipping school, but frankly, something like this?" He turned back and watched as the body began to emerge from the river. "Well, we don't get this kind of thing around here, as I'm sure you are aware."

"No, I suppose we don't." Mrs. Sykes looked over the deputy's shoulder but turned away quickly from the grisly sight. "Can I take my boys home, then? They don't need to be here anymore, do they?"

"You can take them home. I agree. They don't need to be exposed to this any more than they already have. However, I'd like to speak with them tomorrow, if possible. Just a brief statement. I don't think they're up for it today. They're both pretty shaken up."

"Of course. I can bring them by in the morning. I've got second shift tomorrow, so I'll have the time."

"Sir?" one of the officers shouted to Deputy Burgess.

"Thank you, ma'am. I have to be getting back. Please take care of those boys tonight. I imagine they'll be having some pretty unsettling dreams." Burgess tipped his hat and began to walk in the direction of the scene.

"Sir, you need to see this." The officer met him halfway and turned on his heel, heading toward the divers.

"Jesus Christ." Burgess removed his hat and knelt down beside the body. He scanned the swollen figure, shaking his head in disgust and disbelief.

The girl had shoulder-length dark hair. Her face was bloated and discolored, but what struck Burgess the hardest was that her leg had been torn away, leaving only half a thigh with mangled flesh dangling from it.

"Looks like a gator might have gotten to her first," the officer said. "I'm surprised there's anything left of her."

"Did you call the coroner's office yet?" Burgess asked.

"I did. They're coming from Jacksonville. It'll take them a while to get here."

Burgess continued to inspect the girl's body. Her clothes clung to her tightly both from the water and distension. His brow creased as he tried to glean any information based on her appearance. He was neither equipped nor qualified to examine her and, even if he was, it couldn't be done here. "I can't even tell how old she might have been. She must have been in the water for a while."

"And there's something else too." The officer signaled over one of the divers. "You mentioned you thought she might've come downstream a ways, is that right?" he asked the diver.

"I'm not an expert, sir," the diver said, "and I'll leave it to the coroner's office to make the conclusion, but I'm pretty familiar with this area and I gotta tell you that some of the plant material hung up on the body didn't come from down in these parts." He pointed a finger at the girl's hair. "See that?"

"Looks like part of a plant, a flower maybe, stuck in her hair," Burgess replied.

"Well, yes and no. I've seen these before and, to me, it looks like part of a pitcher plant. You know, the flycatchers? It looks like one of its leaves got tangled up here."

"Okay. So what does that mean?" Burgess asked.

"I've never seen one of these down here in this part of the river. These things live in the swamps."

It dawned on Burgess what it was the diver was surmising. "You think she traveled all the way down from the Okefenokee Swamp? That's a mighty long way."

"Well, if she didn't travel that far, then I think she was there at some point, maybe dumped farther downstream and ended up here."

Burgess pushed back up to his feet. "Well, if that's the case, then we better put a call into Charlton County." He began to shake his head. "That's all we need—getting another jurisdiction involved." A brief sigh escaped him. "Let's wait to see what the coroner's office has to say before we go any further. Lord knows I don't want to ruffle any feathers until I have to."

THE LATE LUNCH with Nick meant Kate didn't leave the office until after seven o'clock. Now, as she pulled into the driveway of her small rented house, the day had begun to wear on her. She worried about Nick. Worried about how much time he was spending at the bars. Worried about the effects this inquiry was going to have on his career and even worried about whether he and Georgia were getting along through all of this. Nick hadn't said much about it one way or another and Kate didn't pry. None of this was what she'd expected after graduation. Then again, not much in her life ever really went to plan.

She opened the front door and stepped inside, kicking her shoes off. Once inside her bedroom, she removed her gun from its holster and locked it away as always. A box on top of the closet was where it remained from the time she got home from work until five minutes before she walked out the door in the morning. It wasn't like she had any kids running around, so it seemed overly cautious to lock it up every night. Living alone, she would have been better off keeping it in her nightstand or something to that effect. But she felt safe here. It took quite a while to get to this point, but she felt safe.

Her appetite hadn't returned, thanks to the late lunch, so Kate curled up on the couch for some T.V. So far, in the six weeks she'd been assigned at the WFO, not a single case had been tossed her way. They'd had her doing a whole lot of administrative work—paper pushing, which she intensely disliked. But now that it had finally been resolved and she knew the WFO would be her home, maybe they'd put her onto something with some meat in it.

Dwight would be her mentor as dictated by Bureau policy. The first two years after graduation was a probationary period for a new agent who was learning the ropes. There was a lot to learn and it was mostly bureaucratic political nonsense, but it was all a part of the game. She understood that perhaps now more so than before with everything that had been going on with Nick.

Kate switched on the television, more for white noise than anything else. Living alone was still an adjustment. Loneliness crept in all too often, but she did her best to stay busy and not think about why she was alone. After all, it was coming up on a year now.

"Nope." Kate jumped off the couch, refusing to acknowledge the inching thoughts, and went to the kitchen. A few nibbles, a glass of wine, and a chick flick would keep her occupied for now.

On her return, plate and glass in hand, she glanced at her phone. "Maybe one last check for email." She still held out hope for a speedy resolution to Nick's situation and remained vigilant with those who might offer up information.

"Dammit." No news wasn't necessarily good news, not in her line of work.

She began to search for a good old-fashioned rom-com and flipped through the channels, stopping briefly on one of the cable news stations. It had been a few days since she'd caught the news.

As she listened to the talking heads, the scrolling headlines at the bottom of the screen caught her eye. *"A body was found in the St. Marys River along the Florida side. The Baker County sheriff's department has not released the name of the victim or any details pending an investigation."*

She flipped through the stations again and finally landed on something that would occupy her mind for a while. It was one of her favorite movies.

3

The scent of fear and death lingered on her shirt as he held it to his face and inhaled the intoxicating odor. A smile spread across his lips as he recalled the precise moment of her passing. The moment the light faded from her eyes and her final breath hung in the air just long enough for him to take it in—exciting, liberating. But as quickly as the moment had arrived, it vanished. And now he would have to get rid of her just like the others. Saying goodbye to them was his least favorite part. He loved her—loved controlling her, but it was time to let go.

He folded the shirt and laid it gently on the hand-carved wooden breakfast table. A relic from long ago; perfectly preserved as was the rest of the items in his home. Each piece of furniture, each picture frame that hung on the wall, even the bed in his room. All were exact replicas from when he was a child. The exception was that this house was not his childhood home. He had been forced to leave that place many years ago. This was his reminder of days past.

The tattered wood floor bowed under his weight, both from

age and moisture that had seeped in from the sodden ground beneath the home. Recent heavy rains combined with the high water table being so close to the swamp made the home reek of must and mold. Most everyone had left this town when the wild-fires came, but a few houses were still livable, by his standards anyway. Most had burned up right along with the swamp, but this place suited him just fine. The well still worked, but power came from a diesel generator, not that he used much in the way of electricity. Just enough by which to see at night and to see the look on their beautiful faces before he put them out of their misery.

"It's all right now." He stroked her dark, wavy hair, which was thick with sweat—mostly his. "I'm going to send you home soon, but for tonight, you need your rest."

He pulled a t-shirt over her head with some difficulty as she sat propped up in the dingy green recliner. It was a little small and stretched across her breasts, making the school mascot appear distorted. The letters WJHS just beneath the bird puckered at her waist. She was a slender girl, not skinny like his sister had been, but he stood back and admired his choice of attire. He pushed back his scraggly hair, which was in desperate need of a wash, not that he paid much attention to his appearance, except when he went into town. "You look just like her." A wink and a nod, and Arlen Tucker made his way along the hall to his bedroom. He would get a few hours of shut-eye before making the trip in the early hours of the morning. Weak eyesight made driving at night difficult, but it had to be done when he was sure not to be seen.

THE OLD WIND-UP clock on the nightstand next to his twin bed began to ring. Arlen pulled himself up, groggy from the midnight disruption to his sleep, but ready to face the task ahead. The jeans he wore earlier were crumpled up on the floor. He pulled them back on and buttoned them with ease as they hung low and loose on his waist. The belt was already on its last hole and if he got any thinner, he'd have to punch out a new one to cinch it up tighter.

He reached for the bloodstained undershirt he'd worn during the final phase of his most recent project that awaited him—the highly gratifying part he could only liken to orgasm. In fact, that usually happened afterward. However, it remained damp and he considered that a shirt probably wasn't necessary given the location he'd be heading for, and the lingering heat made it an easier decision.

The bathroom down the hall was his next stop. The mirror was covered in a hoary film and Arlen glanced at his figure through the haze. A skeletal shape of a man and it was no wonder. His entire family had been tall and bony and looked like they'd been stretched like the action figure he played with as a kid. The tattoos helped to conceal the visible ribs. His most treasured, a three-headed beast known in Greek mythology as Cerberus, was also the largest. The heads were that of dogs and spread across the middle of his chest while the body of the snake slinked down to his navel. This particular monster was said to guard the gates of Hades. Arlen considered himself a Greek mythology enthusiast, even if his tattoo wasn't a precise facsimile, which would have included lion's claws and a few other minor details. Still, he believed he was the gatekeeper and could decide who would enter the underworld.

A splash of water on his face, and a deviously fetching one at that, to help wake him, and he headed to the living room to check up on his guest. Her body had stiffened considerably, which made it difficult for him to lift her off the chair and carry her to his truck parked outside.

The passenger door of his 1975 Chevy Silverado squeaked

loudly as Arlen pulled it open. The vinyl bench seat was ripped in several places, exposing the foam beneath. And when he tried to slide her in, her cut-off denim shorts caught on one of the rips.

It took several minutes, but she was in. Arlen jumped in on his side and put the truck into gear, backing out onto the charred blacktop and headed east toward the swamp. He turned the knob for the radio and tapped his fingers to the beat of the music, casting occasional glances at the dead woman and returning his sights to the darkened road ahead.

He'd traveled a long way to find her and she hadn't been an easy pick. But he waited until she was alone, heading home from the coffee shop where she worked. He'd watched her for days and knew it had to be her. She smiled at everyone who came into the small shop a few miles out of town—a last stop before weary travelers hit the highway. It was miles from his job and even more from his home, but Arlen never dipped his pen in the company ink. It was much too risky and he needed the job if he wanted to keep himself in the lavish lifestyle to which he had become accustomed.

Trees lined the roadway that eventually turned into nothing more than a gravel path. He was getting closer now and could smell the decay of the black waters. The sweet smell of degeneration made the heat rise between his legs. Another mile and they would arrive.

Logging was a major industry in the swamp not so long ago and rail lines and other remnants were still visible in some areas. Arlen had spent a considerable amount of time searching for just the right spot. A place that still had pedestrian access blocked off and had only been used when the logging operations were underway, but that would ensure the body would remain in the blackness of the water, beneath the swamp grasses and trees and fallen debris.

Confident that the gators would find them before anyone else did, Arlen believed this was the perfect place in which to dump his used-up projects. He lugged her out of the truck and pulled her along the path. Her heels dragged along the dirt. She'd been wearing flip-flops on the night she met Arlen, but now remained barefooted, wearing a too-small Westmont Junior High School t-shirt and denim shorts. Her appearance was dramatically altered from that fateful night Arlen Tucker crossed her path. She bore the markings of a killer who had squeezed the life from her before doing unspeakable acts to her body, leaving it almost unrecognizable. She'd put up a struggle, but he'd come to expect that. The resulting cuts and bruises on the rest of her were, he believed, of her own doing. All she needed to do was keep quiet and do as she was told.

The edge of the swamp was just beyond the barricade. A couple of steel posts on an A-frame was supposed to keep him out? He pushed through it with ease and continued dragging her down the slope that had turned sticky with black mud. Trudging through, he suddenly regretted not folding up the legs of his jeans. If for nothing else than to make it easier to slog through.

He pulled the small flashlight from his pocket and shined its LED bulb, illuminating the area well enough for him to find the right spot to drop her. He turned the light on the girl. Her shirt was filthy with mud and her legs were covered in thick strips as he dragged her along. She didn't look like the girl he saw smiling last week at the coffee shop.

"Goodbye, Sydney." He picked up a fallen branch and shoved it into her side, rolling her down the small embankment and into the water. The ripples made the swamp floor sway as if it were alive. He stepped closer, careful not to end up in the water himself, and began to ram the jagged end of the branch into her body to shove her beneath the old car rails that carried the logs out of the swamp.

A greenish light rose from the water, ghostly and ethereal. It was only the swamp gasses that had been released as the water was disrupted, but Arlen smiled at the beautiful sight. He shone the light into the water and watched the remaining bubbles rise to the surface until there were no more.

KATE PEERED through the passenger window of Dwight's car. They'd just left BAU headquarters at Quantico after attending a briefing on a new phase of the NGI database soon to be implemented. Training was an ongoing process and, although she'd graduated from the Academy, there were always new systems and procedures being put into place and it was essential for an agent to understand how to use them. But she had been preoccupied. Two more weeks had gone by and still no word on bringing Nick back to active status. He was sliding down that slope at a much faster pace. Dwight had seen it and Kate was sure Georgia had seen it. How could she not? She was sleeping with the man.

"You okay?" Dwight asked.

Kate turned to him with the same look on her face she had every time he asked the question, which was quite a bit lately. "I'm fine."

"Uh-huh," he replied. "Listen, you have to stay focused on your job. Nick can take care of himself. I'm sure you've figured that out already."

"Of course he can. I just—I don't know. He's always been there for me and I can't even return the favor. How much longer is this going to take?"

"I wish I knew, Kate."

"Isn't there something we can do? It wasn't like the suspect was some kind of innocent bystander. He was a damn human smuggler." She stopped. It wasn't going to do anyone any good for her to unleash her frustration onto Dwight. He knew. He understood and if there was anything more to be done, he'd have already done it.

"I'm worried about him too." Dwight faced her. "I've been doing my best to keep an eye on him—keep him in check—but he's just lost without work. He needs it."

Kate knew what that was like. She'd been burying herself in work for the past year.

"Georgia's taking good care of him, Kate. You need to focus on your job right now. These first two years are critical for you and you can't do anything to jeopardize that. That means keeping your head down and nose to the grindstone. Let Nick take care of Nick."

Dwight's cell phone began to buzz inside the console. "Hang on." He pressed the Bluetooth on the steering wheel. "Jameson here."

The voice on the other end wasn't one that Kate recognized as it carried through the radio speakers. "Agent Jameson? This is Agent Lyons out of the Atlanta Field Office."

"Yes, sir. What can I do for you?" Dwight raised his eyebrows and quickly glanced at Kate.

"I was pointed in your direction by BAU headquarters. Actually, it was SSA Scarborough I was looking for; however, I understand he's on administrative leave at present."

"Temporarily, yes."

"I see. Well, I understand you're his right hand and have worked closely with him in the past. As such, I figured you might be able to offer some assistance."

"I've got you on speakerphone in my car and Agent Kate Reid is also listening."

"Agent Reid. I've heard your name mentioned in conjunction with Scarborough. Hello."

"Hello, sir."

"As I was saying, I've been working on a murder investigation that has recently crossed into federal jurisdiction. The body of a missing woman was found in the Saint Marys River a few weeks ago. As the river borders both Georgia and Florida, the local authorities have enlisted our help."

"Okay," Dwight began. "I'm guessing the reason for this call is because you believe this isn't a typical murder investigation."

"No, sir. I don't believe it is."

Nick sliced into the medium-rare steak he'd ordered and stabbed a morsel with his fork. "You and Dwight are flying to Atlanta tomorrow?" He raised the bite to his lips and it slid easily into his mouth.

"We have a nine a.m. flight, yes." Kate waited for him to finish chewing.

"So Agent Lyons wants you two to look into this investigation? For what reason? Can't imagine why BAU needs to be involved." Before she could answer, Nick continued. "You know, I used to work with Lyons when I first started. Haven't talked to him in years, though."

Kate hadn't wanted to fill him in on the gory details, especially considering his choice of entrees. She'd wished Dwight had joined them, but he had his kids tonight and didn't want to tell his ex-wife he'd have to pass on spending time with them again because of work. He'd done it too many times, not by choice. It was just the job. But Kate insisted he didn't need to be at the dinner, and so now she'd have to field Nick's questions on her own.

"He mentioned he was calling for you, but all I know right now is that a few weeks ago, a woman was found in the river by two boys who were fishing. Anyway, from what I gather, Agent Lyons believes that another body recently found farther upstream might be related."

A spark seemed to ignite in Nick's eyes as if he was the one going to Atlanta tomorrow. She could see his face light up because she knew he wanted the case—needed the case.

"What has he given to you so far?" Nick asked before shoving another bite of food into his mouth and washing it down with red wine.

"Nothing yet. We'll get a complete report tomorrow when we meet with him." She could see the light fade just as quickly as it had sparked. She had nothing to share with him and his disappointment was made clear. "How's Georgia doing? I haven't seen her in a few days." An awkward transition to be sure, but Kate didn't know what else to do. A sip of her own drink followed on impulse.

"Yeah, she's okay. They sent her out to consult on an investigation in New York."

"Good. That's great." She paused for a moment. "How's she handling all of this?"

"How's she supposed to handle it?" He finished off his wine. "I don't know. I guess I haven't been dealing with this in a very constructive way and, um, well, I think she's doing her best to steer clear of me right now."

"I'm sorry to hear that, Nick." Kate knew from the very beginning that the two of them were alike. Perhaps now would be the true test of their relationship. Could she handle what might happen to his career? Could he?

"Yeah, well. Things will get back to normal soon enough, I'm sure. She'll be all smiles once I'm reinstated. Georgia likes dating an SSA." He chuckled. "Like I'm arm candy or something."

"Nick," Kate replied. "Come on now. She's not like that and you know it. She loves you and you love her. This is a difficult time for you two, that's all."

"Well, you're right about one thing: I do love her." Nick raised a finger to get the attention of the waiter. "Can I get a refill, please?" He turned to Kate. "You want another glass?"

She glanced at the time. "Sure. Why not?"

The rest of the meal felt uncomfortable as if they had nothing more to say to one another. Kate figured it was just Nick's way of handling what was happening and she didn't fault him. It seemed strange, though—not discussing a case or the office or anything of that nature. While they often spent time together outside of work, everything they discussed seemed to revolve around work. Now, what could she say to him? He'd stopped asking how she was doing a long time ago. Meaning, he seldom brought up Marshall anymore, which was fine by her. She'd made the decision before graduation that sharing her vulnerabilities, even with Nick, wasn't going to help, not anymore. She was on her own to deal with it and she did—day by day.

It was growing late and she had an early flight. The time had come to put the kibosh on this evening which seemed to culminate in a growing silence while Nick downed more wine. "How about I give you a lift home?" What little wine she'd consumed dissipated along with the conversation.

"Sure. Thanks." Nick pulled out his wallet and removed a credit card.

"Why don't you let me get this for once?" Kate retrieved her own credit card and held it up just slightly so the waiter knew they were ready for the bill.

"Look at you, all grown up, Kate Reid," Nick replied.

She tried not to be offended by his comment, which was considerably offensive. He'd had one too many, maybe two, and so she would let it slide this time. "I guess so."

"I should just call a cab," Nick said as they approached her car.

"Don't be ridiculous. I'll take you home. You can take a cab back here in the morning to pick up your car." She pressed the remote and pulled open the passenger door for him.

"That's right. Because you'll be in *Hotlanta* tomorrow, so you can't bring me back here. You got a job to do."

She helped him into the car and closed the door without a reply—his regional reference to the city of Atlanta shrugged off. The engine started with ease and the air blew cold. It was still much too warm, even at ten o'clock at night.

"So you talk to that kid—um—what's his name—Caison?" Nick asked.

"Not for the past few weeks. He's been pretty busy in Louisville. I think he's happy, though."

"Good. Glad to hear it. He's a good kid. Some might even call him good-looking." Nick cast a suspicious eye her way.

"I suppose so." She didn't like where this was going. Kate and Will had remained friends but had seen each other only a couple of times since they graduated. And that was only because he had to come into town for something at Quantico. Some sort of counterterrorism training, he'd said. If Nick was looking to really get under her skin right now, reminding her that she'd slept with Will once was the way to do it. She didn't care to be reminded of her mistakes.

Nick kept his attention on her as she drove out of the parking lot, but didn't say anything further on the matter. Perhaps, even three sheets to the wind, he realized it best not to bring up what'd happened between the two of them.

The rest of the drive back to Nick's place was quiet. Kate

turned on the radio to fill the void. "You need help getting up to your apartment?" She pulled alongside the building's front entrance.

"How drunk do you think I am?" Nick pushed open the passenger door. "No thank you. I don't need any help, but I appreciate the ride." When he closed the door again, Nick leaned into the open window. "Hey, maybe you can give me a call when you get back from Atlanta?"

She could see he regretted his earlier remarks and maybe even regretted having had so much to drink. A tender smile appeared on her lips. "Of course I will. Goodnight, Nick."

"Goodnight, Kate." On his way toward the entrance, a booming voice erupted from him. "Have a safe flight," he said, and a flailing arm waved high in the air.

4

The wheels touched down at Hartsfield-Jackson Airport in Atlanta right on time. Dark clouds hung low, saturated and ready to open at any moment. Kate remained seated, glancing through the small, oval-shaped window and wishing she'd remembered her umbrella. "How are we doing for time?"

Dwight checked his phone. "We'll make it, assuming they let us out of here sometime in the next few minutes." He leaned over the arm of his aisle seat, noting that the passengers were not moving.

Although Dwight, her good friend and now temporary mentor, was sitting right next to her, Kate felt alone. It was the first time she would work on an investigation without Nick. He'd been a part of her life since her old life. He wouldn't be there to lean on. Dwight was senior to her, of course, but the dynamics they shared were completely different. Perhaps it was a good thing. He treated her like a partner, not someone who he felt he had to take under his wing. Things hadn't started out that way with Nick, but since Marshall died, she knew he took it upon himself to guide her.

"Come on." Dwight reached under the seat for his bag. "Looks like they're moving now."

They deplaned and made their way inside the airport. Kate noticed Agent Lyons in the distance as they continued to the terminal exit. She was fairly confident of his identity, considering the fact that when he raised his arm, she spotted his weapon. Any law enforcement officer was allowed to carry a sidearm into airports and even onto flights, assuming they'd been through the required training, so this was of no surprise to her. "I see him over there."

Agent Lyons smiled a broad and welcoming grin. "Agents Jameson and Reid, very nice to meet you." His hand gripped Kate's with firm resolve.

"Pleasure," Dwight replied. "So, where are we off to?"

Lyons led the way outside. "Let's head over to my office first and I'll show you what we've got so far." He stopped and turned on his heel. "I have to tell you. I've got a bad feeling about this one."

Dwight exchanged a glance with Kate. "We've seen our fair share of bad things, Agent Lyons."

He immediately looked at Kate. "I'll bet you have."

It appeared as though he had already done his homework, as far as Kate was concerned. She'd seen that look plenty of times but had learned that her past couldn't be changed. It made her who she was today and if someone had a problem with that, then to hell with them. "Are you working with the Jacksonville Field Office on this too?" A change of topic would solve this little issue.

"They were kind enough to defer the situation to us over here," Lyons replied.

"And you called us?"

"Well, Agent Reid, if this is what I think it is, and from what I know of Agent Scarborough and his team, you all are far better suited to handle this than we are. By the way, I understand Scarborough is fighting his way through some red tape. Happens to the best of us and I hope he gets things sorted out."

"So do we," Dwight replied.

The weather made up its mind and decided to soak the city by the time they arrived at the Atlanta office.

"Sorry about the rain." Lyons pushed his way through the front entrance. "This warm weather's wreaked havoc on us. Had more rain this month than we did in all of July." He shook the water off his arms and pushed his hand through his dampened hair to smooth it back into place. "Probably not much better where you're at."

"No, not much better at all." Dwight hadn't worn a jacket over his shirt and tie, due to the heat, so he now looked as though he'd entered a wet t-shirt contest.

Kate grinned at him as she removed the sweater she'd carried with her on the plane. It helped a little, but she was still pretty damp. "May I use the ladies' room?" she asked Lyons.

"Right over there." He pointed toward his left. "Around the corner from the elevators."

"Thanks." Kate walked away as the men waited, presumably discussing the investigation. She'd seen something in Lyons' face that set her off and taking a moment to clear her thoughts was the only way she could figure out how to handle it.

Maybe it was what he'd said about Nick or the way he looked at her earlier. He was rubbing her the wrong way and she had no idea why. She grabbed a paper towel from the dispenser and dabbed her face to absorb the drops without smudging her makeup. Looking into the mirror, she tried to search her memory for anything that might make sense as to why the disconcerting feeling about this guy, but nothing came to mind.

She couldn't stay in the restroom forever so whatever it was would come to the surface sooner or later. Right now, she was working a case and that had to take priority. Kate tossed the crumpled paper towel into the trashcan and walked out, making her way back to the waiting agents. "Sorry about that. All better now."

"Great. Let's head up to my office." Lyons took the lead once again.

"You all right?" Dwight asked.

She nodded.

Arriving on the second floor, Lyons pointed them in the direction of his office. "Come on in and have a seat." He made his way to his desk and began typing on his computer.

Kate and Dwight settled in for only a moment when another agent arrived.

"Forgive the interruption," he began. "I'm Agent Faulkner." A brief greeting was exchanged. "I work with Lyons and he asked me to sit in on this with you."

"Nice to meet you," Dwight said. "Agent Lyons, you mentioned you believed this investigation was more suited to BAU. Would you care to elaborate?"

"A few weeks ago, two boys found the body of a young woman in the Saint Marys River."

"I saw a little bit about that on the news," Kate added.

"Right. Well, the other day, another body was found farther upstream and it was a woman of similar age."

"And you believe these are connected in what way?" Dwight continued.

A file folder containing images of both bodies and the crime scenes where they were discovered appeared in the agent's hands. Lyons opened it up and began, "According to the autopsy reports, the latter we received just the other morning and prompted my call to you, they indicate both bodies were dumped in or around the Okefenokee Swamp and traveled downstream along the river."

"Do we have an ID on either of the victims?" Dwight asked.

"Not yet. The first victim was in the water for some time. An alligator got a hold of her first, but then fish, floating debris—they all left their mark. We do know that she was already gone before her body hit the water."

"That's why it traveled so far downstream. If the victim had still been alive, the body would have remained at the bottom of the swamp for some time, having ingested water into the lungs," Dwight began. "While I'm confident water did eventually enter the lungs, the reason the body traveled the distance it did was because of the gasses in the abdomen that formed almost immediately upon her death. Probably kept her afloat before water found its way in. She went down for a while along the line until the bacteria in her gut continued to grow and so did the gasses."

"That's right, Agent Jameson," Lyons said. "Buoyancy is inevitable unless she was tied down with bricks and, even then, sometimes that's not enough."

"Okay, so the first victim was discovered quite a ways from the suspected initial disposal site. What about the second victim? I think you mentioned she was found sooner and not as far downstream," Kate said.

"We're waiting on confirmation from the coroner, but the victims matched too closely to be a coincidence. Similar features, hair color, very slender. Aged, we believe, to be between twenty and twenty-five." This time, it was Faulkner who spoke.

"The cause of death in both victims wasn't drowning by your own admission. If that wasn't the cause of death," Kate said. "Then what was?"

Jɪᴍ Lᴀssᴇᴛᴇʀ ᴡᴀs the field coordinator of NCAVC (National Center for the Analysis of Violent Crime). He was Nick's boss' boss. BAU field agents ultimately fell under his direction, and while Nick admired the man, he'd grown impatient by his lack of decision-making with regard to the matter at hand.

The problem, as far as Nick was concerned, was Agent Hughes. He'd testified before the review group that Nick had no cause to shoot the suspect, that the man hadn't raised his weapon.

It was a crock of shit from Nick's perspective. Hughes arrived after the girl had fallen and both he and the suspect believed she was dead. Nick knew what he saw and he saw the suspect raise his gun, ready to fire. Nick put him down just as Hughes would've done. Hell, any of them would have done the same. However, if Nick was being honest with himself, he'd admit that he couldn't be sure the man was about to fire on him. No matter how many times he told himself, he only remembered looking at the girl, believing she was gone and that the suspect had been the one to kill her. So he shot his weapon—it was a split-second decision. Agent Hughes just happened to approach at that very same moment.

Lasseter arrived at the restaurant where Nick waited. He had been twenty minutes late and spotted Nick at one of the tables next to the window. The view of the fountain in DuPont Circle was just outside and Nick watched as a couple embraced for a kiss while the girl was trying to take a selfie. Nick turned away, vexed by the act. Maybe it was because he was on the downhill side of forty and just didn't get it, but it seemed people were living their lives through a lens. He doubted that if people knew what he faced almost daily they'd be so casual about life and making sure they looked good on Facebook.

"Agent Scarborough." Lasseter pulled out the chair opposite Nick's. "How are you? You're looking well rested."

Hungover might have been a better word for it, but Nick didn't correct his boss. "All things considered, I guess I'm doing all right."

"Of course. I understand." He raised a finger to get the waitress' attention. "Have you ordered yet?"

Nick just shook his head.

"What can I get for you two gentlemen today?" The woman was older than one might expect for holding a job such as this, at least around here. This was Washington, a place where people were either on the rise—aspiring politicians, lawyers, federal agents—or people who were already at the top. The middle class didn't seem to exist in D.C. proper. Not to mention that it was far too expensive a place to live on a server's salary.

"I'll take the club and an iced tea," Lasseter replied.

Nick thought a great big juicy burger would help the hangover, but in the presence of the man who could make or break his career, he opted to be a sheep. "I'll take the same, thank you."

"Right away." The woman smiled.

Nick could see her genuine and warm nature in that smile and suddenly felt guilty for passing some sort of socioeconomic judgment against her. What the hell did he know about her life? "So, you wanted to meet outside the office. Should I take that as a bad sign?"

Lasseter folded his hands on top of the small table covered in white linen. "Nick, I'm here because the Incident Review Group finished evaluating the narrative."

Nick's heart pumped a little faster as he waited for the results. After more than ten years as a federal agent, he feared his time was up.

"They're recommending a letter of censure be added to your file."

While Lasseter appeared grave in his delivery of this news, Nick felt a wave of relief. A letter of censure was scarcely more than a written reprimand. Okay, so it would be a part of his record, but it was the least severe punishment he could have hoped for. Well, that wasn't entirely true; they could've dismissed it altogether, but this was his second-best scenario.

"That means you'll be able to come back to work, Nick."

"Thank you. You know, I still don't believe I was in the wrong, sir."

"I know. Your exemplary record over these last several years carried a lot of weight. However, the group simply could not discount Agent Hughes' testimony. I realize he was only witness to a portion of what happened that night, but frankly, it was enough to raise eyebrows."

"He was going to take me down, sir." Nick was still pleading his innocence.

"They've already written their recommendations, Nick. It's over. I understand this is a black mark for you, but know that we are all very well aware of your dedication and high ethical standards. It might mean a slight delay in your rise in the ranks, but it is not the end of your career. I hope you understand that."

"I do. Thank you, sir." He paused for a moment. "Can I ask why you wanted to meet me here and not give me the news at WFO?"

"Because I was hungry." Lasseter chuckled and sipped on his water.

Somehow, Nick didn't think that was the reason and suspected it had something to do with ASAC Campbell. Maybe he'd wanted to make himself look good in the process of trying to make Nick look bad. He knew the man was gunning for Executive Assistant Director and a show of disciplinary action might make him appear more as a leader. Nick also believed it had something to do with the fact that he'd gone around the ASAC to get Kate assigned to the WFO. In fact, Nick had gone straight to the Academy's Assistant Director himself to make that happen.

THE NEW HOME improvement store in Fayetteville was where Arlen Tucker worked as an associate in the lumber department. Hired about six months ago when it opened, Arlen had been the poster child for attendance and customer service. They loved him over there. He knew how to run the saws, knew his wood varieties like the back of his hand, and his long and lean physique paired with his country-boy face scored well with the ladies looking to put up fences around their gardens. Arlen never had much trouble in that department. The girls always liked to look at him. He liked looking back too, but for very different reasons.

Arlen knew how to fly under the radar too. He'd gotten himself a new identity after getting out of the System a few years ago. New name—he'd always liked the name Arlen—new social security number, and even his place of residence was a P.O. Box. But what he liked best about it here was how easily he could pick them off. Of course, he'd had time to master his technique since his first few projects. The hard part came when he had to follow them. Sometimes, it would only take a day or two before he figured out the best place to take them. Sometimes, it would take a week. It all depended on how predictable their schedules were. His only requirements were that they had to have the look—one that bore a resemblance to her.

Arlen pulled the goggles over his face as he flipped the switch to turn on the saw. Five pieces of six-foot-long cypress. Apparently, the customer was building some sort of a deck, which made sense. Cypress didn't rot when exposed to extremely wet conditions. Perfect for this part of the country.

He placed the two-by-fours on a flatbed cart and wheeled it out to the waiting customer. Next to the would-be buyer was a young woman. Arlen figured eighteen and probably living at home because the man appeared to be her father. He glanced at the girl, noticing her cut-off shorts with the white fabric pockets hanging out the bottom. Normally, that would be mid-summer attire, but it was October, although it seemed Mother Nature hadn't realized that yet.

"Here you go, sir," Arlen said. "You putting together a deck?"

"Trying to, I guess. Was hoping to have it done before the weather turned cold, but at this rate, I'm not sure winter's ever going to come." The older man chuckled.

Arlen cast another glance at the pretty young girl before turning his gaze down at his feet. "All right, then. Well, you two have a good day and good luck." His face upturned and a wink of his eye was directed at her.

Her smile faded and a sense of discomfort seemed to appear. The two patrons changed course and headed toward the checkout, pushing their haul.

Arlen stood firm, his eyes never leaving the girl even while their backs were turned. "Maybe." He glanced back to confirm that his supervisor was nowhere in the vicinity and decided to take a walk. Careful not to be seen, he stayed several steps behind and monitored the progress of his customers as they made their way through the checkout. Once they passed through the exit doors, Arlen moved ahead, stopping just short of the doors, and kept an eye on them walking into the parking lot. The girl turned back for a moment, but he didn't think she spotted him because the doors were reflective on the outside.

"Tucker? You need something to do?"

Arlen knew the voice of the man who had approached from behind and a brief scowl appeared as he watched the father and daughter drive away. The sensation that had begun to build as he watched the girl quickly faded upon hearing the words of his supervisor. Arlen closed his eyes and, when they reopened, his pupils had returned to normal, no longer fully dilated and black with desire. A pleasant smile masked his true feelings as he faced the man. "No, sir. I'm heading to the back now." He brushed past his shift boss. "They'll be back."

His shift was ending and Arlen removed his apron and pulled his keys out of the front pocket of his jeans. "Goodnight. See y'all tomorrow." He made his way through the back exit to the lot behind the building where the employees were instructed to park. An hour's drive home was what lay ahead, but Arlen didn't mind. He liked traveling the back roads. They were quiet. Gave him time to think—and plan.

Arlen didn't own a smartphone; instead, he laid his flip phone on the bench seat next to him. It was his only connection, besides his job, to the outside world. He didn't have a bank account and always took his paychecks and cashed them at the grocery store or one of those check-cashing places. He'd learned a lot over these past few years about how to keep a low profile—virtually off the grid. It wasn't so bad once he got used to it because it was the only way to ensure he would avoid getting caught.

Arlen never gave much credit to the police. After his folks' house burned down and his family died, they did all they could do to help him. He was only ten at the time and ended up in the

System, but that didn't last long either. Trouble followed him and the foster parents that did take him in weren't exactly the Cleavers —not even close. Now here he was with a job, a place to live, and those damn cops never did figure out he was the one responsible. Why would they suspect him when his father was so clearly the monster in the family?

5

The news of Scarborough's imminent return hadn't yet reached Kate or Dwight. Busy with the Atlanta field office, it was late in the evening before they arrived back at the WFO.

Kate checked in at her desk and decided on a quick trip to the breakroom for some water. "Hey." She spotted Nick at the counter stirring a coffee. "What are you doing here?"

"You guys just get back from Atlanta?" He smiled at her, apparently wanting to prolong the suspense.

"Just got back from the airport. I was going to give you a call before I headed back home. My car is here, so I had to come back anyway." Kate stepped toward him. "So are you going to tell me what you're doing here or are you going to make me guess?"

"Had a talk with Lasseter earlier today. Looks like I'll be coming back next week."

Kate's eyes widened and her smile matched his. "You are? That's great, but how? When did this happen?"

Nick proceeded to explain the circumstances that brought

about his return, minus the part about how he went around Campbell to get her assigned to his office.

"A letter of censure?" she began. "You shouldn't have been reprimanded at all."

"It's not great and I'll have to mind my p's and q's for a while, but other than that, things will return to normal and I'll officially be back on Monday."

She raised her hands to her cheeks. "I can't believe it's finally over. Welcome back. I can't tell you how good it will be to have you here again." She offered him a brief embrace.

Nick returned the gesture. He missed her, he missed his job, and it was clear he was grateful to be back. It was his saving grace and they both knew it.

With the two at arm's length again, Nick began, "Tell me, how'd it go in Atlanta? Anything interesting?"

"You could say that, but let's go see Dwight first." Kate led the way to Dwight's office until they appeared in his doorway. "Hey, there. Look who the cat dragged in."

Dwight turned away from his monitor. "What are you doing here, man?"

"He's back," Kate replied before Nick could edge out a word of his return.

"What?" Dwight rose from his chair and went in for the man-hug. "Are you serious? Well, what happened? I mean, when did you find out?"

"Today. Met with Lasseter. I'm officially back on Monday. I'll get a letter of censure, but that's it."

"Holy shit." Dwight pushed his hand through his short, crew-cut hair. "I can't believe it. Why the hell did it take them so long to figure this out?"

"I have my own theory, but that's a story for another time." Nick pulled up a chair. "What happened in Atlanta?"

"We met with Agents Lyons and Faulkner. A couple of bodies turned up in the Saint Marys River, and they're pretty sure the deaths are connected." Dwight returned to his desk.

"Did you have a chance to look at their case files?" Nick asked.

"We did and we have a copy of them." He eyed Kate before continuing. "Nick, these girls, from what we know so far, appeared to have died first from strangulation."

"First?" Nick asked.

"Their bodies were mutilated after their deaths." Kate was morose in her reply. "Their genitals—removed."

Dwight turned his monitor toward Nick. "Completely removed." It was a postmortem image of the second female victim. Only a cavernous pelvic region remained.

It seemed Nick had no words for what he was witnessing and Dwight turned the monitor back. Nick continued, "Two of them so far?"

"So far," Kate began. "The victims were redressed afterward in what appeared to be young girls' clothing. Like what you might find a middle-schooler wearing, and then they were dumped."

Nick pursed his lips. "What are the local authorities doing?"

"Because the river borders both Georgia and Florida, the sheriff's departments from the two counties, Baker and Charlton, went to the FBI. Atlanta and Jacksonville deliberated and it was decided that BAU needed to get involved and, apparently, this Agent Lyons wanted to get in touch with you. When he tried to reach out, Campbell directed him to me. And so here we are," Dwight said.

"Agent Jack Lyons," Nick replied.

"Yes, sir. You know him?"

"I do. We were both assigned to Atlanta. That was my first field office. I guess he's still there."

"You two get along?" Kate asked, recalling the unpleasant taste their meeting left in her mouth.

"Well enough, I suppose. After my two years' probationary period, I was transferred to BAU headquarters and then here. To be honest, I hadn't heard from him since I left Atlanta. I'm surprised he thought to contact me."

"Maybe he just hadn't needed to until now," Dwight said.

Kate still thought there was something else to it. The way Lyons had looked at her. Whatever it was, she wasn't thrilled to be working with him, even if it was only in a coordinating capacity.

"Listen, it's getting pretty late. I'm sure the two of you would like to call it a day," Nick rose from his chair. "I've got a lot of administrative bullshit to sort through before Monday and I don't know what's going to happen after that. Campbell might just keep me as a desk jockey for a while."

"You mean you won't work on this with us?" Kate asked.

Nick looked at his partner and friend—the man who'd been there during the Corbett raids. It seemed as though they both knew Dwight wanted to take the lead on this case, and they both knew it wouldn't be up to him to make that call. "I honestly don't know, but it appears as though the two of you have things well under control. Jameson knows what he's doing." He reached out to shake Dwight's hand. "Thanks for everything, man. I'll catch up with you in a few days."

Kate stood from her chair. "I'm glad you're back."

"Me too. Go home. I'm sure you could use the rest. I have a long-awaited date with my girl and I've already kept her waiting too long."

Nick disappeared around the corner and Kate turned to Dwight. "I was really afraid he wasn't going to come back—and what it would do to him."

"Same here, Kate. Same here."

Nick arrived at Georgia's place and waited outside her door, feeling almost nervous. He hadn't seen her in a week and had been holding off on the news because he wanted to tell her in person. Her footsteps were approaching the door from the other side and he smiled, ready to reveal the good news.

Beautiful as ever, her hair cascaded down her shoulders. She'd been letting it grow longer and it seemed the waves framed her face perfectly. His eyes lit up at the sight of her and he immediately regretted what he'd said to Kate at dinner. He'd had too much to drink and, when that happened, his words were not his own. Now, as she stood in front of him, her smile giving him renewed energy, he stepped closer. "Boy, am I glad to see you." He planted a tender kiss on her lips.

"Me too. Come on in." Georgia stepped aside revealing her gleaming apartment. "Housekeeper was here today. You should've seen it before." She closed the door and returned to the kitchen where a home-cooked meal was brewing. "I figured you might be hungry. You haven't eaten dinner yet, have you?"

"No. Not yet." Nick glanced at the clock on the built-in shelves that surrounded her television. It was approaching nine p.m. The day had gotten away from him, but at least it hadn't been spent on a barstool this time. "Smells great. What are we having?"

Georgia approached him, offering a drink she'd just poured. "Lobster Risotto. I have to confess, though, it's not exactly home-made. I did go to the gourmet store and pick it up. I actually have no idea how to make this, but it looked fantastic."

Nick stared at the drink for a moment.

"You okay?"

He smiled and finally took it from her hand. "Great, now that I'm here." He tossed back a large gulp. "So, I've got some news."

"Oh yeah?" She returned to the kitchen to tend to the meal. "What's that?"

"I'm going back on Monday."

She stopped immediately, turning away from the cooktop. "Oh my God. You are?" It seemed as though she couldn't get to him quickly enough and now stood just inches from his face. "It's over?" Her shoulders dropped in relief. "So what happened? What did they decide?"

"It's a bit of a long story, but um, just a written reprimand."

She shook her head. "That's it? All this time and it's essentially been dismissed?"

"You sound surprised."

"No, I just mean that they wasted so much time and, in the end, it turned out to be nothing. Which, by the way, we already knew, and yet, they dragged it out for almost two months."

"I know." He gently took hold of her arms. "But it's over now and I can go back to work. In fact, I stopped by the office to see Kate and Dwight. They'd just come back from Atlanta on a consult."

"Atlanta? What's going on there?"

"I guess a couple of bodies were found on the Georgia-Florida border—a river—and they were murdered in the same fashion. Agent Jack Lyons got the original call and reached out to us. Me, actually, but Campbell mentioned that I was on administrative leave and gave it to Jameson." Nick followed her back into the kitchen. "You know he and I go way back. I haven't heard from him in a long time, but I guess he remembered me."

"Well, of course he did. Who could forget you?" She turned off the flame on the stove. "So, will you be taking the case from here, then?"

"I don't know. Campbell and I have some issues to work through and I just don't know if he's willing to pull me back in so quickly. And I have to tell you, I think Dwight wants this one. I saw the look in his eyes when he heard I was back."

"What does that mean?"

"I know he's got my back; it's not that. I just think he wanted to take the lead. Kate's working with him on it too. He was assigned as her mentor in my absence."

"That's a good thing, right? Dwight doesn't have your experience, but he can take the lead, can't he?"

"Of course. And you know, maybe it's for the best. Kate needs to see how others in the agency work. Not just learn from me. Hell, I'm not perfect. Far from it, actually." He downed the rest of his drink.

"I, for one, am glad the two of them will be working on it together. You're right about Kate. She should spread her wings a little and Dwight will give her that opportunity."

"You don't think I would?"

Georgia reached for the plates in the cabinet. "That's not what I said. I just think it would be good for her. Like you said."

Nick studied her for a moment. "Yeah, maybe you're right. How's that dinner coming?"

THE ENGINE SPUTTERED and Kate realized her car was slowing down of its own accord. She pressed the gas pedal, but the vehicle rejected any notion of moving under her command. "Shit." She eyed the fuel level—half a tank. Her hands turned the wheel and she pulled off the road until the engine eventually died and she rolled to a stop. The time on her dash showed 9:30 p.m.

Only a few miles from home, Kate considered just locking it up and hoofing it the rest of the way. It could be handled in the morning with a quick call for a tow truck. Still, a three-mile walk felt daunting in her current state of fatigue. Her fourteen-hour day apparently was not yet over. Another option would be to call the only person she knew who lived nearby and that was Nick. It occurred to her, however, that he was probably still downtown at Georgia's place and not at home, which would mean interrupting a long-awaited reunion between the two. This wasn't an option she'd wanted to pursue. Unfortunately, the Metro wasn't an option either—not this far out.

Kate inhaled an exhaustive breath and peered through the windshield. She was on the least populated stretch of Colchester Road, so not even a bus stop was nearby. It seemed her options were becoming fewer. She reached for her cell phone and was prepared to dial Nick's number, but stopped short. "Nope, I can handle this on my own." Stepping out of the car, Kate retrieved her belongings, which included a laptop bag, a purse, and her sidearm, which lay on the floor of the passenger seat, still in its holster. The security that alone offered propelled her to move forward with the decision. She would walk the three miles like a big girl.

With the car secured, Kate began to walk along the dirt shoulder that felt soft under her feet. It was a good day to have chosen sensible shoes, for which she thanked herself at this moment. She turned to glance at the beleaguered heap of metal that had once been a reliable, if not enduring, automobile. In fact, it had carried her a great distance, not just in miles, but emotional distance as well. She knew its days were numbered, but had been putting off the decision to rid herself of the only remaining item from a past that felt like decades ago. Seemed a trivial thing, to hang on to something like a car, but now it was possible that she would have to finally let it go. Unfortunately, her funds were low. The Academy had only just afforded her the too-expensive rental house in Woodbridge, but not much else. And now on a probationary agent's salary, the cost of a new car loan might be too much of a stretch.

There was still Marshall's money. She called it that because it had been proceeds from the sale of *his* downtown San Diego apartment. While she might have lived there, it was never hers—and neither was the money. It still sat in a bank account, accumulating a pathetic interest rate that could hardly sustain the cost of the banking fees.

A chill passed through her as she continued along the quiet roadside, only a few cars passing her by, none even attempting to slow down and offer assistance. Not that she would have accepted anyway. It wouldn't be long before she reached the subdivision in which her home resided. The night was revealing signs of a coming fall that was long overdue. Leaves on the ground crunched beneath her feet. The trees from which they fell grew barer by the day. Even in the night sky, she could see their branches becoming devoid of life.

Kate pressed on, unafraid of what was behind her, no longer feeling the urge to check over her shoulder. This was partly a result of her training, partly due to time having passed. Her heart remained hardened thanks to those who had stolen so much from her and it was better that way.

Finally, the community was visible in the distance and a relieved smile masked her face. She was almost home. Hoisting the laptop bag higher atop her shoulder, Kate's eye was drawn to a building on the right-hand side. She must have passed it a hundred times before but never took much notice. Perhaps it was because this was the local school and she had no cause to pay attention to a school. Except now.

She stopped on the sidewalk at the school's entrance. It was gated off and had no way to access it. A sign of the times for certain. In the dim light of a few streetlamps, she could read the sign on the front. Hamilton Middle School. Staring at it for some time, a thought that initiated abstractly began to take form. "Hamilton Middle School," Kate said.

A crime scene photo of the second victim sprang to mind. She was half-emerged from the black waters of the river and wearing a t-shirt. It was too small, Kate recalled, and the words were stretched across her breasts. But upon closing her eyes and focusing on the shirt, wet from the river, Kate began to make out the words. Of course, it would take a second look at the actual image to confirm, but she began to recollect the photo with growing clarity. "WJHS."

When Kate was in school, at least where she was from, it wasn't called middle school, but junior high. "W Junior High School." Although unsure of what the "W" stood for, taking another look at the photo might reveal it. The victim was much older than a middle-schooler; of that, there was already hard evidence. It had to have been something her killer made her wear. This was a clue. The killer had left a clue perhaps deliberately, but there was little doubt in Kate's mind that this was a lead and she would see it through.

6
***

The needle on the fuel gauge had veered pretty far
south and so Arlen figured he'd better stop for gas on his
way home from work. Best not to run out in the middle
of nowhere because one never knows what's out there late at night.
He had to chuckle at the thought.

He pulled into the gas station that would have been the last
stop before the final twenty minutes back home. It was only a few
miles, but the dark and often muddy roads meant he had to take
his time if he didn't want to be digging his way out of a bog.

Hopping out of the old Chevy truck, Arlen closed the driver's
side door, but not without the familiar creaking sound that echoed
beneath the cover of the pump island. There wasn't anyone else
there to take notice anyway. Payday wasn't for a few more days
and, as Arlen pulled open his brown leather wallet that looked
worse for wear, he realized he only had forty bucks in cash. This
old guzzler would eat that up pretty quickly, maybe even before
his next paycheck, and that would leave him with nothing to live

off of. He didn't eat much and probably weighed a buck sixty at best, but he still needed food.

He'd have to split it. Half in gas, half in food, and he hoped that would be enough to see him through. It probably would, so long as he put off his hobby for a while. Not only did it take time to find himself the perfect girl, but it took fuel to drive around doing it. Probably best anyway. He needed to let things cool down for a while. He'd seen on the news that a body had been found while he was on break at work. Didn't own a T.V. himself. They hadn't a clue where it'd come from, just that it washed up downstream and was found by a couple of boys.

At that moment, a familiar feeling passed through him as he recalled the broadcast, bringing about a momentary light-headed-ness. It was as though he'd forgotten something, and now it gnawed at him. Dismissing the sensation, he returned to the memory of the news story and while he couldn't be one hundred percent confident it was his girl, he was pretty damn sure it was. Bearing that in mind, caution would have to take precedence in this matter. But that was okay because he wasn't in a big hurry. After all, it wasn't about the quantity, it was about the quality. And it meant he'd have to take greater precautions about how he handled the girls once he was done with them. He couldn't afford to have them washing up all over the place.

Arlen finished pumping the gas and replaced the spout. "$19.78. Damn close to twenty. It'll do," he said and walked into the store to pay. Sure, he could've bailed on the tab, but it would only bite him in the ass. Drawing that kind of attention for some-thing so stupid would unravel all he had created and it wasn't worth the risk. "Evenin'." He smiled at the kid behind the counter. Some pimple-faced twenty-year-old probably working for his dad.

"Evenin', sir. What pump?" the kid asked.

"Two." Arlen realized they were probably only a few years

apart in age and he soon felt condescension arise from the pimple-faced kid. Like maybe he was better than Arlen. "This your daddy's shop? I been in a few times, but I think he was probably working then."

"Yes, sir. I work second shift, after school." He held out his hand, waiting for Arlen to hand him the twenty that he was rubbing between his fingers.

"College?"

The kid nodded.

"Well, good for you." Arlen's smile faded as he handed over the bill.

"Thank you. You know, I just want to be something someday and get out of this town."

"Oh, I understand that plenty."

The change was returned. "Thank you for coming in. You have a good night."

"I plan to." Arlen stared at the kid. A few beads of sweat ran down the sides of his face and were absorbed by his thickened beard. The outside temperatures wouldn't have mandated such a response, but this was how it started. Rising heart rate, mild trembling, sweating. The idea of the kill was taking hold. Arlen never went after boys or men, so this was a new sensation for him—and it felt good.

Finally, he broke the stare and his smile returned, although his eyes revealed a seething desire for something much more visceral. "Good night." He had to breathe in deeply to calm his pulse as he exited the store. The outside air cooled his skin as it dried the sweat that had formed at his neckline.

Arlen shoved the coins into his jeans pocket and stepped back inside the truck. Hunched over his steering wheel, he turned his head in the direction of the small convenience store where the kid quickly turned away. It was as if he'd been watching Arlen, wanting to make sure he would be leaving.

The sensation started to abate and Arlen laughed as he turned over the truck's engine, and a puff of black smoke drifted from the exhaust past the back window. "Well, that was new." He pulled out onto the paved road and turned on the radio to listen to the static-filled broadcast of the fifth game in the World Series. Reception would be lost soon enough and he'd wanted to catch the score.

KATE OPENED the front door of her home before she even realized she'd made it. Her mind was consumed with the girl in the school shirt and each step was mired in deep thought. Looking at the files again was the first thing she needed to do, considering for a moment to touch base with Nick. "No, I can handle this."

After a quick change of clothes and securing her weapon, Kate returned to the living room and fired up her laptop. She'd have to log into the FBI server and retrieve the files, some of which, however, probably hadn't yet been uploaded. They'd only just received them this afternoon and it was usually her job to update the files. The image might not be there at all, but sleep would not come if she didn't at least try.

Even if she was right and the girl was wearing the WJHS t-shirt, the path from there was ambiguous, but she hoped it would mean something. As far as she was concerned, this was her case, hers and Dwight's, and once again, the chip balanced precariously on Kate's shoulder as she felt compelled to prove herself.

Logging into the system, Kate searched for the file they'd dubbed "Blackwater." The Saint Marys River was born from the Okefenokee Swamp and was considered a black water stream due to the nature of the organic material decay. Despite its name, black water rivers were typically some of the cleanest waters and it was only the tannins produced by those decaying plants and other vegetation that gave the water its blackened color.

The file was there, but not all of the information. "Dammit." No images had yet been uploaded. Kate checked the time on her screen. It was getting late and the idea of calling Dwight at 10:30 to discuss the case probably wasn't the wisest, although she wouldn't hesitate to call Nick, but she didn't have that kind of relationship with Dwight. That was probably a good thing because it meant she wouldn't lean on him the way she always had with Nick.

Kate considered herself independent, but in reality, certain things drove her to seek help. And others, well, she wouldn't dream of ever asking, and they usually involved things in her past for which no help could be offered anyway.

She logged off and closed the lid of her laptop. It was out of her hands and it would have to wait until tomorrow.

KATE APPEARED outside of Dwight's office and waited for an invitation.

He noticed her immediately. "Good morning. Come on in."

"Morning. Did you get the message I left earlier?"

"I did. You should've called me. I would've picked you up." Dwight pushed aside some paperwork and gave Kate his full attention.

"Thanks, but it wasn't too much of a problem. The tow truck dropped me off and I'll take the train tonight to the mechanic and pick it up. I appreciate it, though." Kate took her usual seat. "Listen, I wanted to talk to you about something that I was thinking of last night."

"Shoot." He placed his elbows on the table and folded his hands beneath his chin, ready to listen, but his eyes immediately turned toward the door. "Well, hello there."

Before Kate could utter a word, she spun to see Georgia in the doorway. "Hi."

"Sorry to interrupt."

"Not at all. What's up?" Dwight replied.

"Actually," Kate began. "You might be able to help. You got a second?"

"I only came in to drop off a few things for Nick. I'm leaving later today and I know he'll be in here on Monday, but—um, sure, I have a second." Georgia stepped inside. "Is this about the bodies found in the river? Nick mentioned something about it last night."

"It is, yes. I was wondering if you might consider taking a look at the profiles of the victims. I think our unsub might have left us a clue," Kate replied.

"You know what?" Dwight picked up his phone. "Let me give Lyons a call. We're still missing some information, but maybe if we have a quick pow-wow, it might give you a better idea of what we're dealing with."

Dwight pressed the speakerphone button and waited for the line to answer.

"This is Lyons."

"Agent Lyons, this is Dwight Jameson. Listen, I've got you on speakerphone here in my office and I'm with Agents Reid and Myers. Do you have a moment?"

"Georgia Myers?"

"Yes, I'm here."

"Nice to hear from you. It's been a while," Lyons said.

"Yes, it has. I understand you've been directing efforts on this Blackwater investigation?"

"That's why I wanted to give you a quick call," Dwight interrupted. "I won't keep you, but it sounds like you are already aware of Agent Myers' work. So you know that she's the best profiler we have."

"Yes, I am well aware of that," Lyons replied.

This was a coincidence, Kate thought. Georgia did have a stellar reputation and often consulted on a variety of investigations, but she was unaware that the two had been previously acquainted.

"Good. I was thinking we could have Agent Myers do a workup on the information we have to date, which, by the way, it appears as though we are missing the second coroner's report, if you wouldn't mind sending that over this morning," Dwight said.

"Not at all, and I would be happy to have Myers' help on this. The more eyes the better as far as I'm concerned."

"Great. Thank you. I'll keep an eye out for the second report and, in the meantime, we'll continue working on our end. If anything else pops up, we'll be in touch. Oh, and by the way, Scarborough will be back on Monday. I understand you were initially interested in working with him on this investigation. If that is still your wish..."

"I'm interested only in finding a resolution, Jameson, and if that means I've got Myers and Reid working on the team, then I'm confident a resolution will be in short order."

With compulsory goodbyes exchanged, Dwight ended the call. "Thank you, Myers. We're only scratching the surface of this investigation so far, but with your help, I'm sure we'll move along much more quickly. I can tell you that I have no desire for another body to be found floating along some river. So, the sooner we find the person who killed those girls, the better."

"Of course." Georgia began to rise. "Why don't you send me what you have and I'll take a look at it on the plane later today?"

"Sounds good. Thank you."

Kate waited until Georgia was out of sight before speaking again. "It'll be good to have her helping us out. I had no idea she knew Lyons. Probably should've had her come with us to Atlanta. Anyway, back to what I think might be a clue was the second victim's clothing. Do you have the image Lyons sent over? I haven't uploaded it yet."

Dwight entered a command on his keyboard. "Yes, here it is." He turned the monitor so Kate could see it. "What are you thinking?"

Kate studied the photo of the girl at the crime scene, still in her clothes. Bloated, several contusions, suggesting scrapes from either floating debris or animal life. Evidence of strangulation was determined to be the actual cause of death. Bulging, hemorrhaging eyes, bruising consistent with the hand markings around her neck. "She looks almost as though her skin has been—dissolved or melted away. Does that make sense to you?"

Dwight came around and sat down next to Kate. His brow narrowed as he looked at the screen. "Possibly. We'd have to look at the coroner's report, but it definitely looks eroded in a way inconsistent with injuries or even attacks by whatever lives in that water." He looked back at her. "That's going to make it even harder to pull DNA."

"Right, but there's something else too." She tried to realign her thoughts, as they'd been distracted by this latest concern. "Take a look at her top." Kate raised her index finger and placed it on the monitor, outlining the letters on her shirt. "Looks to me like she was wearing a school t-shirt. WJHS."

"I see it. It doesn't fit her either—too small."

"Yeah. I don't think it was hers. We know the unsub redresses his victims after taking his souvenir, but I think he's putting them in clothes that he owns."

"Interesting. You were thinking about this last night?"

"I was walking home after my car broke down and I came across the school in my neighborhood and it just hit me. I don't know if Lyons has considered this or not, but I think it's worth looking into. The victims' families could probably answer the question as to whether or not the clothes belonged to the victim. And I'm pretty confident the JHS stands for Junior High School. Don't know about the W." She leaned in closer to the screen. "What does that say? Beneath the letters. Can you zoom in on this a little?"

"Sure, hang on." He pulled his keyboard to the end of his desk. "Here, can you read it now?"

Straining to see, Kate began to shake her head. "No. Dammit. It's too faded. It has to be a mascot name or something like that, though. Don't you think?"

"I don't know. It's too damn hard to see." Dwight paused. "Junior High School? I thought it was called middle school now?"

"I think most schools are called that now, but I could be wrong. Maybe it's just newer schools? I don't know, but my guess is, this shirt she's wearing? For one, it's not hers. Secondly, it's fairly old, considering how faded it is and, finally, we need to find out what the W stands for." Kate looked at Dwight. "If we can get the name of this school, we might have a decent lead."

"Okay, let's get started, then." He pulled out the physical files they'd received from Lyons yesterday. "I'd say we need to run a check on the middle schools and junior high schools in the state. Let's cast a wider net right now and see how many of them are a hit."

"Is there a chance the school is no longer open?" Kate considered that this could be a dead end and it wouldn't be the first time.

"I suppose it's possible. Nevertheless, we should still find records of whether or not a school existed. There would have to be something there." Dwight stopped and held her gaze for a moment.

"What?" she asked.

"You might turn out to be better than I am at this job." Dwight smiled.

THE MEETING with BAU headquarters meant that Nick was officially reinstated. It also meant that he now had a letter of censure on his record, but all things considered, that was the best of all possible outcomes. Campbell could have made things worse for him, but in the end, Nick believed Campbell understood that he was a good agent and while he might have circumvented certain protocols, it was only in the interest of ensuring the best for Kate. It was officially over and he would return on Monday. The question remained, however: would he be working on the Blackwater investigation or would Campbell make him suffer a little longer?

Nick pulled out of the parking garage and headed back toward D.C. He'd wanted to go to the office and see how things were progressing with Kate and Dwight, but Georgia's words reverberated in his mind. He needed to let her spread her wings, just like she said. But he would be faced with a fair amount of spare time on his hands until his return. Maybe he could just go back to the office and get his desk reorganized? Naturally, anyone who knew him would see through that excuse in a heartbeat. There would be no denying that his objective was to find a reason to go in. He wanted in on the investigation, but he didn't want to step on Dwight's toes. Knowing his partner's personality, Nick figured he'd bow out of command and offer Nick whatever assistance he needed. That was just the kind of man Dwight was. The thought made Nick feel worse for even considering the idea.

As he drove along the busy streets, a quick call to ensure Georgia had arrived at the airport would offer distraction. A few rings sounded through the speakers and she answered. "Hi. Are you at the airport yet?"

"I just got here. My flight's been delayed a little."

"Oh, I'm sorry to hear that. You want me to come down there and we can grab some lunch or something?"

"No, no. Thank you, honey, but I'll be fine. Besides, it'll give me time to take a look at what Jameson sent over."

"What do you mean?" Nick merged onto the 95. "Sent what over?"

"He and Kate asked me to take a look at the two victims' profiles and see what I can come up with. They don't have much yet, but I might be able to shed some light on the unsub. He's left a hell of a calling card on his victims."

That was putting it mildly. "No doubt. So, Jameson's got you looking into it? And what about Lyons? Is he onboard?"

"So far as I know. Jameson put a call into him this morning and the four of us had a brief chat. They were still waiting on some of the forensics, but he seemed to be happy to have me take a look and offer an opinion."

"Great." Nick fell silent for a moment.

"You okay?" Georgia asked after too long of a pause.

"Oh yeah. I just left headquarters. Got everything organized over there. I was just debating on whether to head into the office—make sure I still have one."

"That's not a bad idea, Nick." It apparently was not lost on her that he'd had far too much time on his hands lately and getting back into the swing of things was probably best. "I won't be back until Tuesday or Wednesday, depending on how things go in Philly, but I'll be sure and send Jameson my findings if you want to give him a heads-up."

She was giving him an even better excuse to go in and Nick was grateful for it. "Yeah, maybe I'll go ahead and do that. Thanks. You have a safe flight and I'll see you when you get home."

"Okay, hon."

"I love you," Nick replied.

"You too. Bye."

It didn't take much prompting to nudge Nick over the fence when he was already teetering in that direction.

He pulled off the highway and headed toward the WFO. Within minutes, he was inside the lobby and making his way to the fourth floor. Nick spotted Kate leaning over the desk of Agent Vasquez. "Kate." He carried on toward her as she turned at the sound of her name.

"Well, this is a pleasant surprise. I didn't expect to see you here today. I thought Monday was the official return?" With a hand at her hip, a wide smile revealed Kate's genuine delight.

"It is. I just thought I'd go through my desk and clean out my office. You know, get ready for the new start." He peeked over Kate's shoulder. "Vasquez, nice to see you."

"This place hasn't been the same without you, Scarborough. It'll be nice to see your ugly mug again."

"Who are you calling ugly?" Nick smoothed his hair and straightened his button-down shirt. "Whatever." He smiled. "It'll be good to see your bright, shining, and lovely face again too."

If Nick was attempting to flirt with Agent Vasquez, he was barking up the wrong tree. She had a girlfriend and there was no way Nick could compete with that, even if he'd wanted to.

"I've got to get back to work. I haven't had a two-month vacation like some people." Vasquez revealed an audacious grin and returned to her computer.

Nick reached for Kate's shoulder. "You got a minute? I'd like to see Dwight, too, if he's here."

"He's here and we can spare some time." Kate led the way to the back offices. "What's going on? Why are you really here?"

Footfalls were all that sounded between them as they approached Dwight's office until, finally, Nick spoke up. "I was wondering if you had heard anything from Campbell."

Dwight was just coming out of his office when the three seemed to spot each other at once. "Scarborough? Thought you weren't coming in until Monday."

"He says he wants to clean up his office," Kate replied with a skeptical smile. "You have a minute?"

"Sure. Let's go inside."

As they returned to Dwight's office, he closed the door behind them. "What's going on?"

Nick leaned against the lateral file cabinets that ran the length of the west wall. "Has Campbell made any mention of how things will transition once I come back?"

"Haven't you talked to him about it yet?" Dwight asked.

"No. Not exactly. I just wanted to get your guys' take on it."

"Well," Dwight moved around to his desk, "he hasn't said much to me about it. I really don't know what he's got planned." A text appeared on his phone and he took a moment to glance at it. It must have jogged a memory because he immediately switched gears. Or maybe he was just trying to avoid the question. "By the way, we talked to Agent Lyons in Atlanta again this morning."

"Georgia mentioned that you all were on a conference call with him," Nick replied.

"We were, yes. Given the similarities of the victims' profiles, I thought it might be a good idea to have her take a look at things early on. I know she's going to be working in Philly for a few days, but I wanted to get her thoughts. So I put in a call to Lyons to ask about some of the remaining information we needed and made mention of it. He seemed completely on board. I don't know if he's worked with her in the past, but the two of them seemed familiar with one another."

"Really?" Nick replied.

"That's how it seemed. I mean, I didn't ask for details."

"I brought up Lyons last night at her place and again this morning. She made no mention of the fact that she knew him. Even when I told her that he and I worked together in Atlanta for a while."

"Maybe it just didn't occur to her to bring it up," Kate replied.

Nick grunted. "Maybe."

7

The saw blade whirled with fierce velocity and sliced through the lumber as though it were nothing more than a loaf of bread. The noise pierced Arlen's ears while he pushed the pine along the table. Most of his colleagues wore headphones—in fact, it was a safety requirement—but no one was around and he likened the sound to that of his victims. He preferred to absorb their high-pitched screams rather than block them out. The pain was his punishment for what he was doing to them.

"Arlen!" the man shouted as he stood at the entrance of the milling area where several saws were lined up. "Shut it down." He made a gesture to reiterate his command.

Arlen followed his supervisor's instructions and cut the switch, watching the blade slow until its sharp teeth came to a halt. "Yes?" He raised his safety goggles. That rule, he followed, not wanting to suffer the consequences of a ricocheting piece of wood flinging toward his eyes.

The supervisor stood feet from him now and placed his hands

inside his orange apron. "I need you to go on an install. This storm's got people freaked out. The chances of it hitting us are slim, but they don't want to take no chances. I need you to put up plywood on some windows. Can you do that?"

"Yes, I can."

"Good. I'll send Pete with you. Go and get loaded up. Y'all are leaving in thirty minutes." The supervisor began to walk away.

"Thank you, sir."

Pete was a useless lump of a man as far as Arlen was concerned. He couldn't figure out how the hell he still had a job here, considering most of the time, he was either late or didn't bother to show up for his shift at all. Arlen rolled his eyes at the thought and then tried to track down the man to help him get loaded up.

"Hey." Arlen tapped Pete on the shoulder as he sat in the breakroom watching Judge Judy and sipping on a Pepsi. "We gotta go put up some plywood 'fore the storm hits. I need your help loadin' up the truck."

Pete screwed up his face and set down the can of soda. "All right. All right." He rose from the plastic chair and hoisted up his sagging jeans from beneath his apron. "Where we goin'?"

"Don't know yet. Boss just said load up, so we best load up."

After too long, thanks to his grossly out-of-shape partner, the truck was loaded with ten sheets of plywood, cut to size according to what the customer needed. The storm was supposed to hit the coast by tonight and it was approaching noon now. Obviously, there were no guarantees it would reach this far inland, but people liked to be cautious and Arlen could understand that.

"Saddle up, son." Arlen jumped into the driver's seat and turned the engine of the flatbed truck. He waited for his partner to pull himself inside the cab and backed away from the great warehouse, watching it shrink in his rearview.

"How far we going?" Pete asked for the second time.

Prepared to answer—for a second time, Arlen began, "Should be there in ten minutes. It's not far."

He was on the mark, once again. Arlen always had a plan, always a path on which to follow. His father taught him that. Bet he wished he hadn't now.

"This is it." Arlen turned down the quiet suburban street filled with older homes that would probably be better off if they were destroyed by a storm. He checked the address written on the ticket once again. "Yep. 183 Hills Lane NW. This is it." With no car in the driveway, he pulled up in order to make the unloading go along a little smoother.

A young woman appeared on the front porch, eyeing the truck as Arlen stopped inches from the garage door.

"That must be our customer." He liked the job already. Stepping out of the truck, Arlen nodded a hello. "Are you Mrs. Hansby?" He looked down at the ticket just to be sure he got the name right.

"No. That's my grandmother. I'm only here to help make sure things go well." The slender woman, not older than her mid-twenties, walked down the porch steps. She wore shorts with a long-sleeved hoodie that was partially unzipped and revealed a skintight tank top beneath. "I'm Lizbeth Hansby." She extended her hand. "Nice to meet you."

"Lizbeth. My name's Arlen and this is Pete." He turned to his partner, whose face reddened from the exertion of getting out of the vehicle. "I suppose we ought to get started."

Opportunities. Arlen was a patient man and, when an opportunity arose, he wasn't the type to squander it. Just such an opportunity had now presented itself. And it would most certainly not be misspent.

Lizbeth walked back inside where her grandmother waited,

peering through the window from her breakfast table. She sipped on her black coffee. "Should we offer them something to drink? It's mighty hot out there."

"Let them get started and I'll go out in a while to check on them." Lizbeth moved next to the old woman. "You sure you don't just want to come back to my apartment until this storm blows over?"

"What's to say it won't hit your place even harder?" Her lips stretched into a smile, almost smoothing out the lines above them that had deepened from years of smoking. "Besides, you know I don't like to leave Granddad."

Lizbeth glanced into the living room where Grandpa's ashes rested inside a brass urn on top of the fireplace mantel. "Okay, Grandma." She returned her attention and then cast a measured look outside toward the skies. "I don't think it's gonna reach us in any event, but we'll get you taken care of, I promise." She placed her hand on top of her grandmother's and smiled.

With each board the men unloaded, Arlen tried to catch a glimpse of the girl, working out whether he thought she'd be an easy take. She fit the bill; there was no question about that. Maybe a little older than the others, but it was her face that sealed it for Arlen. Big hazel eyes, olive skin, and perfect lips—not too full, not too thin. Her hair had obviously been dyed blond, which annoyed him. He often wondered why women changed the color of their hair, especially to blond. Darker hair looked more natural and innocent.

"Arlen, what the hell you waiting on?" Pete tugged on his end of the board, trying to move in the direction of the porch to set it down.

Arlen looked at his partner and shuffled on. If she was to be his next target, a plan would need to be drafted. While the two continued to bring the sheets of plywood to the porch, he noted

Lizbeth's car. Make, model, color, and finally, license plate number. He knew she didn't live with her grandmother; she'd already said as much. But he wondered, would she stay with her until the storm passed? Well, that was the question to which he needed an answer.

KATE'S EYES had grown weary from reviewing the map of all the middle and junior high schools in the southern part of Georgia. There were far more than she initially expected. Out of the approximately two hundred, ten began with a W, ranging from Washington to Warwick to Whitehall. And this was all under the assumption that the school was near the vicinity of where the victims had disappeared. If that assumption was wrong, then none of this information would do them any good, but they had to start somewhere.

She pulled a sheet of paper off the printer and began walking to Jameson's office. It took a moment for her to realize that nearly the entire floor had cleared out. When she stood at Jameson's door, he was staring at his screen with a furrowed brow and seemingly in deep thought. "Sorry to interrupt," Kate began.

Jameson turned away for a moment and blinked hard. "No problem." He glanced down at the paper she was holding. "Is that the list?"

Kate continued inside and set the paper in front of him. "I highlighted the schools that begin with a W. I haven't made it through the entire list yet. This is just southern Georgia."

"So there's about thirty of them." He continued to study the report. "Well, it won't be hard to rule them one way or another. We just need to reach out to the various administrations and find out if the logo on the girl's shirt matches any of these schools."

"What if they don't?"

He pushed the paper back toward her. "Then we widen the search."

She began to rub her eyes with gentle fingertips so as not to smudge her makeup. "So, we find where the shirt came from, then what?"

"It's possible these shirts change, either every year or every other year, I don't know, but if we find a match, then we find out the year it was distributed to the students."

"Then we get a list of those students." Kate finished his thought.

"Right. It's a shot in the dark, but until forensics finds anything, it's the best lead we have to run on." Dwight stopped for a moment. "People like this—they don't just happen overnight. They grow, develop into killers, and leave signs of their transformations in their wake. That's what we'll be looking for—signs." He glanced at the time on his monitor. "It's late. Why don't you go home, get some rest, and be ready for Monday? We've got half a dozen agents and forensics experts working on this between BAU and Atlanta. Something will break soon."

Kate studied Dwight's face and thought she detected a hint of disappointment. "Do you think Campbell's going to put Nick in charge of this next week?"

"I don't know. I guess we'll cross that bridge when we get to it."

Her acknowledging smile had empathy behind it. Dwight was more than capable of handling this investigation and so was she, for that matter. But there were two dead girls—that they knew of. Regardless of how much each of them believed in their own capabilities, they couldn't risk more bodies piling up and they would need everyone on board, even if that meant Dwight would have to relinquish some control.

"Go on; it's damn near midnight," he said.

Her shoulders dropped at the sudden awareness. "I didn't pick up my car and they'll be closed now. I can take a cab."

"Don't be ridiculous. I completely forgot about your car troubles." Dwight shut down his computer and began to pack up. "I'll give you a lift."

"But you live in the opposite direction."

"I kept you here, I'll take you home. Now go and get your things. I should get out of here too."

THE SKIES WERE CLOUDED over and obscured the moon, which usually bounced light onto the bay where Nick's boat remained docked. He'd taken it out twice since making the purchase shortly after he was put on leave. It was an impulse buy, no doubt, and one he'd hoped would see him through the challenges he was facing. While he made it through by the skin of his teeth, the boat still bobbed in the water that seemed rougher than usual tonight.

Nick had recalled hearing about a hurricane that was due in from the Atlantic and that it might hit Florida and parts of Georgia. But it appeared to have brought a disturbance in the weather that now loomed above him as he sat on the lounge chair of his balcony.

It was late, almost midnight, but he couldn't sleep. Monday would bring a lot of issues to a head, both with ASAC Campbell and with his loyal team. He knew Jameson wanted a shot and he wanted to give it to him, but a case like Blackwater was a big deal, especially if things got worse, and things always got worse.

As he tossed back the few drops of what was once a Jack and Coke, Nick wanted to call Kate and get her take on the situation. She'd been working almost solely with Dwight for the past two months. He *was* her mentor.

Nick reached for his cell, which sat lifeless on the small glass-top table between the two lounge chairs. He held it in his hand, the black screen awaiting a decision. Going around Dwight wasn't really his style. He'd respected the man too much to play games. Calling Kate and asking her what Dwight was thinking was tantamount to passing a note in grade school that contained a question with a "yes" or "no" box written on it.

He unlocked the screen and pressed Dwight's contact button. Raising it to his ear, Nick waited for an answer, pretty confident he would pick up. The two were a lot alike in many ways and always being on standby was one of them.

"Jameson here," Dwight answered the call as he pulled into Kate's driveway.

Kate waited inside the car while he held the phone close, keeping the conversation strictly one-sided.

"Yeah, Nick, it's no problem. What's going on?" He turned to see Kate's growing concern at the unexpected call. A raised hand and slow nod suggested there was nothing for her to worry about. Still, she waited, unmoved.

"Hey, look, if that's how Campbell wants it, I don't have any issue with that. Come on, man. You know me better than that," Dwight continued. "I know and it's fine. Blackwater isn't going anywhere any time soon and I think we all know that." He looked at Kate for affirmation. "She's with me now, actually. Had some car troubles earlier and I was just giving her a lift home." Dwight paused again. "Just get yourself to the office Monday morning and this will all sort itself out, okay? My priority is to find out who killed those two girls. Nothing else matters to me right now. Good-night, Nick. Try to get some sleep." Dwight ended the call.

"What was that all about?" Kate asked.

"I don't know." Dwight shook his head. "He's just down, I think. Maybe he's nervous about coming back to work. I know he and Campbell have got some things to work through. But it was pretty clear he'd had a few, so he just needs to sleep it off, I think."

"Should we be worried about that, Dwight? It seems like that's been happening a lot lately."

"Can you blame the guy? He's been on forced admin leave for two months for some trumped-up internal investigation. Nick's the type of guy who needs to work. It keeps him occupied. He'll straighten his act out once he's back in the swing of things."

Kate pushed open the passenger door and stepped outside. "I hope you're right. Thanks for the ride, Dwight. Have a good weekend. You got the kids?"

"No. Not this weekend. Goodnight. I'll see you Monday unless we hear anything sooner."

THE WINDS and rain pounded with equally brutal force, but the brunt of the storm remained on the coast, as the weatherman had predicted. Nevertheless, Arlen was on a mission as he drove down the quiet road with his headlights off. It was late in the season for a hurricane, but Arlen was a firm believer in the idea that there was a reason for everything.

This was it: the old woman's house. He had done a pretty good job convincing Mrs. Hansby that her granddaughter should really stay with her in the event the storm got too bad. Of course, Lizbeth hadn't been in the room when he got to talking to her. Opportunity had presented itself once again.

He was pretty sure he'd had the old woman scared enough to insist Lizbeth stay with her and, as he pulled up to the house, he beamed at the sight of her car still parked out front. The sound of his approach would surely have been drowned beneath the howling winds and whipping tree limbs and the rain would offer even more cover to the noise that he'd have to make to get inside the house.

Arlen made sure he'd gotten the lay of the land earlier today. He knew where Mrs. Hansby's bedroom was as well as the guestroom where Lizbeth would most likely be sleeping. The two rooms were separated by a bathroom and a linen closet. Between the old woman's loss of hearing and the space between the rooms, he'd hoped that would be enough to get Lizbeth out without waking her grandmother. The noise from the storm was a bonus.

There was a reason for everything. He believed opportunities came to those who were patient, who had a plan, and were ready to follow through so as not to disappoint the gods who were kind enough to open the door.

He moved around to the side of the house where he'd left the bathroom window unlocked after he used the facilities earlier in the day. It was a small window, too small to board up, but he'd taped it, which presented no problem as he raised the single-hung frame. He was thin and knew he'd have no trouble slipping through the narrow opening. Pete, on the other hand, would've gotten stuck at his chest.

Arlen slipped through the window with ease but nearly lost his footing as he stepped on the outer rim of the porcelain toilet. The rain had made his shoes slick and it could have cost him his plan. Instead, he regained his footing and made his way inside, closing the window behind him. Covering up his tracks would be the real problem, but he had a plan for that too.

Looking into the mirror, Arlen pushed away his wet hair, but the waves bounced back and fell into his face. He grabbed a towel and patted himself dry. *Dry enough*, he thought. The bathroom door opened quietly and, at that moment, he was grateful the old house didn't creak at every turn. Someone had been maintaining the inside, at least. Perhaps it had been the woman's dutiful granddaughter. What was very noticeable, however, was the smell. It must have been the rain that brought it out because he hadn't noticed it earlier today. The damn place reeked of cat piss and he didn't remember seeing any cats. Maybe they were dead too, along with Grandpa.

He continued along the stunted hall in the darkness, the occasional flash of lightning illuminating his position. Only a few more steps until he reached her room. He inhaled a deep breath and pulled out the knife he'd tucked between his belt and his jeans. The thought of knocking her out with some sort of drug occurred to him, but then he'd have to drag her out. Arlen was well aware of his own lack of upper body strength and so opted to go for keeping her silent with the threat of a slice to the throat. Then, they could walk out together, nice and quiet.

The handle turned easily and he pushed open the door; again, no sound emerged to alert the presence of an intruder. There she was, sleeping on her side, facing the window opposite the door, her slender figure outlined by the light quilt that covered her. Her bleached-blonde hair was neatly pulled back into a ponytail.

His chest was beginning to heave with excitement and sweat formed on his brow. It was the most pleasurable feeling, almost on par with the orgasmic sensation that erupted inside him after he'd squeezed the life from them. Arlen swallowed hard and tried to keep his head on straight. Getting her out would take focus and strength.

Standing inches from her bed, he raised the blade from his side and bent down over her. Her legs moved and her arms flinched, but he continued lowering the blade until its steel rested against her neck. The moment it touched her, Lizbeth's eyes shot open, but she did not jerk her body around to see the intruder. Instead, she seemed to know what lay against her delicate skin and her body began to tremble.

"Lizbeth, it's time to go." Arlen's voice was just above a whisper, almost inaudible beneath the sound of the storm. "Now, just turn slowly and I'll help you up."

She turned to see the person who held the knife to her throat. Her eyes revealed immediate recognition, only second to the fear that came next.

8

F
ive hundred bucks was what they charged her. As Kate swiped her credit card at the cashier's desk, she turned to see them pull her car out to the front curb. Pocketing the receipt, Kate nodded to the woman behind the counter. "Thanks."

A man held the driver's side door open and Kate stepped inside. *At least they cleaned it,* she thought.

"Have a good day, ma'am." He closed the door.

On the drive home, Kate knew she would have to make some decisions—and soon. The date was fast approaching and the mere thought of it sent her to near panic. She wasn't ready to face the anniversary of Marshall's death. Perhaps it was the car trouble that was the catalyst for her current train of thought. Remembering all that had happened in the time she'd owned this little Toyota that, up until now, had been a pretty good car.

But how long could she financially sustain her current situation? Renting a home in an expensive neighborhood and now potentially facing the need to purchase a newer vehicle. These things seemed so mundane and benign in the face of her losses and in light of her current investigation. Nevertheless, an inevitability was approaching.

More than one hundred thousand dollars was sitting in a savings account, profits from the sale of Marshall's apartment in San Diego. Money she had refused to acknowledge, much less spend. And then there were still the occasional publishing offers, although it seemed they were waning, noting her previous rejections to write about her experiences with the notorious Joseph Hendrickson and the case that followed, bringing about the murder of her fiancé.

Yes, they were all interested in the tragic deaths that had followed Kate around for most of her life, setting her on a path she still follows today.

Marshall had never wanted her to write the story when the publishers first came calling and neither had she. So, to consider it out of financial necessity seemed most indecent. Not only that, she would have to reach out to Jarrod, Sam's widower, and while she had spoken to him a few times since leaving California, he'd moved on. Pulling him back into her nightmares—the same nightmares that caused the death of his wife—would be cruel.

The house was just ahead now. To leave this place would send her world spinning once again and Kate was hesitant of her ability to handle such a disturbance. It had taken her months to feel comfortable living here, no longer feeling as though she should look behind every door and walk around the perimeter, gun drawn, to be sure no one was waiting for her behind the trees.

Kate turned off the engine and sat in her car, now parked on the driveway. For a brief moment, she considered going home to see her parents for a few days, the few days that would be the hardest for her to face. But loneliness and grief were things that must be faced alone if she were to conquer them. She wasn't the naïve Katie Reid anymore, clinging on to dreams of a husband and children. For in this life she led, the monsters turned those dreams into nightmares.

THE TWISTED SMILE on Arlen Tucker's face turned grotesque as he slammed his hand over Lizbeth's mouth. "You'd best shut the fuck up now before I get really upset, you hear?"

Tears streamed down her cheeks as she nodded her compliance. No one would hear her screams anyway and certainly not this far into the nearly deserted neighborhood that had never been fully rebuilt after the big fire. "Not enough money," they said. "Economy's in the tank," they said. Never mind that it was now a place for bad people to do bad things.

"Now I'm gonna take my hand away, but if you make a sound, it'll be your last." He pulled his hand from her mouth, having pressed hard enough to leave finger marks behind. "See? That's not so bad, is it?" He stroked her hair, still pulled back in a pony-tail. "Shhh. It'll be all right." He pressed his hands against her shoulders to slow her trembling. "I want to show you something." Arlen reached over to the side table.

Lizbeth's eyes followed his movement as she sat still on the couch, his knees holding her legs in place.

He opened a photo album and set it on her lap, pointing to a picture of a young girl. "You see her? That's my sister. Her name was Charlie, short for Charlene. She's a pretty one, ain't she? Oh yes, the boys liked Charlie. Can you see the family resemblance?"

Lizbeth looked at Arlen but didn't answer, instead casting her eyes back down to the photograph.

"I truly loved my big sister, I truly did. And you know what?

She loved me too. That's right. She showed me just how much she loved me damn near every night." Arlen flipped a few more pages and stopped. A picture of a man and a woman, posing in front of a nondescript building, was the only one on the page.

"But you know, my daddy loved Charlene too, just like she loved me, oh yes he did." Arlen's eyes darkened and he grew silent, studying Lizbeth's features. "You look a little bit like her." He inhaled a deep breath, puffing out his scrawny chest and stroking his heavy beard. "The problem was, you see, Momma never took notice, or if she did, didn't really give a shit, but anyways, I didn't like what Daddy was doing to Charlene. It hurt my feelings." He stroked her hair again and let his hand slide down to her shoulders. He could feel Lizbeth tense beneath his touch. "Girls just don't seem to get me, I guess. Oh, they like to look at me. I'm an attractive man, so I been told. But when I look back, they just turn away." Arlen laughed. "I guess maybe I give them the creeps, I don't know. Do I give you the creeps, Lizbeth?"

With a face full of terror, Lizbeth shook her head. It seemed she thought that if she agreed with him, maybe he would reconsider. But what she didn't understand was that the man now known as Arlen Tucker didn't view her as someone with whom he wished to share any sort of relationship. He didn't view her as a woman, or even a person. Her existence was a minor inconvenience that would have to be dealt with. Once she was devoid of life, he could do what he wanted and that was to control her. That was all he really ever wanted from any of them.

"I can assure you," Arlen leaned in to within inches from her face, "I will before the night is through."

THE WFO WAS quiet as Nick made his way into the washroom. It was still early, six am early, but Nick wanted to get a jump on the day. His return would bring a lot of talk and probably a lot of changes. Straightening his tie and tugging on his jacket, Nick gave himself a final once-over and walked to the door in shoes that echoed on the slate-grey floor.

"Sir?" Nick said as he leaned into Campbell's open doorway.

"Scarborough, please, come in and welcome back." Campbell extended his hand to exchange a mutual greeting.

Nick unbuttoned his jacket and took a seat across from the man whom he believed brought about his preventable absence in the first place. But he said nothing and waited for instruction.

"Listen, um," Campbell scratched at his high forehead, "for whatever it's worth, I think this whole situation got blown way out of proportion and I'm sorry you got caught in the crossfire."

Nick pursed his lips and nodded. "Thank you, sir. I'm just glad to be back at work." He'd preferred to have said a few more choice words about the man's petty behavior just because he went to the Assistant Director to ask that Kate be assigned to the WFO. Instead, Nick wanted to keep his job, realizing now how easily it could all have slipped away.

"I'm sure you're wondering about the Blackwater investigation and where you stand on the matter of mentoring Agent Reid."

"It has crossed my mind." Nick intended a sincere tone and hoped it had been conveyed as such.

"I think it's best if you step back and let Agent Jameson continue to handle this with Reid. I'd like your role to be strictly as a consultant, leaving the fieldwork to the two of them and Agent Lyons in Atlanta along with his team."

"Sir, Agent Jameson has done a hell of a job working with me, but he's not the senior resident BAU agent. I am. And as such, I should be responsible for the investigation." Nick shifted in his seat. "If this is about Agent Reid…"

"Look," Campbell's face hardened in an instant, "whatever deal you struck with the Assistant Director to get Reid assigned here is between you two. Personally, I thought you had a little more faith in me than to pull a stunt like that."

"I wasn't trying to go behind your back…"

Campbell wasn't about to let Nick finish, though. "What's done is done, Scarborough. Agent Reid has proven herself to be an asset to this field office and to the BAU. You shouldn't have stepped in where her career was concerned. Point being, I'm not sure you can be objective when it comes to the Blackwater case. I may not have been in San Diego when it happened, but I know that when her fiancé died, you took it upon yourself to take her under your wing. But you and I both know she can't stay there if she's to become an agent who can make life-and-death decisions. I'd think you would know that better than most, Scarborough."

He was right. Jameson said the same thing months ago when they were in Richmond working on the trafficking case, but Nick didn't listen. Whether or not Campbell had an agenda, an almost certainty in Nick's mind only yesterday, had now come into question. "In all the field ops I've been involved in, never once have you questioned my intent. Why this time? I know what Hughes testified to, but we've been working together for a very long time. I guess I thought you had my back."

"And I thought you had mine." Campbell turned away, masked in frustration. He peered through the picture window that offered a stunning view of the city. "I want you to let Jameson take the lead on Blackwater. If the case starts floundering, we'll reevaluate the situation." He returned his attention to Nick. "You're a good agent—many would say great—but it was *my* call to assign an agent to this office, not yours and not the Assistant Director's.

Mine. I need to know that I can trust you again, Nick. And it'll be up to you to prove it to me."

"Yes, sir." Nick stood up and held out his hand. Campbell returned the greeting. "Thank you, sir." He closed the door behind him.

As he walked along the corridor, his eyes cast downward, Nick spotted a pair of women's dress flats, freshly polished. Attached were legs clad in grey pants, and as he continued to bring his eyes upwards, he noticed Kate's smiling face.

"Welcome back!" Instead of offering a hug, Kate greeted Nick with a handshake. "It's so good to have you back." She glanced at the file in her hand. "Do you have a minute? We should probably go over what Jameson and I have been discussing regarding Blackwater."

"Hang on a second, Kate." Nick thrust his hands in his pockets. "I'm not going to be working with you on this one. Jameson's going to take the lead."

"What? Why?"

"Just—it's time for Jameson to get his shot, okay? And, you will learn a lot from him, I promise you that."

"He's still punishing you, isn't he?"

Nick took hold of her arm. "Come on."

They continued to Nick's office and walked inside. "I'm not being punished." He was, of course, but she didn't need to know that, or how she might not even be at this office if it weren't for him. "Campbell thinks Jameson can handle this. He started it and the two of you, along with help from the Atlanta office and Myers, well, I have no doubt you'll find the man who killed those girls."

"What if we're dealing with more, Nick? I know that with these types of killings—this guy's not going to stop at just two. He's making a statement here and he's only just begun."

Nick folded his arms at his chest. "You see? You don't need

me, Kate. You're smart and so is Jameson." He headed toward his desk chair. "Besides, I've got mounds of administrative bullshit to sort through. I'll be occupied for weeks, I'm sure. I can still be a sounding board if you need one and Campbell said if things aren't developing or if the situation escalates, then he'll reevaluate. If I need to get involved, then I will."

Kate took a seat and stared at him for a moment. "Nick, you know what next week is." She turned away only briefly. "I need you by my side on this one."

"Jeez." He'd been so wrapped up in his own problems, he'd forgotten how near the date was. Now, as he looked into Kate's eyes, he could see that fragile woman he held in his arms only a year ago, trying hard to help her keep her footing when the doctor told her Marshall was gone. "Kate, I'm still here for you, you know that. I am your friend. I just have to step back on this case. But please don't mistake that for me stepping back from our friendship. You have no idea how much you mean to me, Kate, especially these past couple of months. You've stood beside me, you've listened to me whine when I've had too much to drink. I will be here for you whenever you need me."

Kate pushed off the chair. "Yeah, okay." She looked down, a thin white line forming on her lips as they pressed together. "I'd better catch up with Jameson." She began to turn but stopped short. "Oh, I'm assuming he'll want to hear from you that he'll continue to be lead on Blackwater." She reached the door.

"Kate?"

"Yeah?" A quick turn on her heel revealed irritation, or maybe it was just disappointment.

"Never mind. I'll go talk to Jameson."

Only a moment after Kate left Nick's office, his cell phone vibrated on his waist. Sliding it out of its holster, he answered, "Scarborough here."

"Agent Scarborough, this is Agent Lyons in the Atlanta office."

"Yes, sir. Hello. It's been a very long time, Agent Lyons. I don't think we've seen each other since I left Atlanta. How are you? What can I do for you?" Nick switched on his computer.

"It's good to hear your voice, Scarborough. I was informed that you would be back from leave today."

"That is correct." The FBI emblem appeared on his screen along with login fields to type in his credentials.

"Great. Listen, about the Blackwater investigation...."

Nick cut him short. "I'm sorry, Lyons, but it appears as though Jameson and Reid will be handling that investigation."

"Oh. I was under the impression that on your return, you would be taking over things?"

"No, sir. Jameson will be the lead on this one. He's a hell of an agent; don't worry. I have full confidence in his abilities and Reid's."

"Well, okay. I suppose I ought to get in touch with Jameson, then. I have some information I need to pass along. Agent Myers has come up with a very compelling profile on the unsub and he should take a look."

Nick was quiet for a moment. "Right, of course. Jameson mentioned he'd asked Myers to take a look at the file last week. So, I understand that you're already familiar with Myers' work. How do you know her?" He had no idea if Lyons was aware that he and Georgia had been seeing each other and so was trying to disguise any suggestion of the fact.

"I worked with her on a case several months back."

Nick tried to think of when she might have been working a case in Atlanta.

"Just a consult, but we hit it off pretty well and so I was, of course, happy to have her draft something up for me on this deal. I heard she was instrumental in profiling the Highway Hunter investigation you worked on last year?"

"She was, yes. Well, I'll let you get back to it. I'm sure Jameson will be eager to hear of any new information you have on Blackwater. It was good talking to you again, Lyons."

"You too, Scarborough."

Nick set his phone on his desk and began to replay the conversation he'd had with Georgia just the other night when he mentioned Lyons. Not one word from her that she knew him and had worked with him.

He unlocked the screen on his phone again and began flicking through the photos until he came upon his most recent one of Georgia. They'd been out on his boat, only one of the two times, but it had been a great day, that he recalled. Her windblown hair, a sweater wrapped around her shoulders because it was chilly on the water. She was smiling and she looked beautiful as always.

Maybe it had slipped her mind—working with Lyons before. After all, she worked on several cases—some were more involved than others—but she was one of the best profilers they had and so was called upon many times. Yes, that must be it. He'd been sitting at home for too long, and with the conversation with Campbell fresh in his mind, it was just his paranoia. Georgia wouldn't keep anything from him. They didn't have that sort of relationship.

He pressed Georgia's contact and raised the phone to his ear. She was out of town again, although couldn't remember where this time. Philadelphia? Even he was prone to forgetting things and that was all this was.

"Hey, you at work?" Georgia asked immediately upon answering.

"Yes, I am. I just wanted to ask you a quick question..."

Georgia cut him off. "I'm sorry, I'm knee-deep in something right now. Can I call you back?"

"Of course, no problem. I'll talk to you later."

Georgia ended the call and walked out of the hotel bathroom, a towel wrapped around her chest, still dripping from the shower.

"So, I just got off the phone with Scarborough." Lyons was puffing on a cigarette, still lying naked in bed. "He was asking how you and I knew each other."

9

The news Agent Lyons wanted to share with Scarborough, and now Agent Jameson was that his office was able to confirm the identities of the two victims. Jameson was now waiting for copies of the forensics reports. "Kate, you have a minute?" He approached her as she sat at her desk.

"Sure. What's going on?" She turned for a moment and pointed at the screen. "I've been able to rule out the schools whose logos and mascots don't correspond with that on the second victim's shirt, but I'm still going through the list."

"Why don't we talk in my office?" On their arrival, Dwight closed the door while Kate took a seat. "I just got off the phone with Agent Lyons. He's sending the labs over to us now, but it appears as though they've been able to identify both victims." Dwight sat down at his desk.

"Why don't you seem happy about this?" Kate noticed his demeanor. "Oh, you talked to Nick, didn't you?"

"I did."

"Me too. But you know, this is a good thing for you. You deserve to be the front man on this, Dwight." She rarely called him by his first name, especially not at the office. However, over the past couple of months, since they'd been working more closely together, she finally began to feel more comfortable and he always insisted she address him in such a manner.

"It's not that. Not really. Lyons also mentioned that Agent Myers had compiled a profile for our review."

"Great. Where is it?"

"He's sending it over with the forensics." He looked away for a moment.

"What is it, then? I mean, it sounds like we're making progress here, right?"

"We are. I don't know. It was something Nick said earlier. And after talking to Lyons, well..." He turned back to Kate. "Doesn't matter. When I get the information, I'll let you know. If we can find out where they lived, where they went missing, it'll narrow things down for us quite a bit."

"I agree. Okay, I'll keep working on my list in the meantime." Kate stood up to leave.

"Hey, um—if you need a few days off—I'm sure that won't be a problem," Dwight said.

"Nick told you, did he?" Kate returned a doleful smile.

"Yes, but he didn't need to. I was there too, remember? It's not something that could ever be forgotten."

"I'd rather not leave in the middle of an investigation and, besides, I'm better off keeping my mind on work." She headed toward the door. "Thank you, Dwight."

∾

ARLEN PUSHED the comb through his thick, black hair and slapped some aftershave on his face as he stood in front of the bathroom mirror. His beard was slightly more kempt. His shift was due to start in less than two hours. That didn't allow for much time to prepare his guest. Perhaps that would have to wait until tonight. He preferred not to rush these things.

Stepping out of the bathroom, Arlen walked back along the hall and into the living room where Lizbeth waited. "I'm going to have to leave for work soon, so I'm going to need you to keep quiet while I'm gone."

He approached her. "But that shouldn't be a problem, now should it, Lizbeth?" He squatted down. "I'll get you all dolled up after I get home, I promise."

The ponytail she wore was now hanging half in and half out, so Arlen placed his hand on her head to smooth it back. Leaning in to kiss her forehead, he closed his eyes and let his lips take in the salty smooth skin that had already grown cold. As he pulled back, he looked into her lifeless, bloodshot eyes. "Yep. We'll finish what we started when I get back tonight." His hand slid down to her crotch and he squeezed as hard as he could.

Arlen got back on his feet and walked toward the front door, grabbing his keys on the way out. "See you later, sweetheart."

Last night's storm was a distant memory now, save for the mud and silt that covered what little asphalt remained on the neglected street. Turned out not to have been as big of a deal as the weather guy predicted. By the time it hit land, the hurricane diminished substantially and the more inland it traveled, the weaker it became. Just a few inches of rain was all it dropped by the time it reached Arlen's home. Guess the old woman didn't need to board up her windows after all. *Opportunity.*

Arlen surveyed the area and felt like a god. What few houses comprised this burnt-down community were his. No one knew he was here, no one cared. And he could do whatever the fuck he wanted. It was that euphoric feeling that he craved so much. Unfortunately, it didn't ever last long enough and, in fact, seemed to fade much quicker with each victim.

His truck sat in the driveway and Arlen knew it was time to leave. Sure it was risky showing up for work, but it would have been riskier not to. Even if Mrs. Hansby had reported Lizbeth missing, he'd left nothing behind to draw the police to him. As far as they knew, he went back to work after the installation with Pete and left for home at the end of his shift. Arlen parted his lips in a wide grin as he stepped inside his pickup. He was smarter than all those sons of bitches.

The reception on his radio was shoddy this far out, but as he neared town, the music came in clear as he sang along. He began to prepare himself in the event questions were raised regarding the disappearance of the young and beautiful Lizbeth Hansby. As far as he was concerned, the police were much too incompetent to make any sort of connection. Sure, they'd find DNA evidence, fingerprints, and such, that he'd been at the old woman's house, but he was on an install, so no further explanation was needed.

By the time he arrived at work, he'd been confident of his story should the need arise to tell one. And, in the event the heat became too much, he'd simply take up roots, but his arrogance denied any such possibility.

It was the last school on her list and still—nothing. The search would need to be widened, but just how wide? Kate wondered if Dwight had received the information on the victims yet. Perhaps understanding where they were from would help—where they went missing. They needed something more to go on before another body turned up in the river.

The river. Kate began to type on her keyboard with determined speed thanks to an idea that sparked. She opened the case files and pulled up the sheriff's report from Baker County where the first victim had been discovered. Leaning closer to the screen, she read the scanned-in documents. The report indicated the victim had been in the river for a length of time yet to be determined by the coroner's office, but estimated to have been twelve days. It was also assumed that the victim traveled downstream and that the origination of her point of entry was in the Okefenokee Swamp. Indicators such as flora attached to the victim's body suggested this was a fact.

That was why the case had been turned over to the Atlanta office. Charlton County, Georgia, and Baker County, Florida agreed that as it appeared the victim was killed in Georgia, Atlanta should handle the investigation. But what if they were wrong? Kate needed to see the forensics to be sure.

She got to her feet and walked back to Dwight's office, noticing Nick's door was closed. Hesitating for a moment, Kate considered knocking but thought better of it and headed again on the path to her intended destination. "Jameson?" she asked, standing in his doorway.

"Come in, please."

Kate blew out a heavy, exasperated breath as she lowered herself into the chair. "I went through this list. Nothing. Not one of them matches our second victim's shirt."

"Okay." It seemed Dwight sensed there was more coming.

"But what if we aren't looking in the right place? Did you get the forensics and Myers' report yet?"

"As a matter of fact, yes. I was just beginning to review everything now. So this is good timing. Pull your chair over here and let's take a look." Dwight patted the corner of his desk.

"Do we know where the victims lived?" Kate squeezed in next to Dwight.

"According to Lyons, victim number one, who has now been identified as nineteen-year-old Sydney Hawthorne, lived in Valdosta. She was reported missing after she didn't show up for work. That's a fair distance from the swamp, assuming that was where her body was dumped."

"Right. And what about the other victim?" Kate leaned in to get a better view of the monitor while Dwight retrieved the other file.

"Okay, looks like the other victim was a twenty-two-year-old named Ariel Nadal. She's a native Puerto Rican, moved to Georgia with her family back in 2000. Reported missing three weeks ago by her family. They live in Hinesville." Dwight looked at Kate. "That's even further from the swamp."

"Can you pull up Myers' profile of the unsub?" Kate asked.

Dwight typed in a few more commands. "She prefaced this with the fact that it was developed prior to her viewing the forensics report and only having utilized the sheriff's and coroner's information."

"So does that mean this won't do us any good?"

"No. It means she'll go back and modify as needed once she has an opportunity to review the new findings. But for now, this is what she wrote." Dwight zoomed in on the document.

"The first and perhaps most obvious similarity is the age of the two victims. Both are in early adulthood. In addition to that would be the geographic locations in which the victims were discovered. Following along those lines, as well as considering two crucial elements to ascertain whether or not we can label such incidents as

serial killings, one must consider that the killings involved similar sexual mutilation, and a significant "cooling off" period occurred between the deaths. Although each victim was discovered within less than two weeks of each other, it appears as though their deaths occurred within a larger timespan – approximately six weeks of one another. And given the nature of the mutilations, there is clear intent to draw focus on the killer's message. It suggests the killer suffered previous sexual abuse that likely bordered on the extreme. These are prime indicators that these deaths can be labeled serial killings and that it would not be outside the realm of possibilities to consider that this killer, or perhaps killers is/are not finished killing."

Kate leaned back and shook her head. "We know who these girls are now, but as far as you know, there was no foreign DNA found on either victim?"

"No, although I'd like to talk to the coroner and send whatever samples they have to the BAU lab," Dwight began. "But my guess is, because they were in the water for so long, and from what I understand, that particular river—a black water river—contains high levels of acidity, there may not be any DNA to find. Which leaves us with few leads except to talk to the people who were the last to see our victims."

"Do you think Agent Lyons' team has already reached out to them?" Kate asked.

"Possibly. I'll find out. I'd prefer if they just turn things over for us to handle. This is our gig and while we need to coordinate our efforts, we're the ones who should be talking to the families."

"Of course." Kate paused for a moment. "What do you think about this whole thing with Nick? Him not being involved in this. He's the resident agent."

"I know." Dwight shook his head. "It's a crock of shit if you ask me, but if we need him on an advisory basis, and according to Campbell, that's all he'll be available for, then we'll consult with him." He turned back to the monitor and closed the file. "In the meantime, why don't you set something up so we can talk to the victims' families? Maybe someone else saw this guy. It's about all we've got to go on right now."

"Sure thing." Kate stood. "I was thinking maybe we should take Nick to lunch today since it's his first day back. What do you think?" It was a meager gesture, but one she hoped would lift Nick's mood a little. She understood that it was going to be very hard for him to take a back seat to this. If she was in his shoes, she wouldn't handle it well either.

"I think he's got some other things he's working on today. Probably best to leave him to settle back in."

"Okay. I'll get to work on organizing a trip back to Atlanta. Should we plan on heading out in the morning?"

"Yes. Thanks, Kate."

No one raised a single eyebrow, just as Arlen predicted. He knew he was smarter than all of them and this time was no exception. He'd gone about his day, working diligently as always, keeping his nose to the grindstone. Now it was time to head home and finish what he'd started. He could take his time because there would be no pleas for mercy, no screams, nothing to distract him from the precision he needed to do it right.

"I'm punching out," he said to the two co-workers stacking lumber. "I'll see y'all in two days."

A canopy of purple and orange draped over the skies as Arlen walked out of the building and into the parking lot. He shoved a hand into his pants pocket to retrieve the keys and noticed a squad car pulling up to the front. Careful not to appear alarmed, he continued to his truck, nodding to the officers who stepped out. At that moment, he was grateful to not be wearing his apron because he now looked like a customer and nothing more. The officers returned the gesture and walked inside the store.

Arlen picked up his pace, feeling his heart skip a beat. He made it to the truck and inserted the key into the lock. Jumping inside, he turned the ignition, all the while glancing at the store's entrance. "Everything's all right," he told himself. "Everything's all right."

With a final turn of his head; no uniformed men had yet to reemerge and Arlen pulled away. It wasn't unusual for cops to come to the store anyway. Lots of people shoplifted, he thought. That could have just as easily been the situation. He needed to calm himself down. Regain control. Always stay in control. The deep, calming breath set him right again and Arlen continued home to finish taking care of business.

The skies turned to black by the time he reached the turnoff to his little slice of heaven. Thoughts of police officers were beginning to fade as he cut the truck's engine and stepped out onto his driveway. First things first; the generator needed to be refilled. Arlen made his way around the side of the house to a shed and retrieved a couple of gas cans. He always kept five-gallon containers on hand. Once things started to cool down, he didn't use as much. And it seemed with that storm, it might have finally brought the fall weather.

The generator sat beneath the covered patio off the back of the kitchen. It wasn't too loud, at least, from inside the house. If anyone else were to cruise along his street, they'd probably hear it running. But why would anyone ever come down here? He poured the fuel into the generator's engine.

Once inside, he washed his hands and changed his clothes. Now the fun could begin. And as luck would have it, Lizbeth was exactly where he left her. "Come on, sweetheart." He tucked his arms beneath hers and hoisted her from the couch. "Damn, you are heavier than you look."

He carried her into the kitchen where a sheet of plastic covered the floor. "You just lay down right here, okay?" He raised back up. "Now don't you go nowhere." A smile played on his lips— a wicked smile that looked like it came from the devil himself.

A toolbox he kept in a cabinet below the sink rattled as he placed it on the kitchen table. Upon opening it, its contents glimmered beneath the overhanging light. He was nothing if not meticulous about his implements. He bent over to see his reflection bouncing back at him. His face was pale and showed the sweat running down his temples. He reached for the blade that was sharpened with surgical precision and moved to Lizbeth. "I promise you, this won't hurt a bit."

10

Working on this investigation without Nick was a difficult adjustment for Kate. As they prepared to leave the Atlanta office and travel south to speak with the victims' families, her comfort zone had dramatically narrowed. Her reliance on Nick was too great. She hadn't been able to get hold of him last night or this morning, only reaching his voicemail. He wasn't answering any text messages either. This caused a deeper anxiety within her. The topic had been broached with Dwight, but he shrugged it off, a highly suspect reaction coming from him. Something was going on and they were both leaving her in the dark.

"You ready to go?" Dwight asked, peeking his head into Agent Lyons' office.

She'd been waiting for his return as well as Lyons' and had been sitting in his office for an uncomfortable length of time. Kate was more than ready to leave. "Yes." She arose and retrieved her laptop bag from the small conference table inside the office. Lyons' seniority was evident from his plush surroundings and sheer square footage of office space.

"Where are we going first?" Kate followed Dwight into the expansive corridor lined with closed doors.

"We'll head to Valdosta first and speak to Sydney Hawthorne's mother. Her father is deceased." Dwight stepped quickly through the hall toward the lobby. "Lyons is waiting for us out front."

"Have you been able to get in touch with Nick today?" Kate struggled to keep up with his pace.

"No. We'll touch base with him when we get back tonight. I see Lyons up ahead." Dwight stopped and turned to Kate. "Remember that you and I are the lead investigators on this, okay? Not Lyons. He's not running the show here. I am."

"Understood." Something was definitely going on. Dwight wasn't a man to shy away from taking the lead on anything, but he seemed quite adamant about Lyons' place in the pecking order.

"We've already spoken to the mother, and she's identified her daughter," Lyons began, pushing the door that led to the parking garage. "She's also already given a statement. So, let's just remember to go a little easy on her. The woman just lost her daughter."

Kate peered at Lyons as though he was some kind of alien. Did he really think they didn't know how to question a victim's family? From their first meeting, she disliked this man, and he wasn't doing himself any favors right now to change that opinion.

"We're well aware of the situation. This isn't our first rodeo," Dwight replied.

Kate sensed his irritation and unveiled a furtive grin.

THE COMMUTER PLANE landed with ease after the hour-long flight. Kate disliked flying as a rule of thumb anyway, but the fifty-seater, no matter how smooth a flight it offered, still raised the hairs on the back of her neck.

"How far is it from here?" Kate attempted to make conversation after what had been a quiet flight. Tensions were high and fueled further speculation that something had happened within the two federal teams and no one had bothered to fill her in on the details.

"Just a few minutes." Lyons stepped into the aisle as the passengers began to deplane. "I have a car waiting."

It had been a very long time since Kate had spoken to a victim's family. Not since Ashley Davies when she'd gone back to deliver the girl's locket to her family—the same locket that saved Kate's life. And, she'd been with Nick that day. He helped her through it. Now she was about to face a mother who'd lost her daughter to yet another monster. Only this one was still on the loose—and was likely still killing.

"This is the place." Agent Lyons pulled alongside the curb and stopped the engine.

"Does she know there is another victim?" Kate asked.

"She knows," Lyons replied.

"I can only imagine she's not feeling too confident in the FBI's abilities to catch the killer before he takes another life." Dwight pushed open the passenger door and stepped out, peering into the bright noonday sky.

"We're doing the best we can, Jameson," Lyons replied.

"I'm sure that will bring her great comfort."

Kate approached Dwight and waited with him on the sidewalk. "You okay?" His irritation was palpable and she needed to reel him in.

"I'm fine." He turned his shoulder on Lyons while he exited

the car. "I just don't think he needs to be here. This is our deal now."

"It's his town, though," Kate replied.

"Maybe. I just think we'd be better off handling this on our own."

"Shall we go inside?" Lyons asked, locking up the car. He took the lead to the front door of the home and rapped gently on the heavy screen door.

Dwight and Kate brought up the rear, standing behind Lyons when a woman answered.

"Mrs. Hawthorne? Nice to see you again. May we come inside?"

The woman opened the screen door and Kate was able to see her clearly now, beyond the shadowing effects of the darkened foyer. The woman was pale, dark circles under her eyes, and thin. Very thin. She couldn't have been older than forty-five, which would have made her younger than Kate by a few years when she'd had her daughter, Sydney.

"Please, come in."

"Thank you." Lyons turned around. "These are Special Agents Dwight Jameson and Kate Reid. They're with the department that specializes in these types of investigations."

She eyed them as they walked through the door into the quaint country home.

Kate could almost feel the mother's skepticism and couldn't fault her for it. "Thank you, ma'am, and I'm so sorry for your loss." She extended her hand in hopes Mrs. Hawthorne would see that her words were sincere.

The woman looked at Kate's hand for a moment. Her eyes appeared so tired and dry, likely unable to produce any more tears at all. Finally, she returned the handshake. "Thank you, Agent

Reid, I appreciate that. Please, come and have a seat in here." She led the way to the kitchen table.

Kate smiled at the décor. Clearly, the woman was fond of pigs and sheep. It was nice to see something so normal in this world of killers and their prey.

"Can I get any of you something to drink? Water, coffee, or iced tea?" Mrs. Hawthorne opened a cupboard and retrieved some glasses.

"Water for me, thank you," Dwight replied.

Kate walked toward her. "Let me give you a hand." Her smile was warm and it seemed the woman was grateful for the offer.

"You're my guest. You just have a seat and I'll get you something."

"Water for me as well, then. Thank you, Mrs. Hawthorne."

"Of course. Please, call me Janice."

"Thank you, Janice." Kate returned to the kitchen table where Jameson and Lyons were already seated.

The tray of glasses trembled in the woman's hands as she carried it to the table, setting it down slowly so as not to spill, given her nerves that were clearly shot. When she finally sat down, the hard part began.

"Mrs. Hawthorne—Janice, can you tell me when you last saw your daughter and when you realized she'd gone missing?" Dwight maintained a professional yet compassionate tone.

She looked at Lyons. "As I told Agent Lyons, Sydney lived on her own in the apartments on Milner Street."

"Yes, that's right," Lyons interrupted. "We've already collected evidence from the building." He directed his words to Dwight.

"Okay. But she usually contacted you on a daily basis, is that right?"

Janice nodded.

"And you hadn't heard from her the morning of her disappearance before her shift started."

"No. I just figured she'd gotten busy, although it was certainly out of the ordinary."

"Okay. Did Sydney have a boyfriend?"

"She'd recently broken up with a boy from her work at the coffee shop. But that was some time ago—maybe a month prior, at least."

"We've spoken with the ex-boyfriend. He requested different shifts so as not to conflict with hers since their breakup, so he hadn't spoken with her," Lyons interrupted once again.

"Look," Mrs. Hawthorne cast her gaze toward the window that fronted the kitchen and looked upon the quiet street, "I've already answered these questions. Agent Jameson, why are you here? Do you have any leads or any suspects regarding the murder of my daughter?"

Dwight inhaled deeply as he cast glances at both Kate and Lyons. "Mrs. Hawthorne, I can't imagine what you are going through and I'm very sorry to call on you again to answer questions that you've already been asked. However, if I am to be sure I have all of the information, it is essential that I understand the circumstances surrounding Sydney's disappearance." He paused again. "At the moment, no, I do not have any new leads."

Kate wanted to say something about the junior high school shirt victim 2 wore, but that wouldn't help his cause.

"What I'm trying to establish right now is a pattern of behavior. Not your daughter's, but of the person who took her. That's the best place to start. So what I'm looking for is whether or not Sydney's murder was opportunistic or if it was planned. Did she know her killer? Who did she hang around with?"

Mrs. Hawthorne's shoulders dropped and her face softened. Dwight's message was getting through. His intention was not to have her repeat answers, but hopefully to find additional clues. "I understand, Agent Jameson. I apologize."

"You don't owe anyone an apology, Mrs. Hawthorne." Dwight scanned through information on his iPad before continuing. "Where did your daughter attend junior high, or middle school?"

"Let me think. We moved here in '06, so she was ten. The following year, she would've been in middle school, and that would have been," her eyes raised toward the ceiling. "She went to Madison Middle School."

"What about her job? Did she ever mention anyone in particular at work? Maybe someone she didn't feel comfortable around?"

"No, she never said anything to me if that was the case."

"Do we have any video from the coffee shop?" Dwight asked Lyons.

"Yes."

"I'd like to get a copy of the previous two weeks' worth of surveillance. There may be something there that will help." Dwight returned his attention to Mrs. Hawthorne. "If there's anything you can think of, no matter how insignificant you believe it might be, please, don't hesitate to contact me." He retrieved one of his business cards and slid it across the table. "We're going to visit the coffee shop now and we'll be here all day if you think of anything."

A deflated-looking Dwight closed the file on his iPad. "Thank you, Mrs. Hawthorne. You've been very helpful. I think that's all I need today." Dwight pushed back from his seat and stood up. Kate and Lyons followed.

Mrs. Hawthorne walked them to the front door. "Agent Jameson, you have no idea who killed my daughter, do you?"

"No, ma'am. I don't. Not yet." He extended his hand. "Thank you and either Agent Lyons or I will keep you updated on any development in the investigation. Again, I am so sorry for your loss."

She returned the greeting.

The agents returned to Lyons' rental car, stepping inside to leave.

"How old is our other victim?" Dwight asked.

Kate pulled up the information immediately on her own iPad. "Twenty-two."

Lyons started up the car and pulled back out onto the road.

"So, both victims are roughly the same age. Dammit." Dwight turned toward the passenger window.

"What is it?" Kate sensed his frustration, but he couldn't have believed this meeting would have resolved much, if anything. He knew it was never that easy.

"I don't know." He turned toward the back seat where Kate sat. "There's something about the whole middle-school, junior high school—whatever the hell you want to call it—connection. Why would the killer go through the trouble of redressing his victims after he'd carved them up?"

In her mind's eye, Kate saw an image of Sydney Hawthorne— her entire groin area removed with surgical precision. A detail that was intentionally not brought up in front of the mother. She'd already seen the condition of her daughter's body and certainly didn't need to be reminded. "And in a tween's clothing," she added. Although Sydney Hawthorne hadn't been wearing anything so obvious as a school t-shirt, she had been wearing too-small clothing that appeared to have come from the children's section of a department store. That, along with the fact that the clothes were also outdated, brought even more confusion to the case.

"Maybe this asshole was teased in middle school?" Lyons said as he continued along the highway, heading to the coffee shop.

"By girls?" Kate asked. "Maybe. This is a highly charged sexual crime. He's removing the groin to make a statement and it's directed toward women."

Dwight returned his gaze to the front as the car continued along a two-lane stretch of highway surrounded by walls of greenery on either side. "He's retaliating for something. We just need to figure out what it is."

NICK HAD no solid evidence to suggest Georgia had betrayed him. And he was a man who based his decisions almost exclusively on evidence. This time, it was his gut telling him she was hiding something. Her omission of the fact that she knew Lyons was the first red flag. The fact that Lyons seemed to flaunt in his face that he knew Georgia and had worked with her in the past was the second, and that was what really set his mind to thoughts of infidelity. Thoughts that festered all day. With his team still in Atlanta, Nick had nothing to do but dwell upon the idea.

His only choice was to leave the office and go to her apartment. She was coming home tonight after consulting on an investigation in Philadelphia; at least, that was what she told him.

"Stop," he demanded of himself, perched on the edge of her ridiculously long and uncomfortable sofa sectional. Condemning her without hearing her defense wasn't the kind of man he wanted to be. Nick swallowed the last of his drink and waited for her arrival.

The luxurious apartment high above the city conveyed light from below and reflected it inside the windows. Nick sat in near-darkness, except for that light with his back to the front door, now rolling the empty highball glass between his palms. He knew he was drinking too much and had been since all of this started—

maybe even before then. Was that the reason for her duplicity, or was it that he was no longer the golden boy in the WFO? That he'd broken protocol and gone over the head of his ASAC to get Kate assigned to his office. "Stop!" His raised tone did little to squelch the voices in his head.

Finally, the agonizing minutes of being alone with his thoughts ended. The sound of a key in the door had signaled her arrival. Nick debated whether to stand and face her as she entered or to remain seated, his back to her. Seemed absurd to consider something so minute. Of course, this whole situation felt absurd and so to understand how to handle it was beyond his grasp at the moment.

"Hey, sweetheart. I didn't know you were going to be here." Georgia closed the door behind her and began walking toward Nick, arms open. "I can't tell you how good it is to see you."

Nick stood up as she approached. His heart raced at the sight of her. All thoughts fled from his mind. All the words, so abundant as they perpetrated doubt—vanished. His arms remained bent at the elbow and his hands clung to the empty glass that served as a buffer between them. He would have to say something. "Welcome home." He leaned into her embrace without lowering the protective barrier, resulting in an awkward and cold greeting.

Georgia pulled back, her face masked in bewilderment. "Are you okay? Did something happen at the office today?" She stepped back and placed her handbag on the side table, then proceeded to walk into the kitchen. "Looks like you could use a refill. Why don't we sit down outside and you can catch me up on your first few days back?"

Nick had to force his legs to move. His reaction to seeing her face after thoughts of betrayal swirled through his head was more severe than he'd expected, never mind that his expectations were fraught with inconsistencies by this point. He put one foot in front of the other until he reached the kitchen where she stood, smiling, pouring each of them a drink. The words at last came to him. The burning question that begged to be asked was sitting on the edge of his tongue. But he was afraid to know the truth. A man who faced death and danger for the better part of his career was afraid of the words his girlfriend would say. "Why didn't you tell me you knew Jack Lyons?"

There it was— dangling in the air between them—the question she had to know would eventually come.

Only her eyes moved up to meet his, her head still lowered, she set down the bottle of booze. It sounded as though she'd begun to suck all the air from the room, seemingly to prepare a retort, but what came out was a whimper. And then with her eyes closed in a slow blink, she devised an answer.

"I figured it was you he was talking to yesterday morning." She stepped out from behind the kitchen island and was only inches from Nick, who stood half a foot taller. "I won't lie to you."

He'd wanted to roll his eyes because he knew now what was coming—a barrage of excuses as to why she did what she did. "Then don't. Don't lie to me."

"I met him a while back. We were working on a case together. This was before you and I started seeing each other. We made a mistake one night after getting a break on the investigation. It was just the one time and then, after the case was over, we didn't keep in touch."

"Until?"

"Until he called me after he'd heard about what happened with you that night during the raid. I guess he'd heard we were together."

Nick grunted. Word traveled fast in this business when things went south during a takedown. "So, what? You thought since I was out of commission that you would pick things back up with him?"

"No. Of course not." Georgia's eyes glistened. "It wasn't like that at all. It was just—things got complicated. You weren't yourself. Drinking, depressed. For Christ's sake, you bought a boat. I didn't know what to do."

"Well, fucking someone else probably wasn't the best solution." A disparaging grin appeared on his lips. "It wouldn't have been on my top ten list of ideas." He turned away, stepping back into the open living area.

She quietly moved toward him, touching his shoulder as he remained with his back to her. "I'm so sorry. I never meant for this to happen."

He turned back and tried hard to remember why he loved her. "Are you in love with him?" His eyes searched hers for the truth.

"I don't know—maybe."

11

Although standard operating procedure, questioning the families did little to further the investigation. But Kate had been down this road before and understood that no detail could be overlooked. They couldn't rely on the interviews conducted by the Atlanta field office and Agents Lyons and Faulkner. She was sure they were good enough at their jobs, but they weren't BAU.

Kate was in awe of the way Dwight handled the families. They hadn't really worked this closely before and so she'd mainly learned Nick's systems and methodologies. But Dwight was different—perhaps cooler-headed. She understood now why the two of them worked so well together. They were opposites who complemented one another, but her place in this inner-agency triangle remained to be seen as she had yet to carve her own path.

"Can I talk to you for a second?" The breakroom was quiet when Dwight approached Kate, who was stirring sugar into her coffee.

"Sure." On the way to his office, Kate noticed Nick hadn't

arrived yet. His office lights were off and as it was almost eight a.m. Considering this was his first week back and he was prone to starting no later than seven o'clock, it was very curious and only added to the sensation she'd felt yesterday—that her friends were keeping something from her. "Have you heard from Scarborough yet this morning? I'm surprised he's not in."

Without turning, Dwight replied, "No. I'm sure he'll be in soon."

The chance that Dwight wouldn't know Nick's whereabouts was slim at best and only served to confirm what she already suspected.

"I would like for you to run on something." Dwight waited for Kate to head inside and followed closely behind.

"Sure. What is it?"

"After I got home last night from the airport, I couldn't sleep, so I started to do a little work. You remember when I asked the roommate about Ariel Nadal's arrival in the States?"

"Yeah, I think so. What about it?" Kate perched on the edge of his desk.

"Well, she mentioned, as did the paperwork from Atlanta, that her family moved to Georgia in 2000."

"Right, I remember that."

"She also said that Ariel had spent some time in Florida with relatives after the family initially moved. And this would have been around the time Ariel would have been in middle school."

"Her roommate did say she lived with relatives when she was twelve and then moved back in with her parents again after whatever issue they were having financially." Kate considered what he was getting at and she soon began to realize his idea would involve a much wider search.

Dwight leaned back in his chair and folded his arms over his broad chest. "I don't know. I just gotta think there's a reason why both victims wound up being discovered on the Florida side of the river. That just seems—extraordinary, considering everyone seems to think the bodies were dumped in a swamp several miles away."

"The forensics do suggest that. So, what are you getting at? You think the bodies were dumped in the swamp, then recovered and placed in a location that would ensure they were found farther along the river? Seems like a lot of work and to what end?"

"That's the question, isn't it? Assuming I'm right and, at this point, I have no real basis to make that conclusion. However, I wouldn't mind ruling it out. I think you should go down and talk to that sheriff's deputy in Baker County. Maybe he can let us know if we're way off base or not."

"Sounds good. You want me to go on my own?"

"Are you telling me you can't handle that?" He raised his brow.

"Not at all. I can most definitely handle it. When should I leave?" She'd almost blown her first shot at taking the reins on a lead, a mistake that would never happen again.

"Get hold of the sheriff first, tell him what you've got planned, then set it up. I'd like it to happen no later than tomorrow if you can arrange it. We don't have time to sit by while this maniac kills someone else's kid."

"Thank you. I'll get it done." Kate walked out of his office with a confident swagger she rarely displayed. It had occurred to her, however, that Dwight was either unconvinced of the validity of his own lead and thought what harm could it do to have her check on it, or he wanted to give her a chance to handle this on her own and see what she could do. She hoped that the latter was true.

Her concerns detracted her momentarily from the sight of Nick walking into his office. "There you are. I thought maybe you'd forgotten that you worked here." A weak attempt at humor that did not go over well. It was then that the hairs on her neck raised. "Everything all right?"

"I didn't think there was much point in rushing in this morning when I don't have a case to work on."

Over time, Kate had learned to pick up on a few of Nick's cues —his nuances. Although she wasn't yet an expert, something had happened in the twenty-four hours since she'd last seen him. And his façade was transparent. He'd been through a lot these past few months and she thought they were over the worst of it. "Dwight is sending me to Baker County to talk to the sheriff's office about Sydney Hawthorne. They were the ones to find her."

"You're going alone?"

"Yes."

He nodded. "Good. I think that'll be good for you. Listen, I've got to make a call, but I'll catch up with you later. Okay?"

Nick disappeared into his office before she could say another word. "Sure. Okay."

THE BAKER COUNTY Sheriff's office was just ahead as Kate made her way from the Jacksonville airport. She'd booked the first flight this morning after speaking with Deputy Burgess yesterday and arranging the meeting.

It appeared as though the weather might be turning for the worse as Kate looked at the skies through the windshield. She'd hoped Burgess might escort her to the crime scene, but given that rain was in the forecast, it was uncertain whether it would happen today. She wasn't opposed to traipsing through the mud, but slick conditions could make it difficult to safely navigate the area and anything that might have been left behind would be washed away.

For now, the building was visible in the distance and Kate was ready for her first case inquiry on her own. Given the rural location, the facility was impressive. The large building appeared new and contemporary.

Her arrival was anticipated as she spotted a stocky man in a blue uniform step outside. "You Special Agent Reid?"

Kate closed the driver's door after retrieving her belongings. "Yes, sir. Deputy Burgess?"

"That's me." He held the door open and waited for Kate to catch up. "I've been expecting you. Please, come on in."

Kate immediately noticed his eye-catching appearance. He was of average height, but with a build that could rival a top WWE wrestler. With deep-set brown eyes and a clean-shaven face, he was both rugged and slightly boyish. The unexpected twinge in her stomach brought a trace of a grin to her lips. To say it was butterflies would be too generous, but it wasn't far off.

"Follow me. My office is in the back." Burgess led the way along the path between the cubicle walls. "I have to admit, I was surprised to hear from you. I've already spoken with Agent Faulkner in Atlanta."

"Have you been made aware of the discovery of another victim, Ariel Nadal, found in the next county, also in the Saint Marys River?" Kate asked.

"Yes, but like you said, that was in another county and so I haven't had much to do with that. Again, it was my understanding that the FBI in Atlanta had been investigating." Burgess pushed open the office door. "Here we are. Please have a seat." He motioned her inside.

Kate placed her bag on the floor next to her and waited for Burgess. "The Atlanta field office has been handling this investigation. However, after further review of the circumstances regarding not only the discovery of the victims but also the manner in which they were murdered, it has become evident that they were dealing with the same unsub."

"I'm sorry. Unsub?" Burgess asked.

"Yes. Unknown subject. Apologies—the FBI has its own language. But as I was saying, once Atlanta realized that, we were contacted. I'm with the Behavioral Analysis Unit. We generally handle these types of investigations."

"Serial killings. You think we have a serial killer on our hands?"

"Yes, sir."

Burgess leaned back and puffed out his already beefy chest with a deep breath. "Okay, then. What is it that I can do for you, Agent Reid?"

"I understand the first victim, Sydney Hawthorne, was discovered by two young boys. Would it be possible to get hold of their statements?" Kate opened her bag. "Also, we're considering the likelihood that our unsub is targeting a certain age group of female victims. Acknowledging that we have only two victims, what has stood out to us was the fact that both were redressed in clothes that clearly did not belong to them."

"Redressed? So the victim we discovered was found in clothes that were not originally on the body?" Burgess replied.

"No. We don't think so." She retrieved the photos of the second victim, Ariel Nadal, and placed the file on the deputy's desk. "Have you seen the photos from the crime scene where the second body was found?"

"I haven't." Burgess reached for the file and opened it to see the photos of a young woman, badly bloated from the water. "So this girl was also cut up, is that right?"

Kate nodded.

"Good Lord." He began to view each picture carefully. "And these clothes weren't the ones she wore when she disappeared?"

"Not according to the roommate. My partner and I interviewed her roommate the day before yesterday. And, if you'll notice," Kate placed her index finger on the girl's shirt. "Both the shirt and shorts are very small—too small."

"Well, she's swollen all to hell, so that's not hard to believe."

"But it's more than that. The collar of this T-shirt is torn at the back. I viewed the body and the articles of clothing when we initially consulted with Agents Lyons and Faulkner. We assume that the shirt was pulled over the head after the victim's death because the collar was ripped. It's possible it was already in such condition, but given the fact that this is still a child-sized shirt, it's not likely she owned it." Kate was having a hard time convincing the deputy of their theory.

"Okay, say the victims were put in different clothes after they were killed. Of what significance is that, other than you've established one of the killer's habits, his MO?"

"You're correct. This does help us in establishing a pattern of behavior. But in addition to that, and if you'll see here," she pointed to the logo on the t-shirt, "this is a junior high school shirt. Now, I've been searching around the area where the victim lived and could find no such school matching this mascot, and that started with a W, as this school does." She leaned back to make her final point. "My partner believes there was a reason both of our victims were discovered here in Florida, even though they lived in Georgia. Would it be possible to get a list of schools around the area, I'm thinking specifically a fifty-mile radius from the river, so that I can try to find this school? I believe—we believe, our killer could be from the area and perhaps even went to this school."

Burgess rubbed his smooth cheeks. "That's a pretty big leap." He paused. "But I'm happy to get you whatever you need, Agent Reid. Especially if y'all believe this sick bastard is from around this area."

"Thank you, Deputy Burgess. It's just a lead at this point, but we can't afford to ignore it."

"Of course."

"Would it be possible, assuming weather permits, for you to take me out to the spot where Sydney Hawthorne was discovered?"

"Certainly. I think we'll be all right unless we get a torrential downpour, but let's head out now before it's too late. Hard to say this time of year. We can get soaked pretty quickly."

"I appreciate that, deputy. Thank you."

THE IMPULSE to phone Kate crossed Nick's mind more than once today, but he resisted. Dwight did the right thing by sending her on her own and he respected that. And if he was being honest, he'd admit that really what he'd wanted was for her to offer comfort. As much as he hadn't wished that was true—it was. His heart was broken and while he wasn't the type of man to sit at home and lick his wounds, Kate's voice would have been enough to see him through the worst of it.

Dwight had suspicions of his own that arose during the course of the conference call that involved Georgia the other day. So when Nick came to him expressing his own suspicions yesterday, no explanation was necessary. He was smart enough to figure out that Jack Lyons was sleeping with Georgia and Nick confirmed it with a late-night call after he left Georgia's apartment last night.

He glanced at the time, noting that Kate wasn't due back until late this evening, according to Agent Vasquez. The two often worked closely together and it seemed as though she'd become more of a confidant to Kate than Nick had been over the course of his hiatus.

Why it mattered when Kate returned seemed an unnecessary concern anyway. Of course, her safe return was always a concern, but meaning that he had no intention of telling her what happened with Georgia. The primary reason was timing. Unloading this information would only burden Kate more and given that she was about to face an anniversary that no one would celebrate, it seemed almost cruel. Moreover, Georgia still worked in this office, and while bad news always traveled fast within these walls, destroying her reputation was not something Nick had wanted. He couldn't expose her misdeeds. He couldn't humiliate her the way she humiliated him.

Exasperated, Nick knew he needed to shake out of this. What he needed was to work on Blackwater. Finally, he pushed up from his thick leather chair, deciding that something had to be done. ASAC Campbell couldn't keep him behind his desk. He would dry up and wither away if it continued, or drink himself to death—neither was a good option.

Nick marched out of his office and down the hall, catching a glimpse of Dwight, but refusing to stop. Instead, he pushed open ASAC Campbell's door without so much as a knock. It was clear he'd taken Campbell by surprise when he noticed the man nearly jump out of his seat at the disruption.

"Scarborough, have you ever heard of knocking?"

"I'm sorry, but I need to talk to you. I need to be operating on the Blackwater investigation. You're jeopardizing its success by leaving me out of the loop."

Campbell laced his fingers together. "Are you telling me you don't have confidence in your team, Scarborough? That you don't believe Jameson is capable of handling it?"

"Of course he is. But I've got more experience with these types of investigations and you damn well know that. No disrespect to

Jameson, but you need me on this case and I can tell you that my team would stand behind me on this."

"So if I call Jameson in here right now, he'd back you up?"

"One hundred percent." Although stern in his reply, Nick momentarily second-guessed himself.

Campbell seemed to consider Nick's demand, making no mistake that this was merely a request and that alone appeared to agitate the man. "As I said before, Nick. You're welcome to participate in Blackwater if needed as an advisor. It seems to me that Jameson has everything under control. He sent your protégé out on her own without any qualms whatsoever."

Nick closed Campbell's door and moved toward his desk, placing his hands on its edge. "You want me to apologize for going over your head. Is that it?"

"You don't think I deserve an apology?" Campbell seemed to view the question as a personal affront. "How would you feel if one of your subordinates took it upon himself to go directly to me on a situation? Would you not feel the least bit slighted?"

And there it was—the reason behind all of Nick's troubles.

"Do you think I haven't *earned* my position here, Agent Scarborough? Do you think I haven't been in the goddam trenches for years until it was finally my time to be recognized for *my* hard work, putting *my* life on the line as so many of us do?" His face began to soften. "I understand that you feel responsible for what happened to Agent Reid. The loss of her friend, the loss of her fiancé. And I admire that, I do, but you crossed a line."

Nick softened his own stance, taking a seat in reply. "I did cross a line; you're right about that. And I honestly can't tell you why I did what I did. Maybe it was so I could keep Reid under my wing—keep her safe. Maybe I needed her here because I saw the potential in her and I knew—I know what she is capable of accomplishing and I was in awe of her abilities."

"She's a lot like you, Scarborough."

Nick nodded in reply. "I know. Probably better than me—given time and proper training. But you're right. It was your call and I should have made my recommendation and left it at that. For that, I am sorry. I screwed up. But you know as well as I do that this Blackwater investigation won't be a walk in the park. We're dealing with a psychopath who carves his victims like goddam pumpkins at Halloween. It's only a matter of time before this blows up and while I believe my team is more than capable, I have the expertise to guide them. That's why I'm the senior resident agent." Nick took in a deep breath. "Sir—please. I need to help them. We make a good team for a reason."

Campbell looked through his window in silence, appearing to craft a response. He soon returned his attention to Nick. "I'll tell you one thing, Scarborough. If and when it's your time to occupy my shoes, I only hope one of your agents doesn't try to undermine you."

Nick cast down his gaze, sullied by his own behavior, however well-intentioned it had been.

"You can inform your team that you'll be working on Blackwater with them. I'm not sure Jameson will be completely happy with this, but if he's got your back, then I guess you don't need to worry about that. Goodbye, Agent Scarborough."

12

The weather had promised a deluge and it now delivered. Kate and Deputy Burgess had arrived at Saint Marys Cove only a short time ago and were already on their way upstream to the site where Sydney Hawthorne's body was discovered.

Within minutes, the ground sloshed under their feet. This was, after all, swampland that thrived on its damp surroundings.

"Do you want to head back, Agent Reid?" Burgess tugged on his hat to bring further protection from the rain.

"I'd like to continue unless you think we'll get stuck back there."

"We'll be all right; just don't want to hang out for too long." Burgess stepped over fallen limbs and atop swollen soils. "We're almost there anyway."

Kate followed as closely as she could, fearing her sneakers would sink into the ground. To minimize the risk, she tried to walk on top of the slippery rocks covered in moss. The thought that she might slide into the water crossed her mind more than once, but this needed to be done. She had to see for herself, for the investigation, where the body reemerged from the depths of the murky waters. Perhaps something had been left behind. A scrap of clothing, a clump of hair hung up on a branch that may not have belonged to the victim. She was assured Deputy Burgess and his team were more than competent, but she had to see for herself. Kate had developed an ability of sorts, although she hesitated to put a label on it. Whatever it was, she had a knack for picking up on clues that might have otherwise been overlooked. It was a phenomenon that had developed a while ago, although she'd only recently recognized it as a consistent occurrence. She hadn't mentioned this to anyone and figured it would be something best kept to herself. If it helped to solve a case, then so be it. In the meantime, she'd just keep her mouth shut, not wanting to be labeled as a nut job.

"This is the place," Burgess replied in a raised tone. The rains falling in the woods made for a noisy backdrop.

Kate was completely drenched now. Her hair had been pulled back as usual and its length had grown considerably over this summer. The ponytail now clung to her neck and down her collared shirt. She paid no attention to her appearance, though. Vanity wasn't her first concern at the moment. A young woman was dead and Kate was here to find something—anything that might help find her killer.

"Has it rained here since her body was found?" It had been a few weeks and, given the nature of the location, Kate began to doubt that she would find anything, figuring all would have washed away.

"Yes. We got remnants from that hurricane last weekend. Not much, but a couple of inches maybe." Burgess squatted down to where Kate had stopped to observe. "You think we might have missed something? My team is pretty thorough."

"This is just for my own peace of mind, Deputy Burgess. I don't mean to imply any shortcomings of your team. Please understand that." She stood upright once again. "Besides, I believe I may have just wasted your time coming out here. Even if there might have been a shred of evidence left behind, and I'm not saying there was, it would have most certainly washed away. I apologize for taking you away from your work, deputy." Kate continued to peer across the river just beyond the shoreline until the bottom was no longer visible, which wasn't a great distance in any event. The water's depth must have increased fairly dramatically. She retrieved her cell phone from its protective case. Fortunately for her, it was waterproof and began to take a few pictures for her files.

An osprey dove down only feet in front of her, nearly causing her to drop the phone and lose her balance. "Jesus. What the hell was that?" The bird had captured its prey, an unsuspecting mouse balanced on top of a stone just above the waterline. It extended its enormous wings and took flight just as quickly as it had scooped up its meal.

"An osprey."

"Looks like an eagle." She turned to Burgess. "It's got a white head and everything."

"I know. They share some similar features, but no, that was definitely an osprey."

Kate began to consider for a moment the t-shirt Ariel Nadal was wearing. She'd assumed the mascot had been an eagle, but the shirt was faded and stretched. Perhaps it had been something else. "Are they pretty common in this area?"

"Oh yeah. They're everywhere around here." The rain was beginning to let up a little. "Looks like we might get a bit of a reprieve. We should probably head back before it picks up again unless you need to see anything else."

"No. No, this will do, thank you." Kate followed Burgess back the way they came. The brief storm had relinquished some of its earlier strength but still drizzled nonetheless.

Burgess opened the trunk of his patrol car and walked around to Kate. "Here's a towel. I try to be prepared." The deputy smiled.

"Thanks." Kate pressed the towel against her face, careful not to smudge her makeup any more than it likely already was. Maybe she did care about her appearance a little, or was it because of her present company?

She placed the towel on the passenger seat and stepped back inside the car where Burgess returned behind the wheel. "Maybe I could get that list of schools from you before I head back?"

"Sure. You think you got something back there?"

"I don't know. I think I was looking at something that may actually be something else." Her response was vague, but until she could confirm her suspicions, she'd keep her thoughts to herself."

The two hadn't exchanged words on the short drive back to the sheriff's office. Kate's mind was operating on overdrive as she reviewed certain aspects of the case files in her head, working to find something, and simply stared through the passenger window at the still-falling rain.

On arrival, Burgess pulled into the back lot, behind the building. "Listen, um, I don't know when you're due back in D.C., but if you've got time, maybe you want to grab an early dinner or a drink before you go? I mean, if you're up for it. We've got a women's locker room you could use to dry off or whatever."

Kate turned her attention to the deputy, flattered by his invitation. She had time to come to terms with her mistakes of the past. Letting certain feelings get the better of her—loneliness, feeling wanted and desired. She understood that was all part of the healing process. Yes, she knew very well the approaching date and what it was going to do to her to have to relive that day. But maybe just for now, it would be okay to accept a kind man's invitation to share his company. Maybe it was okay for now to remember that she was still a woman. "I'd love to, actually. Thank you. My flight doesn't leave until nine o'clock, so I have a few hours to kill." She noted her drenched attire. "I wouldn't mind using your facilities as well."

"Great. That's great. Okay. Well, let's get back inside. I'll work on the list while you're getting cleaned up." His wide smile complemented his slightly pink-hued cheeks.

"Okay." Kate stepped out of the car and her heart felt lighter than it had in much too long a time. Her reluctance to recognize sincerity had nearly cost her what had become a good friendship with Will Caison. She would not dismiss that rare quality again, even if in her heart she knew this would not go further than friendship. That was something for which she was still ill-equipped to handle.

After a lengthy time in the women's locker room, Kate succeeded in getting her clothes to the point of being only mildly damp. A hairdryer helped to dry her clothes and put some sort of style back into her locks. She'd decided to forgo the ponytail and instead let her dark hair relax upon her shoulders. Makeup refreshed, Kate was ready to head back out and see what Burgess came up with.

She stood outside his office for a moment before he noticed her.

"Well, you don't look at all like a drowned rat anymore. Come on in. Let's go over this list."

Kate appreciated his humor and found it a refreshing change. She sat down across from him.

"Take a look at this." He pushed the paper in front of her. "I've pulled a list of middle schools from here to Jacksonville. So, as you can see, there are quite a few."

"Yes." She began perusing the names.

"So what are you thinking here, exactly?" Burgess asked.

"I can't say for sure just yet and I don't know if this list will help either, but my partner and I thought we'd see where it takes us. It seems our second victim lived in Florida for a while. My team thought that was enough to get me here to check things out." She sat back for a moment. "The fact that the unsub, and for argument's sake, let's assume the unsub is male. The fact that he redresses the victim suggests he's trying to make them appear to be someone they're not. Someone who he had a connection with. A friend, a classmate, maybe even a family member. Not only that, but it seemed as though he intended to make sure the bodies were discovered downstream, on your side of the river."

"He couldn't possibly predict where or when the bodies would turn up," Burgess began. "Or if he anticipated their turning up at all."

"That's a valid point. However, I think if he wanted to ensure they would not be found, he'd have buried them somewhere. Because here's the thing." Kate leaned in once again to make her point clear. "Neither autopsy report showed any signs on the victims of being tied to something—something that would keep them at the bottom of the swamp like a boulder or cinderblock. No rope marks at all. It was like he wanted them to rise and be discovered."

"Why? And how the hell could he know they'd end up this far south?"

"That part, we don't know yet. But that's the reason I'm here. We think the unsub has a connection to this place. It's possible he knew Ariel Nadal, that maybe she went to school here and so did he. The same could be said for Sydney Hawthorne, although he didn't leave such an obvious clue on her. And while it seems difficult to believe, it is possible that he chose to perform his act in one location and then take his victims to another."

"Christ's sake. How do you deal with stuff?" Burgess asked.

"Good question."

HER ARRIVAL at Dulles airport and subsequent drive back home to Woodbridge found Kate preoccupied with thoughts of the investigation, thoughts of the last couple of hours she spent with Deputy Burgess, and how much she'd enjoyed those precious few hours of feeling normal.

The flight had been late to arrive and so there were no thoughts in her mind as to going back to the office. She needed to go home and go to bed. It had been a very long day, one that brought about some positive momentum on the investigation. Kate would delve into the list Burgess provided her with tomorrow morning and see if her theory might pan out. That maybe she'd been looking for an eagle mascot and not an osprey. She was no ornithologist, but it was certainly worth a closer look.

The sight of her home just ahead was a welcomed one. Ideas of climbing into her cool sheets soothed the darker ones that lurked in the recesses of her mind, waiting to appear in her dreams. Hazards of the job.

Once inside, Kate immediately shed her clothing that had been soaked through earlier, only to make her appear as though she had never heard of an iron before, trading them in for a pair of cut-off sweat pants and an old UCSD t-shirt. A quick text to Dwight letting him know she'd arrived home safely and had some information to show him tomorrow, and Kate was already at the fridge, pulling out a bottle of wine. She'd forgone any alcoholic beverages at her early dinner with the deputy. Officially on duty, she could not make the department look bad. Kate chuckled and carried on into the living room. She put on the news for just ten minutes—then it would be off to bed.

Her cell buzzed with an incoming message. She reached for it as it rested next to her curled-up legs on the sofa. It was from Dwight. *"Nick's back with us. Talk tomorrow. Nite."*

"Oh my God." Her eyes widened at the unexpected news. What did he mean exactly? Nick was already back at work, so it could only mean one thing, that he would be working the case with them. She'd wanted to reply, but his final word seemed to imply it was a discussion to be had tomorrow.

Taking in a large sip of wine, Kate was ready to call Nick, but what if he was with Georgia? It was almost midnight and she had made it clear in the past that contacting him at such an hour, especially when he was with her, was generally a bad idea. She wanted to respect that. And, considering that it appeared as though they were on shaky ground, it was probably best to keep her urges at bay. It was good news nonetheless and she hoped Dwight saw it the same way. Nick wasn't the type to push Dwight aside. If he wanted to run on something, Nick was the last person who would stand in his way. He was good like that. She could recall the same behavior from him long ago, shortly after meeting him. He'd let her do what she needed to do, and unless it put her directly in harm's way, he wouldn't try to stop her.

Whatever had transpired to make it possible for Nick to be back on the team, Kate was glad. The work was hard both physically and mentally and having him there to offer up his wisdom meant they might get that much closer to finding the killer.

THE REMNANTS from the hurricane set Arlen's schedule back a day or two, but no matter; he'd gotten what he needed from

Lizbeth and she was of no use to him now. The time had come to rid himself of what had become nothing more than dead weight— literally.

The demons in his head led his hands to do what needed to be done and, for now, they were quieted. Sometimes, it would take a week, maybe two, but they would always claw their way into his thoughts, demanding he fulfill the desire that grew within him.

And now the time had come. The dark skies had cleared and he could see the stars shining brightly on the desolate community —deserted as he had been by a mother and father who were supposed to protect him. He hoisted his quarry from beneath her arms, dragging her as he had with the others, to the waiting truck. He knew Sydney and Ariel had been found in the river and grew uncomfortable with that knowledge. As he looked at Lizbeth, propped against the front seat, he squeezed his eyes shut and shook his head. A moment later, he returned to the task at hand, shrugging off what he'd done. Their bodies turned up miles down-stream, very near to the spot where it first happened. But Arlen couldn't think about that now.

He had to be smart. He knew what they called him—the Blackwater Killer—he'd heard it on the news. And while it had a nice ring to it, making him feel almost invincible, Arlen had to dispose of future projects so as not to be found. He'd been so cautious, ensuring no physical evidence was left anywhere, because there was one thing that scared Arlen Tucker more than failing the beast that lay sleeping upon his chest, driving the demons in his head, and that was getting caught. Life in prison or on death row was not a road on which he wished to travel. So he would remain attentive in order to satisfy the cravings and cool the boiling blood that coursed through his veins each time he set his eyes on his prey. It was a drug—and he had become an addict.

The outside air was no longer stagnant and a chill from a mild breeze walked down his spine as he pushed her inside. The heavy plastic tarp in which she'd been wrapped revealed dangling feet that trailed atop the damp soil surrounding the driveway. Extra precautions had to be taken now that he'd become famous and the tarp offered protection against evidence that might otherwise make its way into his truck.

He had to rethink his plan as he stared at the blue heap next to him. Return to the swamp or find someplace new. The swamp was an enticing place for Arlen. He reveled in the thought that he could feed it—give it life. All the creatures, even the water itself, would devour the bodies as he had done. But there had to be a way to let it feed. The sawmill. Only fragments of it remained yet he was confident it would offer enough cover that the body could be wedged beneath the supports and the machines. It could be done. It would take time, but it could be done. He would need rope, which he had plenty of in the bed of the truck. And he would need his waders because it was going to get messy.

The mills were another half-mile inside the swamplands from where he'd taken the others. It was far from the trails that saw several thousand people each year inside the swamp, walking along wood bridges and curated paths. Deviating from the trails was frowned upon, but Arlen took great pleasure in his knowledge of the swamp. He'd studied it extensively while he still lived with his family. It fascinated him and it revealed its deepest darkest secrets to him.

"Come on, Lizbeth. There's no time to waste." He walked around to the passenger side and opened the door. The cab lighting was poor at best and scarcely illuminated well enough for him to see where he'd placed the knife. He would need to remove the tarp so that nature could run its course and she would not be preserved inside by the cocoon.

The small flashlight tucked inside his belt presented a better view for him to grab what he needed and he pulled Lizbeth out. Her legs had become heavy and the fluids and gasses had already accumulated inside her stomach. He'd taken extra care in putting her back into clothes that had been his sister's, but she no longer looked like the pretty young woman he'd met a few days ago. The tarp was tossed into the bed of the truck to be disposed of later and he dragged her several more feet to the ramp that led to the rotted mill. The shack was small, barely enough for a single operator to push the logs through the blades and out the other side where they would be loaded onto the cars and follow the rail system.

He dropped her through the opening at the bottom where the boards had completely disintegrated, careful not to fall through himself. Arlen had to be quick because she would sink to the bottom pretty quickly. He made his way a few feet into the water to secure her hands to the support beam just below the building. She was now food for all the creatures that lived here.

13

Her early arrival at WFO was prompted by Dwight's short and curt text message after Kate made it back home late last night. The hour had just reached six am as she drove into the parking garage. Only a few cars populated the enormous structure and, as far as she could tell, Nick's SUV wasn't among them.

With her bag tossed over her shoulder, Kate hurried inside to speak with Dwight and get the full story. All of this had put such a strain on her relationship with Nick that she had become almost wary of him—afraid to set him off. He'd also changed as a result. His propensity for drink had grown, and while she knew that it was always a mild concern for everyone, that concern had turned to something akin to worry. However, her hopes that he'd return to his old self again now that he was back at work had begun to fade.

"Good morning, Vasquez." Kate placed her bag beneath her desk and flipped on her computer. "You're here early."

"I could say the same thing about you. How was Florida?"

"Wet." Kate surveyed the area. "Don't suppose you've seen Jameson yet this morning?"

"As a matter of fact, he just came out of the breakroom. I'm pretty sure he was heading back to his office."

"Thanks." She nodded her gratitude and started toward Dwight's office. She hadn't had a chance to fill him in on the progress she'd made with the sheriff's office yet, so that would be her opening line, and, from there, she hoped he would open up about what the hell was going on.

As soon as she appeared in Dwight's doorway, he'd spotted her, holding a mug of coffee to his lips. "Kate, come in. How did things go with the sheriff?"

"It was productive." She took her seat. "I asked Deputy Burgess to compile a list of schools around Baker County. You mentioned Ariel Nadal had lived with extended family around the area, but in addition to that, there was something I saw when the deputy and I were at the river, at the location where Sydney Hawthorne was discovered. I began to consider, after noticing some of the local wildlife in the area, that maybe the mascot on her t-shirt wasn't an eagle, but an osprey. They look a lot alike."

"I see."

"I think the killer wanted those bodies to be found near that area and I think maybe the t-shirt has significance to that effect."

"Okay, good. Let's see where this takes us. He gave you the list, correct?"

"He did. I'll get started on it right away." Kate looked away for a moment, contemplating just how to phrase her next statement. "I got your text last night." She waited for a reaction from him, but he remained unreadable. "It's a good thing that Nick's back with us, right?"

"Yes." His features softened. "It's a good thing. I spoke with

Nick at great length last night. He's going through some things right now."

"I know. He's been going through things for the past few months."

"No. This is something else, Kate, but it's not my place to talk to you about it. I'm sure he'll want to have a word with you later."

Kate's nerves began to tingle. What could be happening that Dwight couldn't say? Her concern over her performance sprang to mind. Perhaps ASAC Campbell wasn't happy with her. It could be a hundred things and now it was all she could do not to sit in Nick's office and wait for him to arrive.

Taking a deep breath, she knew her own insecurities were getting the better of her. "Should I be concerned about this?"

"No. It has nothing to do with you, trust me on that," Dwight replied. "Why don't you get started on that list and keep me updated on your progress? I expect Nick will be in soon enough."

"Okay. Thanks. I'll catch up with you later, then." She left his office without further inquiry. It occurred to her that it was still far too easy to rattle her nerves, especially when it came to her job. It began to feel like her entire existence depended upon this job. Because what else did she have in her life? Where else could she turn?"

Shortly after returning to her station, she began to delve into the names on the list that Burgess had given her. It was a stretch, but it was a lead she had to pursue. It just could not have been a coincidence that the killer dressed Ariel Nadal in that t-shirt. He was making a statement and it was one the authorities could not afford to ignore.

Time had passed by virtually undetected until a tap came upon her shoulder. "Hey. You got a minute?"

"Yes, of course." She noticed Nick's appearance was haggard and grew concerned that he'd pulled some sort of all-night bender.

Arriving at his office, Kate wasted no time in getting down to business. They were after a killer and, while her personal concerns over Nick had grown considerably, she still had a job to do. "I hear Campbell saw his way to allowing you to work with us on Black-water?" Kate wanted her tone to come off as enthusiastic, but she feared her words might have failed her.

"It appears that way. You good with that?"

"Are you kidding? Of course I am. What's going to happen with Dwight? I mean..."

"He'll still be taking the lead on much of the investigation. I'll be at his disposal however he sees fit to utilize me."

This was the Nick she'd come to know—a fair man who saw ability in others and would not stand in the way of their success and, many times, facilitated that success. His seniority meant he could pull the reins from Dwight, but instead, he would comple-ment the team, not run it.

"I'm sure he appreciates the opportunity," Kate replied. "And will I continue to run on tasks he's set for me as well?"

"So far as I'm concerned, nothing here has changed. Except for the fact that I'll be able to help out where I'm needed." Nick lowered his gaze to observe his fingers twisting the pen he held between them.

Kate figured this was it. The reason why she was really here. "Everything okay?"

An expression emerged on Nick's face that she hadn't seen in a very long time, maybe even since Marshall's funeral. He appeared utterly broken and a negligible grin that was trying to disguise his feelings fell far short of its purpose. "Georgia and I are over."

Her eyes blinked slowly as she grasped his words. "Oh my God. I'm so sorry, Nick. I had no idea." She'd wanted to ask why they split, but the intrusion seemed inappropriate.

"Well, it was bound to happen, I guess, sooner or later." After a glance through his window, he soon returned his attention to Kate. "Listen, I know you don't work with her that often, but I don't want your feelings about her—and especially her work—to change. You understand? She's one of the best in her field and she deserves respect."

"I understand and I would never treat her otherwise." His insistence on making such a statement caught Kate off guard. She would never presume to treat Agent Myers any differently because the relationship had failed. It made her believe there was another reason behind his unnecessary declaration.

Kate remained silent, assuming Nick would continue, but it seemed that was all he had to say on the matter. She would not pursue the topic further. "Is there anything else? I'd like to continue working my lead."

He shook his head. "Nothing else."

She began to leave his office, but not before turning a final time. "The three of us should meet so we can get you up to speed on the investigation."

"Sure. Why don't you set a time on the schedule?"

"Will do." Kate continued along the corridor before hearing her name as she passed Dwight's office. Turning on her heel, Kate returned, stopping to peek inside. "What's up?"

"I just got a call from Lyons."

Kate immediately walked inside, folding her arms in front of her. "What did he want?"

"He thinks they may have identified a suspect. A woman who disappeared from her grandmother's home late last week." He waited for Kate to sit down. "I guess the local authorities questioned the last people who had seen the woman. And apparently, two men had been installing storm windows on the grandmother's house the day before the woman had been reported missing. They'd worked for a local DIY store."

"Okay." Her eyes remained fixed on his.

"One of the men hasn't been back at work since the company was questioned and, according to Lyons, the information his employer had on file turned out to be bogus."

"Why does Lyon think this man is connected to Blackwater?"

"Well, they aren't sure yet, but given the circumstances and the area—it's within our search radius—he'd like to dig into it a little bit more. The name and address the employer had on file were both false. Doesn't sound like the guy was on the up and up to begin with."

The unexpected news left her speechless. After she visited with Burgess, she believed that the killer was in Florida. Perhaps she didn't have a sixth sense after all.

"How far have you gotten on the school research?" Dwight asked.

"I'm about a quarter of the way through the names."

"Okay. You continue on that end. I'm going to have a word with Nick, fill him in on this latest development, and then let's touch base in an hour or so and see where we're at."

Kate returned to her desk, unsure now if this was a legitimate lead at all. People went missing all the time and the only thing that could possibly tie this disappearance to Blackwater was the proximity of the occurrence. Okay, it was a little suspect that the man who was on the install turned out to have given a false name and address, probably social security too, but again, that sort of thing wasn't exactly out of the ordinary. There had to be another reason Lyons believed this could be the killer. Perhaps when the local police interviewed the man's co-workers, his behavior was noted as suspect. Regardless of what his reasons were, she had to keep looking for a connection to Ariel Nadal's t-shirt and the schools in Baker County until her boss decided otherwise.

NICK HEARD the knock on his office door and already knew who stood on the other side. "Come in." He continued to scan through his emails.

"Hey," Dwight began. "I wanted to talk to you about a lead Agent Lyons in Atlanta wants us to run on."

Just hearing the man's name made Nick's pulse rise, but he couldn't afford to lose his cool, not when he was under Campbell's microscope. "What is it?"

Dwight sat down and began to fill Nick in on Lyons' man. It was a stretch, but right now, they had two bodies and no foreign DNA. It was only a matter of time before the killer would kill again and so they needed to follow up on any leads that came their way.

"So no one had seen the guy since he left work the next day?" Nick asked.

Dwight only shook his head.

Nick raised his arms and laced his fingers against the back of his head. "What do we know about him? Is he a loner? How long has he worked there? What about any employee evaluations? Do we have anything like that?"

"Not yet. I got off the phone with Lyons only a few minutes ago. He's going to send over the police report and we'll know more after we get that. In the meantime, I've got Kate running on the list of schools to try and find some sort of match to the second victim's school t-shirt. If we can get a break on that, we'll be golden."

"Right. That'll open some doors for us. Did you get any feedback from the deputy down in Baker County?"

"What do you mean?"

"Just how Kate handled the situation. I have no doubt she did a fine job, but I'd be interested in what the locals thought of her."

"I didn't get any complaints. In fact, Kate mentioned she and Burgess grabbed a bite before she headed back to Jacksonville. So, I think she probably did okay. It'll be good for her to start building a rapport with local law enforcement."

"Agreed." Nick lowered his hands and sat upright again. "All right. While you're waiting on the police report, I'll finish getting up to speed on where we're at so far. I need to read Myers' synopsis as well. I need to get a sense of who this guy is."

Dwight hesitated but finally began to speak. "Listen, I can handle Lyons. That's no problem. There's no need for you to contact him."

"Yeah, okay, thanks. I appreciate that, Dwight."

ARLEN SAT ON HIS COUCH, staring at the wall where a picture of his family hung precariously on a nail that had slowly been slipping out of the damp sheetrock. The storm had done enough damage to the badly neglected exterior that the moisture was seeping through the walls. The quiet left him too much time to think about what he'd done. The compulsion to act on his fantasies was ceaseless. Even now, only days after saying goodbye to Lizbeth, the desire returned. It seemed as though with each kill, the satisfaction lasted shorter and shorter. His fever was returning, and his need to serve the demons in his head and the three-headed beast upon his chest, watching his victims as he did, became more powerful. He began to think of the young man who stood behind the counter of the gas station. But he mustn't. It was too soon and much too risky. He'd already missed two days of work and that alone would raise an eyebrow because he hadn't so much as called in sick during his entire employment.

Arlen was beginning to put all he worked for, all he had planned for, at risk to serve him—the beast with a new and seemingly insatiable thirst. Sometimes, he wanted to cut it from him, carve it out of his chest like he carved his victims. But it wouldn't let him. They had to make *her* pay for what she'd done, for what his father had done. Both, however, were no longer around and that was his doing. It didn't seem to matter, though, because the fire in his stomach, the flames of Hades itself would not let him stop.

He closed his eyes and knew what needed to be done, so he made his way to the front door, taking his keys. The truck squealed out of the drive and Arlen sped through the deserted streets. He had to do it before the beast regained control, before the voices in his head returned. There wasn't much time.

Minutes passed and there was only blackness on the road ahead, flanked by shadowed trees as he drove on. His head pounded and he could feel the beast try to rip its way through his gut, back into his head where it could manipulate him again. Burning and clawing and tearing its way, but Arlen pressed on. Control. It was all he ever wanted—over those who had done things to him, over those to whom he had done terrible things.

It was visible in the distance now and the smell carried through the vents of the truck. He was back at the swamp. Arlen pulled on his boots and ran to the place where she was. The flashlight shone in the water until he saw her, still tied to the posts beneath the mill. Knife in hand, Arlen stepped into the water and cut her free of the ropes. Her body was almost too heavy for him to pull from the water as it had become both waterlogged and rigid. But the desire to free himself from the damning thoughts that prevailed forced him to find the strength he needed and, with a severe grunt, Arlen dragged the body to the muddy shore. He fell to the ground and tried to regain his breath. No time to waste; he must continue, for it would come back without warning.

He returned the body to the bed of the truck, tossing over it the tarp he'd tasked himself to destroy. His jeans were damp and muddy, but Arlen jumped back inside and drove west on the road that paralleled the swamp.

More than thirty minutes had passed and Arlen knew he would lose control soon. He had only moments before it returned and so he reached his destination and killed the engine. His vision suffered in the night hours and here, where there were no city lights and the stars and moon hid behind clouds, he struggled to find his footing.

Arlen dropped the tailgate and pulled on her legs, forcing her head to crash against the ground in a loud thud. He dragged her through the leaves and mud to the river's edge. With a firm shove, Lizbeth rolled down the embankment and splashed into the water.

He watched her sink below the surface and cast a look at his surroundings. This was where his father had taken the family when they went camping. And this was where it had all begun.

Arlen returned to his truck, inhaling deeply to slow his pulse from the exertion and the fear that he would not finish his task. He slammed his foot on the gas pedal, smoke rising from the exhaust, and returned to the road to get as much distance as he could from the river.

He'd made it as far as Cheltenham before the headache abated, only miles from his home. It had regained control and, once again, the desire returned.

Returning to his home, Arlen slipped off his soiled clothes and put on fresh ones. In the bathroom, he splashed water on his face, brushed his teeth, and ran gel through his scalp, slicking back his locks, so that they appeared jet black.

Arlen jumped back into his truck and headed northwest to the next town over. A dimly lit sign sat atop an overhang, against the building's rustic wood siding exterior. Several cars were still in the parking lot. A good sign. It must have been a popular nightspot.

He stepped out into the chilly night air. The front door pushed open with ease to the sounds of country music. The smoke in the air from cigarettes obscured his vision, but only momentarily. Pool balls striking one another, laughter and beer bottles clinking together. The sounds of drunk people having a good time brought a smile to his face.

He shoved his hands in his pockets and approached the bar. And that was when he saw her—alone, sipping on a fruity-red drink. He pulled out a barstool next to her and sat down.

She cast a brief look his way, but immediately turned her head.

Arlen knew his looks generally garnered second glances and he counted on that now. The bartender approached him with an inquiring look.

"Coors, thanks." He turned to the young woman, who was trying to be demure, but he knew the true nature of women. "You look like you could use another. What are you drinking?" Arlen smiled and looked at her with a sensuality he conjured up for just such an occasion.

"Vodka cranberry." Her eyes reflected nothing but desire now.

Arlen recognized the look immediately. "Vodka cranberry for the lady, please," he said to the bartender without breaking eye contact with the woman. "So, what's your name?"

14

The information stared back at her, but Kate couldn't trust her weary eyesight. Had she found it? She leaned in closer, just to be sure, and raised her index finger to the screen, pinpointing the name—Westmont Junior High School. And its mascot appeared to be a giant bird, similar to the one on the victim's t-shirt. Confirmation, however, would need to come from the school directly and that would mean reaching out to Burgess because this was his jurisdiction.

Kate immediately got to her feet and hurried to Dwight's office. "I found something." She held the printout of the school's information in her hand and continued inside without waiting for an invitation.

Dwight looked on with interest while she took a seat and placed the sheet of paper on his desk. "What's this?"

"The school." It was all Kate could do to contain her fervor. "Westmont Junior High School—WJHS—and take a look at their mascot." She'd printed a screenshot from the school's website. "That sure as hell looks like an osprey, same as what's on the shirt."

Dwight's lips upturned into a knowing smile. "Okay, now we're getting somewhere." He nodded in triumph. "We should get Nick in here." Upon retrieving his desk phone, he continued to study the information. "Can you come over here? Kate's found something very interesting."

Only moments later, Nick arrived. "So what did you find?"

Elation still surged through Kate's body. "The T-shirt on Ariel Nadal's body, it matches this school here." Again, she pointed to the paper with the screenshot.

Nick picked it up and began to study both the image as well as the image of the shirt after it had been removed from the victim. "Sure as hell looks like the same school to me." He lent his attention to Kate. "Where is this located?"

"About fifteen miles from the Saint Marys River in Westmont, Florida – Baker County." Dwight had been the one to suggest Kate make the trip and her instincts had proven what they both considered—that it wasn't a coincidence these bodies were turning up on the Florida side of the river. And it was in Nick's expression that convinced her further that they were on the right track.

"I think you ought to visit Deputy Burgess again. He's going to be very interested in what you've uncovered," Dwight began. "With the lead from Agent Lyons and now this, I think we'll have to take a two-pronged approach. Nick and I can handle the missing woman in Georgia and I think because you've already developed a relationship with Burgess, you should handle that end of it."

"Sounds good to me." Without hesitation, she jumped at the opportunity. It was exactly what she'd wanted—to run on leads independently, as an equal member of the team. This wasn't training anymore; this was the real deal and success or failure meant lives could be saved or lost. "I can be on the first flight in the morning."

"Nick?" Dwight asked. "What do you think?"

"I think we've got a solid plan."

"Okay." Dwight slapped his desk. "Kate, go ahead and coordinate with Burgess and get your flight booked." He glanced at the time on his phone. "It's getting pretty late. After you get that done, why don't you call it a night?"

She began to rise from the chair. "Are you both heading to Atlanta, then?"

The two senior agents exchanged a glance and then Dwight replied, "Yes. I'll keep you posted and you do the same. Goodnight, Kate."

"Goodnight."

It was going to be a long night because the odds of Kate finding sleep would be slim and none. Ideas continued to fill her head and she just couldn't shut them down. Burgess was on board with meeting with the school tomorrow. She needed local law enforcement with her to suppress any panic on the part of the administrators. No one in the Bureau wanted to call this what it was. No one outside of those who'd read Myer's report had uttered the term "serial killer" yet. And that was not a phrase she intended to use with the school officials either. It was too late to quiet the press, however. Someone had leaked information and they had already begun driving fear into the public's mind. Kate suspected it had come from the Atlanta office. They'd called him the Blackwater Killer. No one else knew that was the name of the investigation. It was nearly impossible to keep these things quiet for long. Fortunately, much of the forensics data was kept from them and she prayed that would thwart any copycat killers.

Kate began to think about her old friend, Marc Aguilar, who

would never let her off the hook. If she knew anything, he'd insist on the scoop. He'd turned out to be a damn good reporter and last she'd heard, he was interviewing with the networks. It was only a matter of time before she spotted him on one of the national evening news broadcasts.

A knock sounded on her door, jolting Kate back into the moment. A quick check of the time showed it was approaching eleven p.m. Her legs tingled when she stood, having had them folded beneath her on the couch for too long. It could only be one person and Kate wondered why he had chosen now to arrive. He'd avoided her for much of the past two days. She guessed he was finally ready to talk about what really happened.

Nick stood on her porch and his appearance was skewed by the fish-eye lens embedded in the door when she peered through it. Kate pulled away, releasing the deadbolt and pulling open the door to the fresh, cool breeze outside. "Come on in." She stepped aside to allow him entry. He was ready to talk. She could see it in his demeanor. "Can I get you something to drink? Have you even had any dinner?"

"Thanks. I'll take a drink if you've got anything. I'm not hungry, though." Nick hoisted his blue dress pants and squatted onto the couch, perched at its edge. "I figured you'd still be up. I know how you get when a theory takes hold of you." He turned his head as she approached with a drink and unveiled a half-cocked grin. "Thanks."

Kate sat down next to him, waiting. She would not ask any questions; only listen.

"Everything all set for tomorrow?" He brought the drink to his lips.

"All set."

"Good. Good." His shoulders finally dropped and a deep sigh

escaped. Nick shook his head before he finally turned to Kate. "She's sleeping with Jack Lyons."

"Oh, Nick, I'm so sorry. Why didn't you tell me this when we spoke earlier?" This was not what she had expected. She figured the breakup had been a result of the internal investigation and now anger was growing, and it was directed toward Georgia.

"I don't know. It's hard to make myself say the words, I guess. And we were at the office, and well, anyway, I'm telling you now." He groaned. "You know I worked with that asshole? Yep. Can you believe that shit?" He tossed back the rest of his drink. "Un-fuck-ing-believable."

"Did she tell you this?" Kate was hesitant to say anything provocative. It was clear Nick was hurting.

"Didn't have to. The son of a bitch called me and practically told me himself. Saying how he'd asked her to profile the Blackwater unsub. And, you know, the funny thing is, I asked her if she knew him. She just glossed over it. Saying nothing."

Kate felt at a loss for words. She was angry with Georgia and didn't understand how she could have done this to him. Especially with all that had been going on with the Corbett raids and his administrative leave. It was like she was kicking him while he was down.

"Listen to me going on." He looked at Kate again, his face masked in regret. "I'm sorry. I know you aren't having an easy time of it right now and then I just burst in..."

"You hardly burst in, Nick." She placed her hand on his knee. "Besides, after all you've done for me, all the times I threw myself a pity party, you were there to pick me up again. Look, you didn't deserve this and I'm so sorry this has happened, but you know—you're my best friend and I don't want you to think that, for whatever reason, I wouldn't be here for you. Just like you've been there for me more times than I can count."

He placed his hand over hers and looked into her eyes. She saw his pain, his anger, and regret; it was all right there, swimming in his dark brown eyes.

"You're an incredible woman, Kate, and I know that, lately, I haven't said so often, but please don't ever forget that you should be proud of how far you've come."

This was bringing too much to the surface and Kate struggled to keep her eyes from stinging. "Can you believe it's been almost a year? It just doesn't seem possible, does it?"

Nick raised his hand and placed his open palm gently on her cheek. "A lot has happened in that year. You're not the same woman I met in California. But even then, I knew who you would become."

Kate pressed her hand onto his and closed her eyes, a rogue tear falling down her cheek. "Thank you."

Silence consumed them both as each seemed to deal with his and her pain. Different, but the same—loss.

Nick soon cleared his throat. "I'm sure you'd like to get some sleep, seeing how you've got an early flight." He began to rise from the couch.

"Stay. Just for a little while. Look, I know you haven't eaten. I think I've got some leftover pizza in the fridge. I mean, how could you turn that down? Come on; we'll talk. And there's no way in hell I'm going to be sleeping anyway. You said so yourself."

"Okay. I'll stay for a little while."

THE DAWN HAD ONLY JUST EMERGED when Kate's alarm dragged her from a wine-induced sleep. While it had been a late night with Nick, it was what they both needed. They talked and even laughed a little. She couldn't recall a time when they'd felt so close to one another, even after her entire life had been turned upside down. They each needed the other's shoulder and each had willingly acquiesced. Nick wasn't the type of man to open up easily, but he did last night and she was so very glad he'd stayed and glad they both eventually found sleep. Although she knew how uncomfortable her sofa was and wondered just how much sleep Nick might have gotten.

In the small bathroom adjacent to her bedroom, Kate snatched a few tablets from the bottle in her medicine cabinet. The water warmed in the shower and, when the steam rose from behind the curtain, she was ready to step inside.

She began to consider the events that needed to take place today upon her arrival back at the sheriff's office. Burgess had set up the meeting with the school and then they'd head back to his office to figure out just how important a lead this was going to be. There were still a lot of variables here, but this was a good start.

The shower helped to sharpen her thoughts and Kate continued to dress while the case churned in her head. On her way down the hall, she inhaled the pleasant aroma. "Good morning. Thanks for making the coffee. How are you feeling?"

"Not bad." Nick poured the black gold into the mugs. "How do you take it?"

"Cream, two sugars, please."

"You don't have much time. You want to take this to go?" Nick asked.

Kate glanced at her phone "I suppose I'd better. Listen, stay as long as you need. You know where the shower is if you want to jump in."

"Thanks, but I'll head out with you and get cleaned up at my place." Nick sipped on his coffee. "Guess I should make this one to go too."

Her car was parked in the drive and she pressed the remote to open it while Nick continued to his own car. "I'll touch base with you after I arrive."

"Sounds good. Have a safe flight."

She waited for him to pull away, feeling confident that the night had done him some good too.

A SMALL DELAY in her flight forced Burgess to push the meeting with the school administrators out an hour. And when Kate finally arrived from Jacksonville, she had no time to get a rundown on who would be at this meeting. It wasn't until they made their way to his patrol car that she'd had a chance to ask. "This meeting is just with the principal, is that right? I'd rather not include the district until we know more."

"Couldn't agree more." Burgess nodded. "It's just the principal for now. He understands what we're dealing with and has no intention of instilling panic in the community."

"Good. I don't want anyone thinking there's a killer out there targeting that school or any other school."

"Got it. We'll be there in a few minutes. Is there anything else you need to discuss?"

"If it turns out that we've got a definite match, we're going to need student names."

Burgess turned south along the single-lane road. "From how many years back? That could be a lot of information and I suspect we'll need a warrant for that type of thing."

"Agreed, and you're right, it'll be a lot of names. I know where I'd like to start, but let's cross that bridge when we get there."

"Understood. This is it up ahead." Burgess pulled into the school's parking lot and stopped in a space in front of the building marked "Administration."

"You ready?" Kate asked.

"As I'll ever be." Burgess grabbed his leather folder. He waited for Kate to get her laptop bag, then locked up the cruiser. "Looks like it's starting to cool down—finally."

It seemed he was trying to fill the silent stroll to the building with benign small talk, but Kate didn't mind. "Sure is. I actually considered turning on the heat last night, but I held off." She turned to him. "It's that San Diego blood in me, I guess. Haven't taken to the cold yet."

The trivial chitchat that brought about a comforting laugh between them eased the anticipation that had been building on the drive over. It was Kate's first time at the helm and it was Burgess' first time assisting on a serial killer investigation. The nervous release was necessary.

On arrival, the deputy stepped forward. "I'm Deputy Burgess and this is Special Agent Kate Reid," he said to the woman at the desk. "We're here to see Principal Whitmore."

The young woman appeared ill at ease by their presence and retrieved the phone. A brief exchange of words and she ended the call, returning her attention to the deputy. "He'll be out in just a moment."

The principal emerged from behind the double doors and, while he seemed poised, his eyes couldn't hide the fear that lurked inside him. "Deputy Burgess, Special Agent Reid, I'm Dr. Matthew Whitmore. Please come on back to my office."

A brief handshake was exchanged between the parties, and Kate and Burgess followed the short, bald man to his office. She knew immediately he would need to be convinced that neither his students nor his school was in any danger. It was a guarantee she would have to offer whether or not she believed it necessary.

"Thank you for meeting with us, Dr. Whitmore," Burgess began. "I know you were only briefly apprised of the reason behind our request for this meeting, so I'd like to turn it over to Agent Reid and she can fill you in with greater detail."

"Thank you, Deputy Burgess." Kate turned her attention to the principal. "As you may have heard on the news, a few weeks ago, a young woman was found in the Saint Marys River. Not far from here actually—in the Cove."

"Yes, I did hear that." His face was masked in lament.

"And on that young woman was a t-shirt that we believe came from your school." Kate retrieved the image of the shirt from her bag and slid it across his desk.

Whitmore placed glasses on his face and began to study the photograph. "Yes." He nodded his head. "This is old, but yes, it's from our school."

"How old?" Kate asked.

He removed the glasses and looked at Kate. "I'd have to check our files, but it was before I was the principal here, so at least ten years ago."

"I see." Dates began to run through her mind as she tried to piece it together.

"Do you believe the young woman who was murdered was a former student?"

"That's what we would like to determine." Kate hesitated to explain fully and crafted a response that would omit the gruesome nature of the discovery. "We believe this article of clothing was placed on the victim post-mortem and that it could have belonged to either a former student, the victim, or possibly even the perpetrator. However, our current line of thought leans toward the latter."

"So you think the killer went to this school?" Whitmore appeared distressed by the inference.

"It's just too early to say right now, Dr. Whitmore. But I think we'll need to obtain a list of students who attended the school during the time this particular image would have been used on school gear."

"I'm afraid I can't just give you student names, Agent Reid. I'm sorry."

She raised a preemptive hand. "Don't be. I understand this will require a warrant and I will act accordingly to obtain the proper paperwork so that we can delve into this further. In the meantime, if you could find out when this particular design was used, it would help us tremendously in narrowing down a time frame."

"Of course. I'll help out in any way I can."

"And, there's one other thing, doctor." Kate hesitated. "We'd like to keep this as quiet as possible, as I'm sure you can understand. There's no point in panicking parents or students when we don't know what we're dealing with yet. I'm sure you're a very busy man, but if it's all the same to you, I'd prefer it if you could handle this directly, meaning no one else on staff should be made aware."

Dr. Whitmore pursed his lips and nodded. "Of course, I understand completely."

"Thank you for your help." She extended her hand.

"Certainly. I'll do what I can." Dr. Whitmore returned the obligatory handshakes.

Kate and Deputy Burgess returned to the deputy's patrol car.

"How well do you know the district judge?" she asked, stepping inside the vehicle.

"Fairly well. I don't anticipate any problems obtaining a warrant."

"If we find something, it's going to become more difficult keeping this quiet," Kate said.

"Yes. It will." Burgess started up the car and pulled away from the school.

Kate began to consider what Burgess had said at their last meeting. That it seemed incredible that both bodies were discovered so near one another when it appeared as though each had originally been dumped in the Okefenokee Swamp. What were the odds of such a thing happening? She was missing something and it was beginning to whittle away at her thoughts. The intense volume of the dispatch radio as a voice crackled through it startled them both. "Deputy Burgess, please come in."

He tossed a glance to Kate, then retrieved the receiver. "Burgess here."

"Mike, we've got another body in the river."

15

It was an event that changed the entire course of the day in a single moment. Another victim in the Blackwater investigation had been discovered and Kate was on her own. Nick and Dwight were already in Atlanta, following Agent Lyon's lead. They were tracking down the man whom Lyons believed to be responsible for the disappearance of Lizbeth Hansby and Kate was in the process of heading to the scene where a body had just emerged. If it turned out to be that of Lizbeth—then they had their killer.

"First thing we need to do is find out who this person is," Kate said. "Her identity is going to be critical to the rest of my team, which is currently in Atlanta following a suspect in the disappearance of a woman."

Burgess turned to her. "I suggest we get the coroner out there right away. In the meantime, I'll get one of my guys to work on the warrant. Although at this point, I'm not sure how important that still is."

"Until we get some clarity regarding the victim's identity, that information is still valuable, I believe. Even if we do find out who the victim is, from what I understand, this lead in Atlanta is a man who had given his employer a false identity. The school information may be our only indication of finding out who this person really is."

"I'm not sure how easy it is going to be to keep this quiet. Three bodies in this river inside of a month?" Burgess began to shake his head. "Unless you pull some strings on your end, I don't think we'll be able to keep this one out of the press. And people are going to start getting nervous around here." Burgess turned onto the dirt lot that led to a remote part of the river. "This is it, just ahead."

"This isn't where we were the other day, is it?" Kate asked.

"Nope." He shifted the car into park. "We're about three miles upstream."

The two stepped out of the vehicle where three other officials, looking as though they belonged to the sheriff, were standing nearby. They approached the scene where the other deputies huddled in conversation.

Burgess greeted his colleagues. "This is Special Agent Reid. She and I were working on a lead when the call came in."

"This has something to do with the other two bodies that were pulled from the river a while ago, doesn't it?" one of the officers asked.

"I would assume so, but if you could show me where the victim is, I'll be able to make a better assessment," Kate replied.

"Right." He waved his hand. "Follow me."

It was another fifty feet down the river before they came upon the victim. Kate knelt at the shoreline where she'd been placed. "Where exactly was she before being pulled from the water?" She examined the body.

"According to the people who found her, they were on their

boat, doing some fishing, and saw something floating by close to shore. When they steered towards it, well, it didn't take them long to figure out it was a body."

"Did they pull her out?"

"No. The call came from them while they were still on the river. They dropped anchor and waited, keeping an eye on the body, but never touching it."

"Good."

"Coroner's on the way now," Burgess said.

Kate retrieved her phone. "Any CSIs here?"

"On the way."

She began to snap pictures of the victim. First her body, then closing in on her face. "I need to send this to my team and see if she's a match to the missing woman near Fayetteville."

ARLEN SLAMMED the palm of his hand against his head as he drove on. This wasn't supposed to happen; it was too soon. But he couldn't stop it and now there was another body. He needed his paycheck first and then he'd have to leave—get the hell out of the state because Lizbeth's body would be discovered soon enough. Every law enforcement official in the state would be looking for him when that happened.

He felt as though his skull was splitting under the weight of his mistake. He'd listened to the serpent—listened to it hissing in his ear that she had to die. It was too soon and Arlen had lost control. He had jeopardized everything because he could no longer manage the impulse. With virtually no money, he needed what would most certainly be his last paycheck.

The woman would have to be dealt with later and so she waited in his house, her blank stare and cold body bloodied by his desperation. He'd tried to choke the life out of her, just as he had the others, but she just wouldn't die. So he had no choice but to thrust a knife into her stomach and then her chest. Blood was everywhere and cleaning it up, leaving no trace, would be almost impossible. Arlen roared in anger. The man he had convinced himself he was had begun to unravel.

Arriving at the store, Arlen glanced into the rearview mirror to double-check his appearance. The last thing he wanted was to look nervous or agitated. He had to maintain his cool in order to pull this off. As he walked inside, a co-worker spotted him and approached.

"Dude. Where you been? You know that lady went missing after y'all left her grandma's house, right? Dude, everyone's been looking for you since you didn't show up for two days."

Arlen stopped short. "What do you mean, 'everyone'?"

"I mean like the boss and some cops. They came in a few days ago after she disappeared. Didn't anyone call you?"

He shook his head. "No phone."

"No phone? Who the hell ain't got no phone? I don't know, dude, you'd better go see the boss before shit turns serious."

"Thanks." Arlen nodded and waited for the co-worker to disappear from view. He wasn't going to go and find the boss and he could kiss his last check goodbye. The cops from the other day. They must have been there to ask about Lizbeth. In his arrogance, he'd convinced himself they had been there for another reason, but it seemed he was wrong. Now he had to leave before anyone else spotted him.

The garden area was his best chance. He meandered back so as not to draw any more unwanted attention. They only ever had one guy working back there at a time and he was usually watering something or stocking something else. Arlen could sneak out through that exit and head straight back to his truck.

A clear path out of the building was what he needed and his pulse quickened in search for one. The idiot he just ran into probably wouldn't waste any time spouting off his mouth that he'd seen him. The thud of giant fertilizer bags being tossed around echoed near him. That meant whoever was manning the garden area was at the back. He'd just been given his chance and wouldn't waste the opportunity. With careful but urgent steps, Arlen moved covertly through the outdoor area. A glance over his shoulder to ensure no one noticed, and he was out the door, speed-walking back to his truck.

The risk was now too great to even go back to his home. He would have to leave everything behind. A shooting pain ripped through his head at the idea he could not finish what he'd started. The beast would not be happy and Arlen would have to atone. "There'll be others, I swear it. There'll be others."

First and foremost, Arlen needed money. The gas station. The kid at the gas station he'd been drawn to. That was where he needed to go. The kid would give him money whether he wanted to or not. Turning the truck south, Arlen drove toward the lone gas station that was near his home. It was morning and he couldn't be sure the kid would be working. It might be his father and that would be a tougher set of circumstances, but there wasn't much choice right now.

Several minutes passed until Arlen pulled alongside the front of the gas station and reached into the back storage area of his truck for the gun. It wasn't his weapon of choice, not for his victims. But he'd found it inside the purse of his most recent victim. Inside, the kid stood behind the counter and Arlen began to feel that something had finally gone in his favor.

"Good morning," the kid said.

Arlen didn't reply, only approaching the counter and glancing up. No cameras. "Do you remember me?"

"Yes, sir. I've seen you a few times. How are you?"

The sensation grew inside him once again and he had to force it back down. There was no time. He slowly pulled the gun that had been tucked inside the back of his jeans. "I'm only going to say this once. Open the drawer and give me the money."

The kid's eyes widened and he began to tremble, fumbling with the keys on the cash register to get it to open. "Please don't hurt me."

"You have no idea how I've wanted to hurt you, boy. But if you stay calm and just give me the money, I'll leave and you'll never see me again."

A nod was all the boy could muster and he returned to the machine that still refused to open. "I'm sorry." He trembled with greater ferocity.

"Calm down. Take a breath and open the fucking register." Arlen peered outside. No one had driven into the station, but he knew he didn't have much time before someone did.

The kid seemed to calm down, appearing to understand that Arlen would follow through on his word. The register finally opened and he pulled out all the money inside. "This is all we have."

Arlen looked at the cash he placed on the counter. There couldn't have been more than a couple hundred bucks there. "That's it? That's all you have?" He slammed the side of his fist against the counter and the kid recoiled. "Fuck!" He raised his gun to the boy's forehead. "You have no idea how fucking lucky you are." Arlen quickly walked out and jumped in his truck, roaring out of the gas station. The cops would be notified, but that didn't matter now. Distance was what he needed and he figured he could gain a fair bit of it if he just kept going.

$\sim$

THE CORONER'S team raised the body and placed it on the stretcher. If there had been any doubts as to whether this woman was a victim of the Blackwater Killer, they had all but vanished when Kate viewed the destruction of the body. Exactly the same as the others. Beneath the clothes in which the killer redressed his victims was the bloody, hollowed opening he'd created by removing the genitals.

"What kind of goddam monster does this?" Burgess asked.

"The world is full of monsters, deputy," Kate replied as she watched them carry the stretcher to the waiting ambulance. "It's our job to find them—and stop them."

"Any word back from your team in Atlanta?"

"I'm waiting for official confirmation, but off the record, it appears to be Lizbeth Hansby, the woman who went missing last week." Kate paused for a moment. "You know, I thought I had this guy pegged, but now this one. He'd been waiting for weeks in between and now his MO has changed. Why?" Kate turned to Burgess. "Excuse me for a minute, would you? I need to make a quick call." She stepped away from the busy scene and retrieved her cell. "Agent Myers, it's Reid." For a moment, she expected Georgia to say something about Nick or somehow defend her actions, but there was silence on the other end. "The preliminary report you built on our Blackwater unsub—it appears as though we've just found his latest victim. What are your thoughts as to why he would accelerate his attacks?"

"There could be several reasons," Georgia began, "but the most logical one is that he appears to be an opportunist. Randomly selecting his victims based on ease and accessibility. Your latest victim could have just been in the wrong place at the wrong time and he seized the opportunity."

"That makes sense," Kate agreed.

"There could, however, be less obvious factors as to why the cooling-off period would become abbreviated. He could be losing control of his compulsions, or there could be a sense that his time is running out and he feels he may be close to getting caught."

Kate was angry with Georgia for what she'd done to Nick, but she would never question the woman's ability as an agent and certainly not as a profiler. She considered the reasoning behind this latest finding and pondered in silence.

"Kate, listen, I'm really sorry about—you know—about what happened between Nick and me. I'm sure he told you. He tells you everything."

That rubbed her the wrong way. "It's none of my business, Agent Myers, but thank you for taking my call and answering some questions. It was very helpful." She could hear Georgia sigh on the other end.

"I see. Got it. Don't hesitate to contact me if you need anything else, Agent Reid. Goodbye."

A pang of regret surged in her stomach as she ended the call. Kate hadn't wanted an adversarial relationship. They'd been through a lot together and she did admire Georgia a great deal. But what she did—it just seemed incomprehensible, especially at the lowest period in Nick's career. Perhaps in time, Kate would see her way past it because it was Georgia who defined the Highway Hunter killers. She set them on the path to Edward Shalot and the others. She was the best.

Just as Kate was about to rejoin the others, her phone buzzed in her hand. "Nick? Do you have him?"

"No. We're talking with his employer now. Apparently, he came in shortly before we arrived and one of his coworkers saw him. I guess he took off. Just means that we're after the right guy. I'm sure of it."

"So he's gone?" Kate's stomach dropped.

"Afraid so. We'll have to coordinate with state police and the FBI field offices and have a BOLO issued."

When Nick paused, Kate felt that a shoe was about to drop.

"The problem is, we don't have a name. He was going by an alias, but we do have a personnel file with his picture in it. So, we'll get that out over the wire as quickly as possible. How are things going down there? Coroner arrive yet?"

"He's here. They're taking the body now."

"Well, there's no doubt you've just found Lizbeth Hansby. I'll have to arrange for the family to come and identify her. Jacksonville, right?"

"Yes. They're taking her to Jacksonville. What can I do now?"

"Just hang tight. Get copies of everything they're collecting down there and get that warrant. We have a face. We need a name."

"Got it. Oh, I reached out to Agent Myers. That's not a problem, is it? I needed to ask her a few questions now that the unsub has altered his patterns."

"Of course not. Do what you need to do, Kate. You're in charge down there and, right now, this rests on you getting that name."

"Understood. I'll be in touch as soon as I have anything." She rejoined the other officers, most of whom had been standing around while CSI collected evidence. There wasn't much more for them to do at this point.

"Any news?" Burgess asked.

"Looks like Lizbeth was a victim of the Blackwater Killer. We'll need to get information from the coroner's office as soon as it becomes available. In the meantime, getting that warrant is our priority."

"But you know who the guy is."

"He used a false identity. We know what he looks like and a

BOLO will be issued as soon as my team coordinates with state police. Right now, we need a name so we can dig up whatever history we can find on him that might point us to where he's going." Kate shook her head. "He may be feeling as though he's losing control of the situation. If that's the case, he'll become more unpredictable and anything we thought we knew about him is going to fly right out the window."

"What are you going to do about the press?" Burgess asked.

"Once the BOLO goes out, there'll be no keeping it quiet. Let's try to get on top of the media before they trample all over us." Kate began to walk toward the patrol car. "We'll need to issue a statement. I'm sure your sheriff will want to address the press first and that's fine. I'd prefer if the FBI not be mentioned, although I'm not sure that's possible at this point. But my goal would be to keep the coverage localized. Once it goes national, I have a feeling the killer will feed off the attention, amplifying his control issues."

They reached the car and Burgess opened his door. "You think he'll go on some sort of killing spree? I mean, worse than what he's done already."

"Honestly, I have no idea."

They made it back to the sheriff's office, where Kate proceeded to fill Sheriff Conroy in on the latest details.

"Where are we at on the warrant?" the sheriff asked Burgess.

"Deputy Grimes is getting it signed by the judge now."

Sheriff Conroy placed his hands at his waist. "Good. I'll have PR work on a statement for the press." He turned to Kate. "When are your people going to issue that BOLO?"

"Within the hour."

"Okay. That doesn't give me much time, but obviously, we can't afford to waste any more of it. Agent Reid, I'm sure you and Deputy Burgess will be able to deliver the warrant to Principal

Whitmore and I hope to hell he's already got the names ready for you."

"Thank you, Sheriff," Kate replied. "We'll keep you abreast of any new developments." She reached into her bag and retrieved a business card. "This is my information." She began to scribble on the back of it. "This is the contact information for the resident agent. He'll be happy to answer any questions you may have."

"Thank you. I appreciate that, but you seem to be doing a fine job and I'll let you do it. I've got a lot of work ahead of me." Sheriff Conroy left the room, leaving Kate and Burgess to process the warrant.

Within an hour, the two had arrived back at the school and waited for Dr. Whitmore inside his office. He'd gone to collect the much-needed information and soon returned.

"Okay, this is what we've got." Whitmore walked around his desk and sat down. "I have the names of the students from the years ranging from 2000 to 2008. Our logo hadn't changed in that amount of time and so I think this is what you'll be most interested in." He pushed the documents toward Kate.

There were several pages and Kate began to flip through them. Many names that would require a lot of time to research. She began to deflate at the sheer magnitude of the task. "Thank you, Dr. Whitmore. Now that we have a face, we hope to match it up with a name. Even though these are old photos of young kids, this will help us out." Kate stood on weary legs. "We'd better get started on this. Oh, and the sheriff is going to be making a statement regarding our investigation. However, please rest assured that our meetings and concerns will not be made public. We don't know anything for sure yet, so there's no need to raise any red flags."

Dr. Whitmore rose to meet Kate. "I appreciate that and, while

I hate for you to waste your time, I certainly hope you don't find a connection between this madman and our fine school."

"So do I, doctor."

16

I t was only a matter of time, once the BOLO was issued for the man they thought to be Arlen Tucker, that the press would pick it up and it seemed that time had come. Nick's phone rang incessantly with calls from WFO about questions from reporters. All he could do was tell them that a statement would be issued at the appropriate time, as their primary concern was finding the suspect.

"We have to get a handle on this, Nick." Dwight walked alongside him as they left the Atlanta office. "You know the media will put a spin on this and scare the shit out of the public."

"Maybe they should be scared," Nick replied.

"Come on; you don't mean that. You're just frustrated, same as me." Dwight stepped inside the car while Nick slipped into the passenger seat.

It had been a visit earlier today by one of Lyons' agents to the post office where Arlen Tucker's P.O. Box was registered that led them to a street address. "Let's just see what we can find at his place," Nick started. "We know he took off in a hurry, so there may be something he left behind that would give us an idea as to where he might be going."

Dwight backed out of the parking garage. "You know, you handled yourself well today with Lyons. Frankly, I don't know that I could have. I'm just sorry the son of a bitch is tagging along with us."

"It still involves his office. Not much I can do about that." Nick squeezed the door handle. "Besides, if he wants her, he can have her. We've got a job to do."

The drive to Tucker's home was long and quiet, save for Nick's phone buzzing endlessly with calls inquiring about the case. He eventually shut it off.

It was Dwight's phone that rang this time, surprising the both of them.

Nick looked at it resting in the console. "You sure you want to get that? Probably another call from the media."

Dwight looked briefly at the caller ID. "I'd better get it. The number's local." He picked up the call. "Agent Jameson here."

The speakerphone muffled the voice for a moment due to a weak signal, but it soon regained some strength. "It's Lyons. I tried Scarborough, but it keeps going straight to voicemail."

The two exchanged a knowing look.

"I got a call from Fayetteville Police. A robbery occurred earlier this morning at a gas station just a few miles from Tucker's residence. When they heard the BOLO and saw the picture, it matched their suspect in the robbery. They'd already spoken to the victim."

"So it was our guy. What do we know? Did he say anything to the victim?" Dwight asked.

"Just that he said the kid was lucky. But more importantly, the kid said Tucker headed south along the frontage and onto the high-way. I've confirmed that the state police have placed a roadblock, but no one matching our unsub's description or vehicle has tried to pass."

"You think they already missed him?" Dwight's shoulders dropped in defeat. If Tucker made it out of the state already, things just got a hell of a lot more complicated.

"I think he's long gone," Lyons replied.

Dwight slammed his palm on the steering wheel and began shaking his head. "Are you heading to the house now?"

"Yes. I'll be there in ten minutes. You?"

"We're just in front of you."

"Okay. Fayetteville Police will be there too."

"Ten-four. See you there." Dwight ended the call. "Where do you think this guy's going?"

"I don't have a damn clue." Nick appeared as disgusted as Dwight had. "I hope to hell Kate's having better luck than we are."

"WE'VE GOT to be able to narrow this down." Burgess rubbed his eyes as he sat at the conference table that was covered in sheets of paper filled with names. "There's a killer out there and all we have is a face and a fake name."

"I'm just as frustrated as you, but..." It suddenly occurred to Kate a more expedient way to address the problem. "You're right. We have a face." Kate thought about the personnel file. "Dr. Whitmore had to have pulled this information from some sort of database the school or district maintains."

"Right," Burgess replied.

"I'd need to check with one of my colleagues in D.C., but she would know, if it was at all possible, how to get that information uploaded to our facial recognition database."

"Okay, but these photos are from up to ten years ago. They're just kids. We're looking for a man."

"That's right, we are. So we can eliminate the females in this group. Deputy Burgess, this could save us valuable time."

"It's worth a shot."

Kate immediately called Agent Vasquez and asked if this was even a possibility. "I'm sure the principal will give us access. We have a warrant and I know he's just as anxious as we are to find a resolution. Whether his school is involved or not, he wants to put this to bed." Kate waited for a reply as she paced Burgess' office. "Okay, thanks, Vasquez."

Her smile revealed that she'd received the answer she was hoping for. She ended the call and turned to Burgess. "I'm going to get in touch with Dr. Whitmore and get access to the district's database. I'm sure he'll need permission from the school board, but I can't foresee that as an issue, all things considered."

"No. I don't think the board would want to come across as uncooperative in this situation," Burgess said. "So, what do we do in the meantime? Just wait?"

Kate wasn't really sure how to answer him. It seemed they would be at a standstill until the data could be analyzed. "Vasquez will work as quickly as possible, but it will take some time. Not only will she have to cross-reference the names and faces with any records we have, but we're also dealing with the age aspect. There will likely be some markers she'll look for and probably from there, implement the aging program to come up with the possible matches."

"I wish we had access to that kind of technology."

"You do. The biggest problem I've seen with local authorities is that they just don't have the manpower to utilize what's available to them."

"Sounds like you speak from experience."

"I spent a few years working for the San Diego Police Department in evidence collection. I spent time on a few cases as well."

"So you decided to move on up to the Federal Bureau of Investigation, huh?"

Kate glanced away for a moment, not feeling up to elaborating on her short law enforcement career. "You could say that. I'd better get on the horn to Dr. Whitmore and get the ball rolling. Excuse me for a moment."

THEY ARRIVED at the derelict shack that Tucker had called home for at least the past six months, according to the post office. The first on the scene, Dwight and Nick pulled into the driveway from the cracked asphalt street inside the neglected community.

"So this is it." Nick surveyed the area. "Can't wait to see what's inside." He followed Dwight as the two approached the front door. "Don't suppose anyone's home?"

Dwight turned back, pressing his lips together.

"Just a thought." Nick held his hands up as if in surrender. "Just open the door."

Dwight turned the handle, but it was locked. "Guess we'll have to go in the old-fashioned way." He walked into the front yard and retrieved a stone. On his return, he threw the stone into the small glass insert in the door. "There you go." Pulling the sleeve of his button-down shirt over his hand, he inserted it into the broken section and disengaged the deadbolt.

The smell nearly knocked them to the ground, but with guns raised, they entered the small mudroom.

"Jesus. What the hell?" Nick crinkled his nose and closed his eyes as if that would stop the assault on his senses.

They both recognized the odor and knew death would make its presence known.

"Scarborough, over here." Dwight had been a few steps ahead and was standing in the living room.

He was looking at something and Nick had already figured out what it was, but approached anyway. "Aw, hell. Goddammit."

"I'll finish with the sweep, see if you can find any identification for this girl—what's left of her." Dwight continued to check the other rooms in the house, which didn't take long but stopped short when he arrived inside the first of the two bedrooms. No matter how many times he'd been in this very situation, Dwight never got used to it. As much as he'd wanted to close his eyes, he just couldn't.

The room was covered in pornography and not just any pornography—bondage and sadomasochism. However, that alone was not the reason for his revolted stare. The images showed women with a particular body part having been removed, that same part having been removed from all of the killer's victims.

In the distance, he heard Nick's voice. "Are we clear?" The words reached his ears and Dwight tried to blink and remember what he was doing there in the first place. "All clear. You'd better come in here and take a look."

Nick stepped away from the body, not having found any identification, and as he began to walk toward the bedroom, footsteps sounded behind him. He turned to see Agent Lyons and one of the local cops.

It seemed the smell had still been extremely pungent, although they'd left the door open.

"For God's sake, is there a body in here?" Lyons asked.

"Over here," Nick replied, tossing his head in the direction of the latest victim of the Blackwater Killer. "She hasn't been dead long, from what I can tell. Maybe not even twenty-four hours."

"Scarborough, you need to see this," Dwight shouted from the bedroom.

"Excuse me." Nick walked into the darkened hall and toward the only room with a light turned on. Upon entry, he could only shake his head as he looked around the room—the walls papered in debauchery. "We gotta find out who and where this guy is."

"Was that Lyons and one of the locals I heard?" Dwight asked.

"Yeah. Let the circus begin." He paused to consider the meaning of what they were both seeing. "What do you think he's done with the cutouts?"

It seemed Dwight understood that Nick meant both what was on the walls and what had come from the victims. "I have a feeling we'll find everything right here. Somewhere." He looked at Nick. "He's not done. Not now that he knows we're after him. I think he's planning on leaving a whole lot of bodies in his wake."

"I hope to God you're wrong."

"Come on, let's start working with those guys and see if we can get any useful information from all this shit." Dwight started back into the hall, Nick following behind, until they met the others.

"Where are we at on the BOLO?" Nick began. "Anything come up yet?"

"Not yet," Lyons replied. "I just got off the phone with state police; they've extended the BOLO to include South Carolina, Alabama, and Florida. Someone's bound to spot his old beat-up truck somewhere. He couldn't have gotten that far yet."

"What can I do?" the officer asked.

"Get a coroner down here to collect the body," Nick began. "In the meantime, help us search this place for any clues as to where he might be going." He turned to the others. "There's a pretty good chance we'll find tissue from the other victims here somewhere. We're pretty confident he was keeping them as trophies."

Several hours had passed with no news from Agent Vasquez. Kate glanced at the time on the wall. It was approaching six in the evening. The two had been at a virtual standstill since the information was forwarded to Vasquez, although Kate had spoken to Nick during that time and he filled her in on where they were, which hadn't been much further. Still, no one had spotted the vehicle or the man himself and that seemed unbelievable, considering four states were looking for him.

The news had already broken and it wouldn't be long before it reached the national level. In fact, she expected to see a special report break through at any moment. But there was nothing more they could do right now, except sit in the breakroom of the Baker County Sheriff's office and wait.

"Dammit," Burgess said. "How much longer is this going to take? With the millions of dollars in resources you people have, you'd think things would move along a little faster, considering a goddam killer is running around." His anger was directed toward Kate, but she didn't flinch. It seemed that was enough to settle him down. "I'm sorry, Agent Reid. I just feel completely impotent right now."

"I understand. No apology necessary."

"I just can't help but think of those two young boys who found the first victim. They should've never had to see something like that, you know? I'm supposed to be the one they look to for help and what have I done for them so far?"

"Mike, it's not in your control." Kate stopped short when her cell phone vibrated on the table. She looked at Burgess and picked it up. "Agent Reid."

Burgess could only glean the direction of the conversation by

Kate's facial expressions and she appeared to be pretty good at hiding them.

"No, thank you, Vasquez. You've saved us a lot of time." Kate exhaled a breath as her eyes slowly met with Burgess'. She only shook her head.

"Nothing? They found nothing? No match?" Burgess appeared ready to explode.

"I can't believe it. I thought for sure this was how we were going to find him, find out who he really is," Kate said.

Burgess began rubbing his forehead. "What the hell are we going to do now?"

Kate considered several directions but was nearly at a loss herself. "Let me think." She stopped again, dropping her eyes to the floor. "If he didn't go to school there, it had to be someone he knew. Someone who had harmed him in some way."

"Well, hell, that could be anyone," Burgess replied.

Her instincts could not have led her astray. They'd been so reliable up to now. Kate was missing something and she had to figure it out fast. Her mind spun with all sorts of thoughts, images of the victims, the crime scenes, the clothing. Everything she could possibly think of that would lead her somewhere.

She snatched up her phone and dialed a number while Burgess looked on with curiosity. "Yes, can I speak with Dr. Kinney?"

Burgess furrowed his brow.

"Dr. Kinney, this is Special Agent Kate Reid. We met the other day. Yes. I know. We're still looking, but I needed to ask you a question. The t-shirt on Ariel Nadal's body. Is there any way you can tell me if the tag on that shirt indicates a size? More specifically, if it indicates a gender? Thank you. I'll hold."

Burgess folded his arms. "What are you thinking?"

Kate raised an index finger. "Yes, I'm here. Okay, yes, that's all

I need for now. Thank you very much. And same to you. Good-night." Her chest began to heave as a renewed excitement welled inside her.

"What is it? What's going on?" Burgess appeared on the edge of his seat, waiting for an answer.

"It was labeled "girl's medium.""

"It wasn't his shirt," Burgess replied.

Kate shook her head. "It was a girl's shirt." She almost jumped from her chair. "I need to get the names of those girls from the school over to Vasquez." She started to walk out of the room and Burgess had to jog to catch up to her. "I shouldn't have held them back. How could I have been so stupid?"

"It's still a long shot, though, right?" Burgess still struggled to keep up with her. "I mean, if he didn't go to school there, but a girl he was after did? That still doesn't get us any closer to finding out his identity."

"It does because I don't think it was just some girl." Kate stopped in her tracks. "It had to be someone who had a deeper relationship with the suspect. Someone who had intimate access to him on a regular basis. Given the nature of the mutilations, this person had to have done great harm to him. I think he has a sister—and I think she might have abused him."

17

Precious **time still** ticked away and they were no closer to finding the killer's true identity. The names of the girls were sent to Vasquez and she was working double-time to find any identifying markers that would match closely enough to whom they knew to be Arlen Tucker. It would still take time if one of the names was a match to track down this person, but it would get them a step closer.

Burgess returned with two paper bags in his hand. "You need to eat." He placed the grease-stained bags of food on his desk. "Sorry, there isn't much around here, but these guys make the best burgers in town."

Kate pulled her attention from scrolling through her phone, hoping new information would appear with each refresh of the screen. "Thanks. I guess you're right. We haven't had anything all day." She reached into the bag and retrieved a burger and fries.

"Has your team made any progress in Tucker's home?" Burgess reached for his food and unwrapped the enormous burger.

"Last we spoke, the coroner had just arrived, and they were

still searching the house, but nothing so far that would indicate where he was headed. The closest they have is the statement from the gas station robbery victim that Tucker was heading south and it appears that state police missed him."

"So he could be anywhere."

"Four states are looking for him. He won't be able to stay hidden for long." Kate raised the burger to her lips and took a mouthful.

"You know, this has taken a much more dramatic turn than I could have ever imagined. When that body turned up, Sydney Hawthorne's, my first thought wasn't that it had been the work of a serial killer. In fact, I can tell you that never in my fifteen-year career have I come across such a horrific case." Burgess seemed to study Kate for a moment. "I don't know how you're able to maintain the level-headed approach you've displayed so far. I find it both amazing and a little unsettling at the same time. No disrespect."

A thin smile briefly appeared on Kate's lips. She'd felt as he did on more than one occasion in the past. "None taken." It had been the loss of Marshall that ultimately forced her to view the world around her in harsher, more black-and-white terms. Because it didn't matter how much one was loved, or how much compassion one had for the plight of others. There will always be someone out there who believes it to be his or her responsibility to destroy lives. To take what was not theirs for the purpose of causing pain to others. And it took a callous mind to find those types of people. While she hadn't believed herself to have become so callous, perhaps she had. "Let's just say that I've seen what people like Arlen Tucker are capable of, and it changes you. It makes you realize that you must see the world, at least partially, as they do in order to anticipate their next move."

"Well, I guess I'm glad I don't have to see the world that way," he now appeared indebted. "But I'm glad there are people like you who do."

An image popped up on the screen of Kate's phone. A call immediately followed. "Agent Reid." She placed it on speaker.

"The picture I just sent you is of a thirteen-year-old girl named Janelle Durham."

Kate flipped back to the image. "Who is she?"

"She attended the school in 2005 and her facial markers are similar enough to Arlen Tucker for me to conclude that they are related."

"That's great." Kate smiled at Burgess. "That's got to be his sister. Where is she?"

"She's deceased, Kate. Died in a house fire a year later with her family," Vasquez replied.

"Wait a minute." Burgess leaned in with interest. "Did you say 'Durham'?"

"Yes."

Kate looked at him. "Do you know who this is?"

"The fire. It happened here in Baker County, about twenty miles away. There was one survivor. A boy."

"Oh my God. What happened to him?" Kate asked.

"He was put in foster care, but honestly, I didn't keep track of the case after that. The files would be in archive, but it wouldn't take long to get them."

"Thank you, Agent Vasquez. Thank you so much." Kate ended the call. "Let's get those files."

NICK MARCHED with deliberate speed toward Dwight, who was outside, pointing a flashlight into the shed. "Vasquez turned up a match."

Dwight turned on his heel. "We know his real name?"

"Not yet, but Kate's close. I just got off the phone with her and she and Deputy Burgess are looking up the files from some fire that happened back in '06. Turns out the girl whose facial markers matched the closest to Tucker died in that fire and so did the rest of her family. Except for a boy."

"Arlen Tucker, or whatever the hell his real name is," Dwight replied.

"We think so. The boy was put into the system shortly after the fire."

"Then he'll have a file. It shouldn't be too hard to confirm an actual identity, but that doesn't get us any closer to finding him."

"But it does. We're dealing with someone obsessed with taking some sort of revenge on his female victims. He had a sister who died in the fire. Now, I can't say what type of relationship he had with his sister but look at the ages of our victims. They're all in their early to mid-twenties. That would have put each of them in middle school in 2006."

"Sure sounds like he's after victims in the general age range of what his sister would be now." Dwight's brow narrowed as he seemed to consider their current options. "I say we start looking in Florida, particularly in Baker County. He might be going home."

"It's about the best we can hope for at this point. I can coordinate with the Florida State Police and talk to Kate and Deputy Burgess again. I'm thinking we need to get down there with her as quickly as possible."

"Hang on," Dwight began. "There's something in here you'll want to see first." Dwight turned his flashlight inside the dark shed and illuminated a grisly discovery.

"Oh God," Nick replied. "This was where he kept the parts."

A set of steel shelving units bolted on the back wall of the shed revealed the horrific sight. Large glass containers, similar to those that would hold flour or cookies, were placed on those shelves, each containing the parts of his victims that had been removed.

"There are six containers." It only took a moment for Nick to realize that meant there were more victims than had yet been discovered. "Get forensics in here to collect these." He turned away, repulsed by the display. "I'll phone in for the helo. We need to get to Baker County ASAP."

A CONFLICTED MIND split in two, each half struggling for control made the road ahead appear divergent. Arlen's vision suffered the effects of the war that raged inside him, and the beast that seared his chest was calling. His work was not yet finished.

The two-lane road was familiar to him, though, and so navigating its twists and turns came by way of memory. The truck continued along the highway as the sun faded from view, leaving behind only nightfall.

Aware that they were all looking for him, he intentionally traveled the back roads, avoiding detection. Arlen considered a destination that would offer a reprieve if only a brief one. A place where he could gather his thoughts and determine his final destination because being captured wasn't something he could abide by. He knew what happened to men like him in prison and surviving more than a week there would take an act of God, and he realized he wasn't a man who deserved a miracle.

Arlen rocked back and forth as he gripped the steering wheel tightly. His breath was heavy and beads of sweat spilled down his temples. He stared at the roadway lit by the truck's faint headlights. In an instant, his body shot upright and his eyes fixed ahead with deadly precision. The answer appeared and the beast had again resumed control.

He pressed hard on the gas pedal and the old truck's engine sputtered and finally roared into gear, sending him reeling down the highway, his destination fully in sight. He'd already been on the path without realizing it, but it was all too clear now. Arlen Tucker—Zachariah Durham—was going home.

DEPUTY BURGESS RECOVERED the case file sent via email from the archive department. It was already after-hours and so he had to pull some strings, but considering what was at stake, it wasn't a difficult task. "This is him." He dropped the papers onto his desk where Kate waited.

She began to compare the employee ID against this new image of a ten-year-old boy known as Zachariah Durham who was the victim of a fire that killed his family. "It sure as hell looks like him, but let me get this to Vasquez to run the age progression program. She'll be able to confirm it."

"What do we do after that?" Burgess asked. "I'm concerned this community will turn to panic."

"He's on the run right now. I need Agent Myers to shed some light on where he might be heading. Given what we know now, she could assemble a more comprehensive profile." Kate knew what she had to do. Myers was top in her area of expertise and her feelings for what she'd done to Nick couldn't stand in the way of finding Durham. "I'm going to request that she come down with the rest of the team. It's got to be all hands on deck if we stand any chance of finding Durham before he kills again."

Kate made the call and Myers would be on the same chopper as Nick and Dwight. She'd given Myers the new data so that she had time to review it and would hopefully be prepared with a solution upon her arrival.

"Can we take a drive over to where the Durham house was? I'd like to see what's there now," Kate said.

"You think he might show up?"

"I don't know, but I'd feel better if I knew what we were dealing with in terms of population in the area. Depending on what the team and Sheriff Conroy want to do, they may consider setting up a patrol, just to be safe."

"Sure. It's not far. I don't often have to travel there as they have a local police department. Which, I suppose if we implement a patrol, they're likely going to want to be involved."

"I agree." Kate followed Burgess outside where the air had cooled considerably and the earlier breeze had quieted to an eerie calm.

Burgess started up the engine as Kate stepped inside. "You really think he'll come back here after all this time?"

"From my limited experience, it's entirely feasible. And I'm not sure he's been gone all that long. They found additional— items—in a storage shed behind Durham's home near Fayet-teville. That means we have more bodies to uncover and they could be victims from around here." Kate immediately thought of Hendrickson and his parents' home where she'd been held captive along with so many other children who were not as fortunate as she. "Can you radio back to your office and have them run a missing persons' report for the past, say, twelve months? We might get hits on similar victims." She paused. "He might have been active for much longer than we originally thought."

"That's what I'm afraid of." Burgess eyed the road ahead and drove southeast to the small community of Briar. Zachariah Durham and his family had lived there until a fire that originated in the garage killed all of them, except the boy.

"I don't want to sound like a creep or anything, which is kind of what I feel like right now by asking something so absurdly inappropriate at this given moment," Burgess said.

Kate turned to him before he could continue. "You know, someone once told me it was best to stay detached from an investigation. And by that, I mean, keeping the grim nature of it separate from who you are as a person. Because if you don't, you'll never lead a normal life."

"Hmm. That's pretty sound advice. This person must have been very wise indeed."

"He was." Kate smiled. "So you were saying?"

"I guess what I was trying to say was that maybe after this is over and we put this son of a bitch behind bars, maybe you and I could get together every now and again. I mean, when you're not busy, which I know is probably a rarity in any case."

"You seem like a good man, Mike, and I appreciate the offer. Can we revisit this conversation? And I'm not dismissing you. It's just, well, I'd like some time to consider it." She could not deny that there had been a spark between them at their first meeting. And now that she'd spent some time with him, his authenticity was transparent. Maybe it was time to move on. It didn't have to be anything serious, but the thought of spending time with someone again... was a nice idea—something that resembled normalcy. And that was appealing in and of itself.

"There's a coffee shop just ahead." Burgess raised a finger from its grip on the wheel and pointed to the shop. "You mind if I pop in and grab a cup? It's been a long day and I could use the pick-me-up."

"Sounds good to me. I wouldn't mind one myself."

Only five miles from their intended destination and approaching 7 pm, Deputy Burgess pulled into the parking lot of a place called Ground Control. Apparently, they had the best coffee this side of the river.

"Just a plain coffee, or do you want one of those fancy drinks?" Burgess asked.

"Plain but with cream and sugar if you don't mind."

He nodded and stepped out of the car.

Her eyes followed him as he went inside. He was a decent guy —down to earth, and she liked that about him. Kate soon directed her focus away from the building's brightly lit exterior to look through the passenger window at the oncoming traffic, which was hardly significant. Her thoughts turned to the investigation and the endless possibilities surged through her mind as to where Myers thought Durham might go. It was going to be difficult with Nick and Georgia's now contentious relationship, but lives were at stake and neither would ultimately let it get in the way.

Ahead, a vehicle approached. Its headlights cast a yellow glow that shone in her eyes momentarily. As it continued to draw nearer, she began to recognize it as a truck. But it wasn't until it drove past at a speed noticeably greater than what had been posted that she realized what type of truck it had been. Her mouth fell open and her heart jumped into her throat. It was him. The plate number, however, had been missed as she focused on the make of the old Chevy. But she had to assume it was the same truck as identified by the BOLO. It had to be.

Kate glanced inside to see Burgess still waiting for the coffees. She had only a moment to make her choice. She leaped into the driver's seat of the running patrol car and yanked the gearshift into reverse. With tires spinning, she saw Burgess turn and begin to charge toward the door, but there was no time to wait or to explain. If she didn't trail, he would be lost to them.

Making it onto the road, Kate drove in darkness—no head-lights. She couldn't risk Durham knowing he was being followed. But she'd caught up to him. His old Chevy pickup truck rumbled ahead of her. A call immediately came over the radio.

"Kate, what the hell are you doing?" It was Burgess.

She picked up the receiver. "I'm sorry. It's him. I have to follow him."

"What? No. Let me call it in. We can get help." His voice was elevated in panic.

"There's no time, Mike. I have to keep on him or he'll get away. I'll be fine for right now and, as soon as he stops, I'll radio you with our location."

"Shit." A short pause. "All right. But as soon as he stops, call it in."

"I will." Kate replaced the receiver in its cradle. She believed for a moment that he would insist she stop, but she was no longer a civilian going rogue. Kate needed to remind herself that she was a highly trained federal agent here to do a job. It seemed Burgess realized that too and didn't presume to circumvent her decision.

Kate continued to trail along the darkened road, suspecting that she'd remained undetected as Durham hadn't attempted to veer away. Her whereabouts, though, were unclear. All that lay ahead seemed to be more dark roads. Where was he going?

The team was heading her way, but undoubtedly still out of reach. Kate was on her own, following the Blackwater Killer.

A few more miles of straight single-lane roads. No traffic was coming from the opposite side and so wherever he was headed had to be sparsely populated. He began to slow. Kate fell back and waited. He made a right turn. It was a narrow street, lined with trees that she could just make out in the shadows. No street lights.

Finally, he'd made a left and stopped. She hung back a half of a block, hoping he hadn't seen her. His headlights flicked off and a dim light inside the cab of the truck illuminated. Durham was stepping out. He was parked in front of a house, but she had no idea if this was in the same neighborhood where his family home burned down. He circled to examine the area and stopped in her general direction.

"Shit." Kate had almost forgotten to breathe, believing that he'd seen her, but he continued. Confident he'd gone inside the home, she slowly rolled forward until reaching the house next door. Kate immediately grabbed her cell phone to get a location and radio it in. "Are you kidding me?" The top of the screen showed no bars. Without a signal, she picked up the radio. "Mike, I'm in a neighborhood." Her eyes surveyed her surroundings. "I have no idea where. I checked my cell, but I don't have a signal to get GPS."

He answered immediately. "What's around you?"

"Tall trees. The houses are old, maybe from the fifties or sixties. I'm east from where you are, but I don't know how far."

"I can track the vehicle. Give me a couple of minutes and I'll send some units to back you up."

"I'm going in," Kate insisted.

"Please, wait for backup."

"I have no idea if anyone is in that home, Mike. I can't risk him killing someone. Just find me and get me some backup." She dropped the radio receiver and slowly got out of the car. The cabin light illuminated like a beacon. "Damn it." Kate got out as quickly and quietly as possible, gently closing the door to extinguish the light.

With her hand on her sidearm, she cautiously approached the door of the home. No lights were visible from this vantage point, but she had to assume he'd gone inside. There were no sounds, except her own heightened breath. In the darkness, she could see no evidence of forced entry. No broken glass, no damage to the front door. He might have gone around the back to enter the home. But she feared occupants were inside and tried the front door in the event people around here didn't feel it necessary to lock them.

Her relief that her assumption had been correct quickly diminished as she proceeded to push the door open. Her throat turned dry and her heart beat rapidly.

With hands guiding her through the room, her vision had been compromised by darkness. Any sound she made might mean the end of someone's life—maybe even her own—so she advanced with discretion. A hallway was on the left with a small night light that lit up a bathroom at the hall's end. Still, there were no sounds. Was the house empty? Was he hiding and waiting for her? Kate moved again, her gun pointed directly ahead of her. She heard a moan, like someone whose mouth had been gagged. Her movements ceased in an instant and her hands gripped her weapon with white-knuckled strength. She turned in the direction of the noise. A closed bedroom door was on her left. That was where it came from.

"FBI. Identify yourself." Her voice carried easily through the cramped corridor. If anyone was in this house, they would have been alerted to her presence. He was inside. He had to be.

"FBI. Identify yourself." Again, she waited until finally...

"Help me," the voice cried.

With her gun still at the ready, she pushed open the door, using it to shield her as much as possible until what was inside had been revealed. Standing in front of a window, holding an elderly woman down on her knees—there he was—a gun pointed at her temple.

"Drop the weapon, now!" Her voice raised and echoed firmly inside the room. She was a good shot, but in this dark room, if he refused, a clean shot would be tenuous. He had the upper hand.

"Do you know who I am?" he asked.

"Zachariah Durham." Kate watched as his shadowy figure came into focus.

"Very good. I didn't think you people would figure that out so quickly. He pulled the trigger. A loud clap erupted and the woman dropped to the floor.

Kate instantly returned fire. The spark of ignited gunpowder momentarily lit up his face and she knew she'd struck him. But as the woman fell, he lunged toward her. Wherever her bullet had struck, it hadn't been enough to stop him and he tackled her to the ground.

"You can't kill me. It won't let you."

18

A **gust of** wind scattered the fallen leaves from the ground as the chopper descended in front of the sheriff's office. Deputy Burgess stood just outside the entrance, shielding his eyes from the lights and blowing debris. The blades slowed to a halt and a door opened. Agent Scarborough was the first to emerge and he wasted no time making his way toward Burgess. A close second was Agent Jameson and, finally, Agent Myers.

"Deputy Burgess?" Nick extended his hand. "I'm Special Agent Scarborough." He turned to Dwight. "This is Agent Jameson and Agent Myers."

"Pleasure." Burgess returned the greetings. "Please, come inside." He pushed open the glass door and led the way to his office. "We're still trying to locate Agent Reid." Burgess turned a shoulder but continued. "Has she made contact with you?"

Nick came to an immediate halt. "I'm sorry? What are you talking about? You're trying to locate her?" His face was masked with alarm. "I thought she was here with you."

Burgess furrowed his brow. "No. We were on our way to take a look at Durham's childhood home and we stopped briefly. I went inside a coffee shop and was placing an order when Agent Reid spotted the suspect's vehicle. Agent Scarborough, she went after him."

Nick reached for his cell phone.

"I'm sorry. She called me on the radio. There's no signal out there. I thought she would have reached out to you while she was in pursuit. I tried to persuade her to wait for backup, but when the suspect pulled up to a home, she went inside after him."

Nick pushed his hand through his hair. "Damn it. Where the hell is she?"

"We're still trying to locate the vehicle through our GPS. I just returned myself and I was heading to see if we'd made progress."

"Why would it take this long to get her position?" Dwight asked.

"We recently installed a new software system and not all of the vehicles had been updated. Unfortunately, mine had not been."

"Where's the sheriff?" Nick asked, turning his head in every direction. "I need to find my agent now."

"The situation has obviously escalated quickly over the course of the past couple of hours. Sheriff Conroy has been getting updates from state police and myself. I informed him of the situation and he is coming in now from a meeting with the governor."

"Where's the tech who's working on finding Agent Reid?" Nick asked.

"Follow me." Burgess carried on along the corridor to the elevator. "They're on the second floor." On arrival upstairs, he led the way to an open area—a bullpen—where his techs were positioned. "Where are we at on locating my patrol car?" He approached one of the officers.

"The system will be updated in a matter of minutes. We'll be able to see it shortly thereafter."

"You mentioned the two of you were driving out to Durham's childhood home," Nick began. "Why? What's out there?"

"Agent Reid figured out that Durham's sister attended the middle school that was shown on Ariel Nadal's clothing. And after she'd sent the information to one of your other agents, an Agent Vasquez, I believe, she discovered that the facial markers between her and the suspect were the same. We then began to search through our archived files and discovered that the man who we believe to be the suspect, Zachariah Durham, survived a fire that killed his family. He was ten."

"That's how you discovered his actual identity." Myers shook her head. "Agent Reid contacted me and asked that I revisit my original profile and go over this new information in hopes of locating the suspect. Apparently, she didn't need me to do that."

"I got it!" The officer whipped his chair around to Burgess. "She's at 637 Marlin Street."

Burgess revealed a dire look. "That's almost thirty minutes from here."

"You stay here," Nick said to Georgia. "Jameson and I will go get her."

Georgia stepped aside while they walked on. "Agent Scarborough."

Nick stopped and turned back.

"You mentioned on the way over that you found three other victims based on the contents Durham had in the containers in his shed."

"That's right."

"Given what we know now, and that he appears to be growing desperate for escape, please keep in mind that if Agent Reid hasn't taken him down, he won't care that she's a federal agent. At this point, he won't care about his own life."

Nick studied Georgia's eyes, knowing that she would never risk another agent's life or mislead them in any way. "Thank you."

"I'd like to come with you." Burgess started toward them. "This is still my town. You need a car and I can get you there faster."

Nick turned to Dwight, who gave a nod of approval. "All right. Let's go." He pushed through the exit and headed toward the helicopter pilot. "I'll need air support. We've got an agent in danger."

"I'll stay on you." The pilot waited for the agents to clear before firing up the blades.

KATE WAS PINNED BENEATH HIM. His shoulder trickled blood down his arm and onto her body. The gun was pointed between her eyes and Kate trusted that this wasn't going to end well for her. She was losing the fight, and after fighting for the past few years, maybe she was ready to call it quits. She'd come in here fearing he'd take the life of whoever was inside this house and he did. And she was powerless to help the old woman. "Who was that woman to you?" Her words struggled to materialize as she squirmed beneath him. "She didn't deserve to die."

Durham glanced back momentarily and then returned his attention to Kate. "She was my first foster parent. Not a very good one either."

"I'm sorry you lost your family in that fire." Kate noticed his eyes flinch just for a minute. "I lost some people who I loved very much."

"Is this supposed to be FBI psychology 101?" Durham smiled and shook his head. "Don't pretend you know anything, you stupid bitch. I'm the one with the gun pointed at your head, not the other way around."

"You're right about that, but don't think for one second that I'm afraid of you. I'm not one of those young women you pretended was your sister. What did she do to you anyway?" Her eyes locked onto his. Even in the darkness, she could see he hadn't expected this. Her words came as a surprise to her as well.

"Don't you worry about that. She got what she deserved and so did those other girls. Just like you're about to."

"Is this you talking? What did you mean by 'it won't let you?' Who's 'it?'" Her tone grew firm and she had no idea where this strength was coming from but was grateful for its manifestation.

"I could shoot you right in your pretty little head, bitch, so I'd keep my mouth shut if I were you."

"You think you're the only one who's ever threatened me?" Kate smiled. "You think I haven't faced death before? What you don't realize is, if you kill me, they won't stop until they kill you. There'll be no judge and no jury."

A faint sound, deep and throbbing, began to arise from a far-off place. Kate shifted her eyes toward the window. She recognized the rumbling noise. "They're already here."

Durham turned in the direction of the window and that was when she struck. Kate raised her knee and slammed it into his back. He swung in return toward her with a face twisted in pain. She reached for the gun that was no longer pointed at her head but could still do damage if she couldn't seize it from him. It wasn't long before he regained his breath and realized Kate had her hands wrapped around the gun, working to pry it from his fingers. Her right knee raised and struck him again.

This time, Durham took to his feet with powerful strength in his legs, rising as if propelled by an unknown force. Kate flipped to her side as he tried to flee, taking hold of his leg and he came crashing down again and dropped his gun. She held on as tightly as she could, but her arms tingled from the weight of his knees placed upon them for too long. Her fingers began to slip from his torn jeans until he broke free.

The helicopter sounded much closer now and Kate began to hear the rumbling of a car's engine too. But he was going to get away and she had to stop him. She scrambled to her feet, lunging toward the gun that he'd bolted over without attempting to grab. His fear of capture led him to make the grave mistake of not retrieving it and so Kate seized the unexpected opportunity.

With her weapon back in proper hands and his secured in her waist, she pushed to her feet and sprinted after him. The noises grew louder, the blades slicing through the air and sirens screaming down the quiet street. They had to be only seconds away, but that might still be too late.

Kate raced out the back door and spotted him leaping over a fence and into another yard. She followed him, jumping over the wooden slats. Snagging her shirt, she yanked it off the splintered wood and pressed on. He was just ahead, taking flight over yet another fence. His face turned back toward her and she could have sworn he was smiling, his white teeth shining in the dark, clenched tightly.

Behind the housing development lay a marshy river that flowed from the larger Saint Marys. She had to get to him before he reached it; otherwise, the search would become nearly impossible, allowing Durham not only the cover of darkness but also cover in the terrain over which he was likely a good navigator. He could not get the upper hand.

She was fit and she could keep up with him, but a sharp pain was nagging at her side and worsening. When she slowed for a moment, Kate realized that a cut was oozing blood. It must have happened when the shirt was snagged. *Don't let him get away.* He was gaining ground on her. It was then that Kate knew she had to turn back. All was not yet lost and she knew the helicopter could continue the search, shining a light, refusing to let him hide in the tall grasses and cypress that covered the area.

Turning back, she pressed her hand against the wound and made her way back to the house, climbing over the fences more slowly this time, until she returned. Shouting could be heard up ahead. They must have been inside by now and might be calling for her, but she couldn't discern the words, or the voices.

The final crawl over the fence and she was in the backyard again. She called out to make her presence known and to ensure there would be no confusion as to her identity. The back door that had remained open was now consumed by the shadow of someone she immediately recognized.

"Kate?" the voice bellowed.

"It's me. I'm okay." She appeared through the darkness and into the reflection of the light that had been switched on inside the home. "He got away. I tried to chase him, but..." She removed her hand which was now covered in blood. "I couldn't keep up."

"Jesus." Nick reached out for her hand and cast his eyes to the wound. "Get inside." He followed behind her into the kitchen where Dwight and Deputy Burgess had arrived. "Are you hurt anywhere else?"

"No. I'm fine." Kate peered beyond the back door, until closing her eyes at the knowledge that he'd slipped away. "We can still go after him, Nick. I saw the helicopter. We have to get in there and look for him before it's too late."

"She's right," Dwight replied. "If he's out there, we can find him. We can't afford to let him slip through our fingers."

Nick looked at his colleagues and nodded. "Okay. Burgess, you stay here with Kate and secure the scene."

"I don't think so." She slowly pushed off the chair. "I'm not staying here. I just fended off that son of a bitch. I know what he's capable of and I'm sure as hell not going take a back seat on this."

"Okay, okay," Nick conceded. "Burgess, do what you need to do. We need to leave now if we stand any chance at all of tracking him down."

"Understood."

"Let's go. There's a first aid kit in the chopper. We can at least put a bandage on that gash." Nick reached for Kate's arm, but she pulled it away.

"I got this."

He held her gaze for a moment, but seemed to realize now was not the time to coddle her. Instead, he continued past the others and walked outside to the waiting helicopter.

As Kate moved to keep up with him, Burgess stopped her. "I can't believe you did that. I don't know if you're the bravest person I've ever met or the most reckless."

"I'm somewhere in between. We'll keep you posted." She reached for his arm. "Thank you, Mike." Kate continued outside where the chopper was ready and waiting for them. It was an odd sight as it sat in the middle of a neighborhood street.

Several residents had emerged from their homes to witness the ambush of the FBI in their rural community. Burgess must have called for backup as well because several patrol cars were roaring down the street, lights flashing and sirens blaring.

"Kate, come on. We need to go." Nick waved her over, shouting above the noise from the chopper.

She jogged toward them and jumped inside. The last time she'd been in one of these, Marshall's life had been hanging by a thread, and so had hers.

"Which way was he headed?" Nick reached for the kit and pulled out the bandages. "Lift your shirt."

"As far as I could tell, he was heading to the river," Kate held her shirt above the wound while Nick began to dress it. "What about the houses here? We should get Burgess' team to canvas them. Make sure he hasn't slipped inside one of them."

"Good call," Dwight began. "I'll let him know." He reached for the radio just as the chopper began its vertical ascent.

"I'm not going to bother asking why you went after him, Kate," Nick pressed the surgical tape against her bare skin. "I think I know you better than that, but you have to know that it wasn't the right call. You understand that, right?"

She nodded. "I understand, but if we'd waited for the sheriff to respond, he could have easily dumped the truck somewhere and we'd never have known where he was going. I didn't intend to approach him without backup. But when he went inside that house, I couldn't be sure he wouldn't hurt whoever was inside."

A reluctant nod of approval from Nick followed. She'd risked her safety, but only in hopes of saving someone else, despite the fact it hadn't quite gone to plan, and now there was another in a string of deaths that Durham had left behind.

They were over the river now. The chopper's light cast a menacing glow on the cloudy waters. Green algae blanketed the water's surface beyond the shorelines, reaching nearly halfway into the river, leaving only a narrow path. These were protected waters, not generally traversed, which meant there were likely few if any designated paths on which a pedestrian could travel. It would be hard for him to hide here, especially as they had an aerial view. "He's wearing blue jeans and a dark grey t-shirt," Kate said.

Nick moved to the seat next to the pilot and placed the headgear on for communication with ground units that were arriving from the sheriff's office.

"You all right?" Dwight glanced at Kate's freshly dressed wound.

"I'm fine. It's not bad."

"That was a crazy stunt you pulled, Reid, but it was a hell of a good thing you did."

Kate smiled, appreciating the vote of confidence, especially because Nick might reconsider plans for some form of punishment for her rash behavior. She returned her attention to the front. Her vantage point wasn't the best, but she could see the light moving along the river. So far, they hadn't seen him. There was no way he could have gotten that far that fast. From the time she last spotted him to now couldn't have been longer than fifteen minutes. Then again, the chase seemed to make time stand still. All she could see was him. All she could recall was the gun he had pointed at her head and the body of the old woman slumped against the bedroom wall. A woman she failed to protect.

After several more minutes, the pilot turned to Nick and shook his head.

"Keep going. Head downstream another mile, then we'll turn around and make another pass." Nick looked back to Dwight and Kate. "We're going to keep at it."

They both nodded their agreement.

On the ground, Burgess was fielding calls from the press, and his boss, and being approached by the neighbors. This was a manhunt and there was no way to stop the snowball from mounting.

"Where are you?" Burgess radioed one of his deputies.

"I'm a block to the west. Still nothing. What do you want to do?"

"I don't know yet. They're still searching and about to make another run at it, but I think it might be too late." He paused to consider his next move. "Go up to the next block north, then head back. I have to let the sheriff know where we're at. He'll have to get in front of the media sooner rather than later." Burgess stepped outside the home as the body was being carted out of the house and into a waiting ambulance. Neighbors with craned necks tried to catch a glimpse of the old woman they'd known as Beatrice Gustafson, a sixty-seven-year-old who lived in the house alone. A background check confirmed that she had been the first foster parent that Durham had been assigned to live with. Why he chose this house, this poor woman, Burgess couldn't fathom. Was it possible he might target another of his foster parents? It didn't fit his MO, but nothing had fit his MO in the past few hours. Durham was shaping a new path now that had yet to reveal a pattern. Would he go after someone else, or would he just seek to get as far away from here as he could in hopes of escaping justice? Burgess considered the options. He remembered reading the file. It was as though the man had dropped from existence once he turned eighteen and left the System, only to turn up four years later, killing young women and dumping them into the swamp.

Burgess looked ahead; his eyes were clear and his mind sharp. An idea had ignited, one that Kate initially kindled, but only in passing. Now that Durham's former foster parent had been murdered, perhaps she had been on the right track after all. He raised the radio to his mouth. "Agent Scarborough, it's Deputy Burgess, come in." The radio crackled.

"Scarborough here. Burgess, you got something?" His voice seemed to rise slightly as though anticipating a positive reply.

"He might go back to the place where it all started for him. Back to the home he burned down. Agent Reid mentioned it in passing earlier and now that he's killed again, I think she may have been onto something."

"Is there anything there?" The static fractured Nick's response.

"The land's been cleared, but I haven't been there in a long time. The family lived on three acres. He might've built something makeshift." Burgess paused. "You said there were three other victims at his place near Fayetteville."

"That's right."

"What if there's more? What if he's coming home to collect his final treasures?"

Nick looked over his shoulder at Kate. "Burgess says you thought Durham might go back to his family's property."

"I said it was a possibility, but I don't have anything to base that on."

"What about now? He thinks maybe there are more victims buried there. What do you think? Does he have something?"

"We've lost him, Nick. We've been up and down this river for the past hour," Dwight began. "We got nothing else to go on."

Kate nodded. "He's right."

Nick took in a deep breath and turned back. "Get your people down there and we'll go there now. Scarborough out."

19

The **deep thud** of helicopter blades faded into the distance and Durham emerged from beneath the cover of a large tupelo tree that had shielded him from view. His biggest concern had been the gators, but so far he hadn't seen any, although they were master concealers. Going back to his truck wasn't an option any longer. The place was teeming with law enforcement.

Durham cringed and placed his hand over his chest, gripping it as though he was experiencing a heart attack. But it was the beast that controlled him and it was demanding he kill again. With a pounding head and a thirst that demanded equal attention, he was beginning to feel as though he might split in two, but one thing was certain—he had to leave this place now.

The boots on his feet were soaked through as he trudged along the river's edge. All sense of time eluded him, and the moon offered just enough light by which to see. He knew he was heading east. The shoulder that had been grazed by the agent's bullet throbbed and continued to ooze blood. Recalling the words she spoke, Durham's anger swelled. She hadn't been afraid of him. She'd been ready to die. In fact, she'd almost encouraged him to kill her because she knew that would mean his certain demise. He couldn't control her the way he could the others.

Inside his head, an image began to burn. The boy he used to be had all the power taken from him. She'd done unspeakable things to him, just as their father had done to her. He squeezed his eyes shut to rid himself of the painful memory. Everything changed for little Zachariah after the fire. The fire no one discovered had been intentionally set by him and was an all too easy task. His father had been a welder and Zach, as he was called, watched him work, learning how the soldering iron worked—and the gases it used.

It had been deemed an accident and only Zach Durham survived. He'd been forced to live in several foster homes, running away from most of them until he finally left the System at the age of eighteen. But the compulsions started much earlier than that. Even before his family died, thoughts of killing and maiming prevailed in his mind—a consequence of his extreme abuse. He practiced on animals first and the excitement he derived from that grew.

There had been a part of him, after the first human kill—the girl who lived only miles from his old home—that knew it was wrong and wanted him to confess. That small piece of him still struggled to survive as it now existed only in a cage beneath the power of the beast that had taken over. The little boy had grown to become a killer and at times, that small part managed fleeting control and did what needed to be done to ensure the madness would be stopped. The beast couldn't find out what he'd done, though. It couldn't know that he had moved his projects, his victims, to the spot where his sister abused him for the first time. He forced that knowledge to the back of his mind where the task could remain buried.

Durham continued east as the river widened. He had to be approaching the end where it would divert into another stream. He needed to get back onto the road and find a car. Several minutes ticked by and he made it to a single-lane road but did not know where he was, only that he needed to get the hell out of there.

Walking along the shoulder, a few cars passed by and although he'd tried to hitch a ride, no one stopped. It wasn't until Durham turned to face the direction of the cars that one finally began to slow. His shoulder, still dripping blood, seemed to get the attention of the driver.

The car rolled to a stop and the passenger window lowered. A man who looked to be in his late forties peered out. "Are you okay? Do you need a doctor?"

"Yes." Durham sounded out of breath. "Please, I've been carjacked and was shot in the shoulder." He knew his face had been all over the news and hoped this man hadn't seen it.

He hesitated for a moment and Durham thought that he'd been recognized. But he leaned over and pushed open the passenger door. Durham slipped inside. "Thank you. I've been out here walking for more than an hour and no one has stopped."

"Haven't you heard?" the man said. "There's some serial killer on the loose. I'm not surprised no one stopped." He looked at Durham. "There's a hospital about twenty miles away. I'll have you there as quickly as possible."

"I can't thank you enough, sir."

"Please, call me Hank."

Durham looked at the road ahead and his lips curled with a wicked smile. "Thank you, Hank."

❧

THE GROUNDS below offered a clearing with enough room to land the helicopter. Burgess and his team waited, having arrived only minutes before the FBI. With four patrol cars lined up along the gravel drive in front of the structural remains of the Durham family home, Burgess and his team began to approach the emerging federal agents.

The late hour and insufficient light would only hamper the search, and the general consensus among the sheriff's department staff seemed to be that this was a shot in the dark anyway.

Nick was the first to step out of the chopper. He pulled open the rear door and Kate and Dwight followed. The three moved to Burgess.

"So this is it?" Nick asked.

"Yes. This was the Durham home that burned down." Burgess looked over his shoulder. "We haven't started our search yet."

"Then let's get started," Nick replied.

"I'll take Agent Reid and one of your men," Dwight said. "We'll head to the north end of the property and start from there."

"Burgess, why don't we pair up and go south and the rest of your men can start on the east and west ends," Nick said. "We've got three acres to cover. I sure as hell hope we find something." He started south and Burgess jogged to catch up with him.

Meanwhile, Kate and Dwight approached one of the deputies.

"Better get started," Dwight said to the man, and the three began to travel to the north end of the property. "Looks like it might have been cleared recently."

"It's been in probate court since the incident and so the State has retained possession of the property. Since the only remaining heir hasn't claimed it, the State's preparing for its sale."

"Have they ever tried to locate Durham?" Kate asked as the lights from the patrol cars faded from view and the skies grew even darker.

"I assume so," the deputy replied, "but he's been going by a different name for how long, I don't know, but that would make it pretty hard to find him. Anyway, we're coming up on the spot where the workshop was situated." The deputy shined his flashlight over the area.

The only remaining indication that a building had stood in that spot was the foundation. This whole situation was bringing back some disconcerting memories for Kate and she was glad no other evidence of the fire remained.

Nick, along with Burgess and another of his team continued south toward the front entrance of the property. "I'm not feeling very confident this psycho's going to come back here. At least, not tonight. Almost the entire southern part of the country is looking for him."

"I wasn't initially inclined to go along with Agent Reid's hunch until I got to thinking more about it," Burgess started. "But she was the one to discover his identity so even if she wasn't entirely sure he'd come back here, I think that woman's got some sort of sixth sense and I'm not going to dismiss her hunches."

"Maybe you're right." Nick shone his light a few feet to the left of where they'd been walking. "What do you suppose that is?" What appeared to be a slight knoll in the ground caught his attention. "This piece of land is pretty damn flat and you got this little mound tucked between these trees back here. I don't know if it's anything, but I'd like to find out."

Burgess pressed the button on the radio receiver attached to the top of his uniform. "Higgins, we need a shovel. We're about two hundred yards due south of the main structure."

"On my way."

Moments later, the deputy arrived with two shovels in hand. "Sorry for the delay. We were already pretty far west on the property."

"Thanks." Burgess grabbed both shovels and handed one to Nick. "Let's get to it and hope that you have the same sixth sense as your Agent Reid."

The deputy held his flashlight over the mound where the other two began stripping away the pile. At least four feet wide and eight feet long, it would take some time to make a dent, but the two pressed on with as much speed as they could muster.

"Wait." Nick raised a hand. "I hit something." He lowered the shovel back into the ground, only inches deep, and began to push the soft, moist soil around with its pointed tip. "I can't see a goddam thing." He looked at the deputy. "Shine that light closer, would you?" He continued to slowly pull the dirt back until bones appeared. "Son of a bitch. We got something here." Nick knelt and wiped the material from the bones. "Whatever this is, it's been here a while. Nothing but bone left." He began to use both hands to scrape away from the outline of what was beginning to look like an arm. "We got fingers here." He glanced at Burgess. "This has to be one of the three other victims."

"We'll need to get forensics out here," Burgess replied.

"Guess you were right about his treasures. Now let's see if he comes back to collect them." Nick pushed off the ground and got back on his feet. "If this place gets lit up with cops, we won't stand a chance of Durham returning here at all." He retrieved his cell phone from his pocket. "Let me make contact with Jameson and Reid—see if they've turned up anything yet." He turned away for a moment to make the call. "We just found another victim down here and we need to decide whether or not to lay low a while longer and hope Durham shows up. But, I need to know if you two have found anything."

"What's that? Hang on Nick, I don't have shit for a signal." Dwight walked several more feet. "You said something about finding a victim?"

"Yeah. You guys find anything?"

"No. We've almost reached the property's northern boundary and, apart from the foundation of an old workshop, we haven't seen anything unusual or anything that would indicate he'd been here recently."

Nick looked at Burgess and shook his head. "All right. Why don't you all meet us here? We're a couple hundred yards south of the house, near the property's main entrance." He ended the call and placed the phone back in his pocket. "We'll regroup and decide where to go from here. They've got squat so I told them to meet us."

"We can't sit on this for long," Burgess replied.

"I know."

DURHAM FOCUSED his attention on the man at the wheel. "Could you pull over for a minute? I'm sorry, I just feel like I'm gonna toss my cookies."

The man's eyes widened. "Of course, yeah." He pulled across the lane onto the shoulder.

Durham pushed open the passenger door and leaned out. When he was confident Hank had shifted the gear into park, he raised his left leg and, with his heavy, sodden boot, struck the man in the head. The older man was slow to react and released an excruciating bellow.

Zachariah Durham was anything but slow and, with his wiry body, drew upright again and began to pummel the man's face, looming over him with the beast in his eyes.

Hank tried to shield himself with his bulky forearms, but could not slow the assault. His lips moved as if trying to speak, but the blows to his head made it impossible for words to form.

"You know who I am?" Durham shouted. "Who am I? Who the fuck am I?" He needed to dominate the man, just as he had the others. *Kill him. Kill him.* The voice in his head filled him with even greater strength until finally, Hank fell unconscious.

Durham's eyes shifted wildly, ensuring no other vehicles were approaching, and reached for the keys still in the ignition. He looked back at Hank, whose mouth hung open, spilling blood—swollen eyes and cheeks. Durham had to finish him and drove one of the keys with brute force into his throat and blood spewed from the hole. A few gurgling sounds erupted as Hank seemed to regain consciousness, but it didn't last long. Pushing back the hair that had fallen into his eyes, Durham looked at his own hands, covered in blood, and his shoulder wound that seemed to have widened in the attack.

An overwhelming desire came upon him in a frenzy. He'd never killed a man before, but that didn't suppress his need to release the energy that built up after a kill. Durham unzipped his pants and rested his knees on the large man's thigh. It only took moments for him to reach full excitement and release it over the body of the dead man.

He began to recover from the rush, slowing his breath and dropping his head. His eyes shot up toward the driver's side door. Durham reached for the handle and opened it. He pushed the man out. Hank Greene of Palmdale, Florida, fell to the blacktop. His plump body smacked on the ground. With haste, Durham stepped out of the vehicle and dragged the nearly 250-pound man around the back of the car and down the slight slope of ground. There was no time to try and hide his body further from view. Durham was being hunted and so what did one more body matter?

He stepped back inside the car and wiped the blood from the keys. Turning over the engine, Durham pulled away and continued along the back road leading him toward the river, only he slammed on the brakes and spun the car around in a 360. He wasn't going back there. The question remained: where would he go?

THE TEAM HAD CONVERGED and now stood over the remains of at least one additional victim of the Blackwater Killer. It was approaching midnight and, so far, Durham remained on the loose.

"I let him slip through my fingers," Kate said, standing over the bones of the victim. "I took my shot and missed."

"No one blames you for that, Kate," Burgess said, seemingly preempting the words that were about to come from Nick's lips. "If you hadn't gone after him, albeit, by abandoning me, we wouldn't have a damn clue as to where he was at. At least now we know he's close and coming here was a logical step."

"He's right." Nick cast a look at Burgess. "I can only assume we'll find all three victims here. There could be more, and that means Durham has been at this a lot longer than any of us believed."

"The key is to pinpoint his next move," Dwight said. "But then, if we could do that, none of us would be standing here right now."

Burgess' radio crackled. "Deputy Burgess, come in, please."

He pressed the receiver. "Burgess here."

"We got a 911 call stating a body had been found on northbound State Route 257. Fresh tire marks were also found near the body and it's assumed the victim's car was stolen."

Burgess looked to the team. "It's gotta be him. It has to be." He pressed on the receiver again. "Do we have the make and model of that car? Plates?"

"No sir, but the man still had identification."

"Run the ID through MVD and get his registration information ASAP."

"Ten-four." The radio went silent again.

"How far away is State Route 257?" Dwight asked.

"It runs north and south and the nearest junction to here is about ten miles due east," one of the deputies replied.

"Let's inform state police and get some air support in place," Nick began. "How soon before we confirm make and model?" he asked Burgess.

"Only a matter of minutes."

"Okay." Nick placed his hands on his hips and cast his gaze down, seemingly to work out a solution to this new break. "Can we keep this location quiet until we track down the vehicle?"

"Yes," Burgess replied.

"Good. My team will stay here with me. I'll send up the chopper once we get confirmation and you and your team can coordinate with state police and try to keep him from getting off that highway."

"Got it." Burgess began to direct his team back to their vehicles. "As soon as I hear..."

"Thank you," Nick replied.

Once the others were out of earshot, Nick turned to Kate and Dwight. "Look, we have no idea how long he's been on the road. We've been searching this place for almost two hours. There's no telling when he found his way out of the river and hoofed it to the highway. It's possible we might have already missed him."

"But you don't think we have," Kate said.

"I'm trusting your instincts, Kate. This is not a rational man. He's impulsive and beyond reckless."

"That makes him unpredictable and even more dangerous. He's never killed a man that we know of," Dwight said.

"There are no guarantees he killed this one, but I think it

would be far too coincidental in a place where these things just don't happen, and then two deaths in one night within a twenty-mile radius?" Kate began. "It's Durham and, yes, I believe he will come back here. He may even be counting on us already assuming as much."

20

Headlights beaming in the rearview mirror made it almost impossible for Durham to ascertain whether or not the vehicle behind him was a police car. He assumed, however, that if it had been the police, he'd have seen flashing red and blue lights by now. Nevertheless, he accelerated and switched lanes in an effort to remove his car from the glow of those headlights because he'd also been listening to the car radio. Just about every station cut into regular programming several times to broadcast an alert that detailed the license plate, make, and model of the car he was now driving. While the car behind him wasn't the police, it could have been someone who'd heard those same alerts and was perhaps on the phone right now to 911.

Desperation could make a man dangerous, but it made Zachariah Durham positively lethal. If he couldn't get out of this alive, then he would be sure to take down anyone and everyone in his path. And especially the FBI agent—the one who had been so defiant. The one who left the bleeding wound on his shoulder.

She'd taken away his power, his control, and he would make her pay for it.

Durham figured they would have found his other victims by now. They already knew his true identity and, from there, it would have only been a small leap to piece together his past. He realized, too late, that it had been a mistake to go to the old woman's house, but he didn't know he'd been followed. He had planned to stay there until the feds gave up searching the area and moved on, but she followed him.

The war that had erupted inside him, splintering what cohesive thoughts he still possessed, continued to rage. The part of him that sought to make him suffer the consequences of his actions had wrangled control from the beast and nearly offered him up to the authorities on a silver platter by way of moving the bodies to the river. And he began to wonder if it had been that part of him that drove him to the old woman's house. He could no longer decipher who was running the show and the conclusion meant no one was safe.

The first thing he needed to do was to ditch the car. He'd been traveling for the better part of forty minutes, heading south toward Orlando. An exit was just ahead to a small town thirty miles north of Orlando called Lakeside. He could leave the car and find another vehicle, by force, if necessary. Waiting them out was what he had to do. But with his face all over the news, it would not be easy to hide in plain sight.

Durham turned right to exit the highway and came upon the stoplight. The red glow began to sting his eyes as he stared and the burning in his chest worsened. He closed his eyes for a moment and, when the light turned green, they opened again, only this time, a force previously unknown had taken hold. Something new had emerged from his shattered mind. And it was about to bring devastation to all those who encountered it.

As he pressed the gas pedal, the tires spun and the car veered to the left, driving back onto the highway. The FBI agent could not be allowed to live and he knew exactly where she would be.

EVERY INCH of the land where the Durham home once stood had been traversed. A small shed had been located by Burgess' team on the far west end of the property, along with another concrete slab nearby. A few pieces of equipment remained inside the shed beneath dusty blankets. Perhaps this was where the father welded on occasion. However, nothing else of any significance was inside. Kate stood in front of that shed now with Nick. Dwight had been posted near the property's entrance where the remains had been discovered.

"It's been almost an hour," Kate said. "I'm starting to think I might have been wrong. What if he's out there killing again?" She looked at Nick with doubt in her eyes. "We can't stay here any longer. We need to do something."

Nick seemed to ponder her request. According to local law enforcement, there had been sightings of the vehicle they suspected Durham to be driving, but as of yet, they had not caught up with him.

She waited for him to speak, but her patience was wearing thin. "What does Agent Myers think? Have you spoken with her? Given what we know now, does she believe he will come back here?" Kate needed something other than her own suspicions to confirm they were on the right track.

He appeared irritated by the questions Kate was launching at him. "I haven't had any updates from her." Nick rubbed his face as though it might clear his mind. "I don't know what the hell to do right now. Why the hell can't these guys find him?"

"Nick." Kate reached out to him. "We have to find Durham. We just can't risk him taking another life."

He peered into her eyes. "I thought he'd come here too. I really did."

In the distance, a faint light appeared. Both turned in the direction from which it came. Nick raised his phone and called Dwight. "Do you see that? What is it?"

"It's a car," Dwight replied. "I—I can't tell." He paused for a moment. "Yes, it's heading this way. Nick, this could be him."

"Can you see if it's his car?"

Another pause. "It's him! It's him!"

"Son of a bitch." Nick beamed with certitude. "He's here." Returning his attention to the call, he continued, "We're heading over to you now." The call ended and Nick dropped his phone back into his pocket. "Let's go. This is it."

It took several minutes to make it to the front of the property and as they approached, something appeared out of order. No gunshots had been heard, no yelling of demands, only Dwight standing at the driver's side door of what they believed had been Durham's car, with no weapon drawn. It was the look on Dwight's face as he turned toward them that forced Nick to conclude something had gone awry. "Slow up," he said to Kate.

"Who's inside that car?" She was the first to speak as they drew nearer to Dwight.

"She was abducted from the diner where she works." Dwight handed Nick a note. "He took her clothes." That explained why Dwight was no longer wearing his jacket. She'd had it draped over the front of her. "He told her to drive here and give this note to the FBI bitch."

"Miss, are you okay?" Nick leaned into the car.

"She's scared, but it doesn't look like he hurt her," Dwight replied.

Her frail voice arose. "He told me that he wouldn't kill me if I came here to give you the note. I was at work and he said if I called the police or told anyone else, he'd come back for me." Her tone was barely above a whisper as she spoke through quaking nerves. "He came in just as I was closing and grabbed me." She wiped a tear away with her hand.

"What does the note say?" Kate's expression fortified in an instant and her steely eyes demanded a reply.

Nick handed her the scrap paper that appeared to be from the diner.

Kate opened the note and began to read. "I'm coming for you next." She looked at her colleagues and a scathing grin formed on her lips. "Guess he won't be here tonight after all."

"We'll go back to the sheriff's office," Nick began. "We need to get her to a hospital first and have her checked out. Jameson, call Burgess and let him know we have the car. He can call off the air support, but keep the troopers posted at the roadblocks. I don't know what this son of a bitch is planning on, but we'd better figure it out damn quick."

THE SUSPECT's car was being towed back to the sheriff's office and the young woman who had been threatened remained at the hospital. The four federal agents stood inside Sheriff Conroy's office while Burgess filled him in on what they had so far.

"So we still have no goddam clue where this guy is?" The sheriff paced his large and plush office.

"He's issued a threat against Agent Reid," Dwight began. "There's a possibility we can use this to our advantage."

"Jameson's right." Agent Myers pushed off the credenza that rested against the wall. "From what we know of Zachariah

Durham, and from what I've read in your archived files, this man needs to be in control. As a formerly abused child, this is fairly characteristic."

"There were no incidents of any abuse in the Durham home, Agent Myers." Sheriff Conroy wrinkled his brow as though insulted by the comment.

"I'm sorry, Sheriff, but did you read the files? Protective Services were called out on four different occasions based on concerns expressed by Durham's school teachers at the time."

"Yes, but they'd been determined to be unfounded once CPS interviewed the family." The sheriff was on the defensive.

"This happened more than ten years ago. I'm not trying to point the finger here. I'm simply stating that there were problems inside the Durham home. And the fact that Zachariah Durham dismembers his victims the way he does—well, sir, I can tell you that I've been doing this long enough and have studied sociopaths enough to understand that this type of behavior does not simply appear one day for no apparent reason." Myers cast a glance at Nick, seemingly to ensure she hadn't crossed some boundary of authority. "Getting back to this situation, Agent Reid has become his next target because she denied him control over her as he had had with his previous victims."

"He's obviously become emboldened by this latest action—and erratic," Nick said. "Agent Myers is right. We can use this opportunity to draw him in."

Kate wasn't about to object. She'd been a target before, albeit for different reasons, but a target nonetheless. And this would probably not be the last time either. So, if there was a way for her to draw Durham out again, then she wouldn't hesitate. The difference this time was that she was a trained federal agent, not a fearful young woman. "Look, whatever you need me to do, I can handle it."

Dwight raised a hand. "If we're going to do this, we'll have your back the entire time."

"Agreed," Nick added. "He knew we would be at his former home. He must also know that we found the other victims." He paused for a moment. "Agent Myers, why do you think he chose to go to one of his foster parents' homes?"

"I think he sees that his lifestyle has been compromised—that he believes he's reached the end of the road and there is nowhere left for him to turn and so why not exact retribution on those who had perhaps treated him the way his own family had? I think we all know by now that the fire that killed his parents and sister was intentionally set by him." Myers looked at Conroy again, who appeared as though she was still on the attack. "There were other incidents in his case file from the state that indicated his abuse carried on with other various foster parents, including Mrs. Gustafson, the woman he killed when Agent Reid attempted to thwart his efforts."

"You think it's possible then, that he might seek out any others who abused him?" Burgess, who had been quiet up to this point, seemed interested in Myers' theory.

"First of all, Durham won't hunt down Agent Reid, even if his threat indicated as much. That would be tantamount to a death wish if he were to just waltz in here and attack her. And, while I don't believe he's of a particularly high intelligence, he can put two and two together."

Myers walked to the center of the room. "Our immediate assumption was that because he'd sought out his first foster parent, he could potentially seek out the others, at least the ones from whom he'd suffered some form of abuse. I believe he will also come to that conclusion. So, to answer your question, Deputy Burgess, yes, I think he might seek out his other abusers, which in turn means that he will expect us to be there when he does, thus giving him access to Agent Reid, which might be his end-game."

"Look, whatever it is that you people need to do to get this crazed psycho off my streets, I'll trust you to do it." The sheriff's impatient tone wasn't lost on anyone, least of all the FBI agents in the room who were supposed to be trained on how to capture serial killers. "I've got the media hounding me and a community afraid to leave their homes. It's one a.m. now. Put your plan in place. I want this asshole off my streets by morning." Conroy stormed out of his own office.

"I'm sorry. He's normally a pretty decent guy to work for and a great sheriff. This just isn't something that happens around here and with the media attention and scared citizens, it's starting to get to him." Burgess moved toward Kate but looked at Myers. "What else was in that file about the other foster parents? I apologize, but I didn't get through it before we left for Durham's home."

"In the seven or so years Durham was in the System, he had a total of twenty foster homes. After he turned eighteen, the state lost track of him. While you all were trying to track him down, I had our team back in D.C. run a background check and he's essentially been a ghost for the past six years. No tax returns, and no bank accounts in his name. However, the social security number he was using to obtain employment was registered to a man named Arlen Tucker, who died in 1987."

"Okay," Nick began. "Going back to the foster families, after Gustafson, who was the next family he had problems with?"

Agent Myers retrieved her iPad and pulled up her notes. "According to CPS, he went to live with the Sutter family two years later and that was the second time an incident, later deemed unsubstantiated, was filed." She looked at Nick. "Could be where he's going."

"Or he could already be there," Dwight replied. "There's no telling how much of a head start he's got on us right now."

"Do we have an address?" Burgess asked.

"Yes. During that time, the Sutters lived in McLeary," Myers replied.

"That town backs up to the river, further east than where we were looking by about six miles."

"He's got a thing for the river. Might be the first place he'd go," Dwight replied.

"Let's put a plan in place and then we'll head out." Nick began to walk out of the room and raised his phone to his ear, but before he could make the call, Georgia approached.

"Can I talk to you for a minute?"

Nick cast his gaze left and then right, ensuring no one had noticed that the two were speaking to one another. "Yeah, I guess, but only a minute." He continued along the corridor, spotting an unoccupied office. He flipped the light switch and closed the door after Georgia entered. "What is it?"

"Listen, I know this is awkward, but I really appreciate you not letting it get in the way of the job." She raised her eyes to meet his.

Nick folded his arms, trying hard not to be provoked. "I think finding a serial killer is more important than pointing out the fact that you cheated on me with a former colleague."

"I'm sorry, Nick. I truly am. I didn't mean for it to happen."

"Yeah, you know what? You said all this the other night. I really have no desire to hear it again. I've got a deranged man who wants to kill one of my agents, so I should really get back and try to figure out how to keep him from doing that." He began to leave the room.

"Damn you, Nick. Don't you see it? You almost cost yourself your career for her. You think I don't know what you did to get her assigned to WFO? You think shit like that doesn't get around?

Everyone knew that was why all those allegations started popping up after the Corbett raids. Okay, yeah, so Hughes instigated it, but that was all Campbell needed to put you in your place. You know as well as I do that nothing would have come from that shooting incident if you hadn't screwed Campbell over." Georgia appeared at her wit's end. "All this time and you still don't see it."

"What the hell are you talking about?" His contempt could no longer be contained if she insisted on hurling unwarranted accusations. "You thought I was on my way down, so you decided to kick me in the gut by fucking around with that asshole Lyons. And then what? You fell in love with him?"

"My God." Her eyes widened with astonishment. "You really don't see it, do you? After Marshall died, you practically dragged Kate to Washington and made sure she got into the Academy. Even then, you made certain she got all the help she needed to pass. And then to top it all off, you went around Campbell to the Director and got her assigned to your field office."

"Because *I* knew what she wanted to be. What she'd wanted to be since the day I met her, but she'd stayed back because that was what she thought *he* wanted. Even if he'd insisted she go, Kate would never have left him."

Georgia inhaled a deep breath. "That's because she loved him. And I think, at some point after Marshall died, you fell in love with her."

Nick threw his arms into the air. "Oh, here we go again."

"There were times when I'd picked up on it and I thought, 'No, he's just looking out for her.' She'd been through a lot, God knows. But during the Corbett investigation and her training, it just became so obvious, and yet I still tried to deny it."

"I don't need to hear any more of this." Nick reached for the door, but Georgia grabbed his hand.

"When you were put on leave, I was there for you. I supported you. But I realized then that I was too late. I'd lost you—to her."

"You don't have a goddam clue what you're talking about, so don't try to blame Kate for your mistakes."

She released his hand and he pulled open the door. As he began walking out, Georgia leaned into the hall. "She'll realize it too, Nick. If she hasn't already—she'll realize she's in love with you too."

Nick's back was already turned to her, but he stopped at her final words. He froze, unable to breathe, and almost looked back over his shoulder. His legs found their purpose again and he continued—walking away from Georgia for the last time.

21

The white Toyota compact Durham had hijacked from the girl at the diner sputtered along the country road until he'd reached his destination. At the end of the long drive, he slowed to a stop and killed the headlights but left the engine running.

He remembered this house as if he'd lived here only yesterday, except that it looked different now. Even in the darkness, he could see that it had been painted some hideous color and that they'd mowed down all the shrubs that had once lined a path to the front porch.

It was obvious that the Sutters no longer occupied this residence. It had, after all, been nearly eight years. And Renee Sutter might have been a chain-smoking, bleached blonde whore of a mother, but Andy Sutter took pride in his home. He took pride in his own children too, but not young Zachariah, and probably not the other unfortunate kids this hellish family took in. No, he had a special place for kids who were not his own.

Nonetheless, this was where the FBI would find him. He'd

chosen this place as his last stand, so to speak, knowing they would bring her here, also knowing they would not let him leave.

The old car idled forward, slowly rolling over the gravel beneath its tires until Durham reached the top of the drive. The house sat atop a slight mound of property where the nearest neighbor was an acre away. He didn't know how much time he had before the FBI would come for him, so he had to act quickly. The car rolled to a stop and Durham cut the engine. The pebbles beneath his foot as he stepped out crumbled under his weight and the sound was louder than he'd expected. Perhaps it had been the dead silence surrounding him that amplified his own echoes.

His first mistake after the skirmish with the female agent had been rectified. A gun he took from the manager's office at that God-forsaken diner would come in handy. He slid it into the back of his pants and closed the car door. It would be too easy if they'd left the front door unlocked, but Durham couldn't dismiss the fact that they were way out in the boonies and that type of behavior was pretty common. People who believed they could trust other people were the easiest targets. Just like Hank. Old, fat Hank who was kind enough to warn him that a killer was on the loose.

The girl at the diner was trusting too. She'd already been in the process of closing up shop when he pressed his hands against the door, twisting up his face and pretending that he had to take a piss. His expression begged for her to let him in just this once. He figured it had something to do with the fact that he was an attractive man and, well—she wasn't an attractive woman. It took all the restraint he had not to kill her. The beast had wanted her desperately, but he needed the girl to deliver the message and dump the car.

It was always that side of him, the side the beast controlled, who needed the kill. In fact, it wasn't his favorite part at all. No, once they were gone, that was when the real fun began. He'd had absolute control over them. He could do anything he wanted and wouldn't have to listen to them cry and whine and beg him to stop. That was what gave him the gratification he needed.

With cautious steps, he climbed the few treads that led to the wooden porch. And although the worn deck creaked with alarming noise, he continued until reaching the door. His hands grasped the handle and Durham put faith in his own god that it was unlocked, and the handle turned. "Too easy," he whispered, appalled by naïveté. He walked inside with his gun now drawn because there was no telling if someone might be in the kitchen sneaking food or getting a drink of water. The thought occurred to him that if it had been good ol' Andy Sutter, he'd have been sitting on the couch with the light from his laptop shining on his face and his dick in his hands, watching porn.

Durham's senses would need to guide him through the darkened house until his eyes could adjust to the negligible light. The interior drew into focus and he began to remember the layout now. The furnishings were different, but everything else was the same. For a moment, he'd wished no one had been home because he only wanted the agent right now. But never mind, he could take care of any problems that arose. As he entered the hallway, he recalled which one had been his room. The first door on the right past the bathroom. He walked past that door. Any adults in the house would have to be taken care of first, so he continued to the end of the hall. That was where Mr. and Mrs. Sutter shared a room and he figured the people living here now also shared that room.

Durham stopped at the entrance and leaned his ear to the door, believing he heard whispers. The room's occupants had been awakened and while that would make things more difficult, it would not be impossible. He released the safety and aimed the gun straight ahead, ready to take down anyone who might charge at him, or maybe fire at him. Everyone carried a gun in these parts. They left their front doors open, but they carried guns.

He pushed hard on the door and it slammed into the wall, the knob catching the drywall and knocking a hole into it. A woman screamed while lying in the bed with blankets up to her neck as if that would stop a bullet. The man stood next to the bed in only boxers with his hands in the air.

"Please take anything you want, just don't hurt us," the man said.

Durham's first inclination was to laugh. "Unfortunately for you, what I want is for you to be dead." He fired the weapon and the man collapsed to the ground.

The woman screamed at the top of her voice until he turned the gun on her. "Stop that. There's nothing anybody can do for you now, okay?"

She fell silent but trembled violently beneath the covers.

"Is there anyone else in this house?" His tone was calm, almost soothing.

Her head gently moved side to side, while her eyes remained locked onto Durham's.

"Don't lie to me now. You ain't got kids living here? 'Cause it sure looks like you do, based on those pictures I saw."

"They're not here."

"All right. I guess that'll make it easier on me anyways."

THE SHERIFF'S office had been overtaken by bustling FBI staff and other deputies preparing for the confrontation with Durham. Kate and Dwight were plotting the locations where support vehicles would be placed so that Durham would remain under the impression that she was arriving on her own. Although no one believed he lacked so much intelligence as to assume they would send her in alone.

When Nick entered the room, he'd made it clear to those inside that his fuse was nearly burned out. The argument with Georgia not only distracted him, it had pissed him off. "Where are we at?" He approached Kate and Dwight as they huddled around the monitor, a satellite zoomed in on the location.

"We're almost ready to head out." Kate knew something had happened, but it was a discussion for another time. "A family is living here now and it's not the same one as when Durham lived there."

"Do you think he'll still go there?" Nick asked.

"No doubt." Dwight placed his hands on his hips. "He'll be there because he knows that's the only place we'd go."

Georgia walked past the room, briefly glancing inside. Kate caught her gaze, then looked to Nick. "Where's she going?"

"Back to D.C." Nick's curt reply was enough to let her know to move on. "We've got enough information now. She won't be of any further use to us here."

He'd made his point and Kate continued, "We were strategizing on team placement." She pointed toward the screen. "We'll need backup here and here." The two points on the screen flanked the north and south sides of the property and, according to the satellite image, would be obscured by trees.

"Let's get you equipped with a wire too," Dwight said.

"What about a body camera?" she asked.

"I don't want him to catch on and realize he's being recorded, but you will wear a jacket," Nick said. "Video, if he spots the camera, might entice him to behave even more erratically. This is a man on the brink, knowing there's no escape for him. I don't think he'll hesitate to take as many lives with him as possible. And if it was on video, so much the better, according to him."

Burgess entered the room and headed toward the agents. "I've just contacted state police. They've indicated full support for our operation and will remain on standby." He looked at Kate. "I'm praying to God y'all get there before he does. I don't know if the family is home or not, but if they are, he'll kill them. I tried Jenny Sykes' cell phone, but she didn't answer. Tried her employer too because she works odd shifts. She's not there either. They did give me the number of the boys' father and I contacted him. He said the boys are with him this weekend. Thank God. But you got to get down there now and save their mother. Please. Those boys have been through enough already."

"I just can't believe it's the same damn house," Kate began. "I know it's a small town, but for God's sake. It's like he planned this or something. Like he knew it was those boys who found her."

"It's just one hell of a coincidence, Kate. It has to be. No one could have predicted this." Nick glanced at his watch. "It's 3:00 now. The sun will be up in a few hours. We need to get in and get out before then. Better to operate under cover of darkness."

Kate refused to believe it was merely a coincidence. There had to be an explanation. Either Durham was watching the boys when they found the body or had read something in the papers about it. Whatever it was, this wasn't a coincidence, and she would find out the truth.

Dwight checked his weapon before sliding it back into its holster. "We'd better get a move on. There's no telling how much time we have before he shows up there and I won't risk more lives. Deputy Burgess, I think it's best if Agent Reid takes a personal vehicle. Durham's expecting us, yes, but I don't want any curious neighbors approaching because they see a patrol car there. Do you have a suitable vehicle?"

"She can take mine." One of the deputies held out his keys. "It's not much, so I don't mind if anything happens to it." He looked at Burgess. "Maybe the department will buy me a new one if something does?"

"Thanks. We'll be sure no damage comes to it," Nick replied, swiping the keys from him.

As they exited the building and everyone scattered to their vehicles, Nick pulled Kate aside for a moment. "You know we'll be right behind you, right?"

"I know," she replied. "I'm okay with this—really. It has to be me this time and I'll do what it takes to bring him down. You know, I saw something in his eyes, Nick. I've faced down some monsters, but this man," she shook her head, "there was nothing behind his eyes—only blackness—and death. He won't get away from me this time."

Nick studied her face and placed his hand on her shoulder. "I know he won't. None of us will let that happen."

Kate began walking toward Dwight, who still held the keys to the compact car owned by one of Burgess' deputies. "I got it from here." She reached for the keys and stepped inside the blue Ford.

Dwight closed the door and slapped the roof of the car. "We'll be right behind you, Kate."

With a final nod, she turned the ignition and drove to the end of the parking lot. Looking into the rearview, she made sure the others were poised to leave. She would have a three-minute head start and on her word through the headpiece, she would signal when it was time to get her the hell out of there.

Kate pulled out onto the road and disappeared in the distance.

"Reid, can you hear me?" Dwight asked through the earpiece.

"Affirmative. I got you, Jameson."

"Okay. We'll see you soon. Jameson out."

She focused on the road ahead, softly lit by the amber glow of the older car's headlights. She remained undaunted and began to realize that she'd lived in fear for a long time. Not just fear of malicious people in the world, but fear of loss. Kate began to recall what she'd said to Will Caison that day after her run-in with James Corbett. She'd told him that there was nothing left for anyone to take from her anymore and she figured that made her invincible. Perhaps it had because her breath was even, her hands were steady, and she feared nothing—not even death.

It was in that moment too, that Kate realized what day it was and maybe that was the real reason for her audacity. The night had passed with such momentum when the clock turned beyond midnight, it had turned without notice. Now that she was alone, planning her confrontation with the killer, the strength of her resolve arose from something ethereal. He was with her now. Marshall was still protecting her.

The manufactured home sat atop a mild incline and appeared in the dark of night as nothing more than a shoebox on an anthill. Kate turned off the headlights and pressed the button on her earpiece that would keep it activated. "I'm here and I'm heading up the driveway now. There are two cars parked in front of the building, but there are no interior lights visible from this angle."

"Ten-four. Proceed with caution, Reid. We're only blocks from your twenty and approaching," Nick said.

Durham knew she was coming. He probably knew they were all coming. Kate slowly rolled up the narrow dirt driveway until she reached the other vehicles. She recognized one as belonging to the young woman from the diner, meaning Durham was already inside. "Damn." Kate's head sunk in defeat. "He's already here." This setback could mean that Jenny Sykes and her husband were already dead.

"Stay focused, Kate. You don't know anything yet."

Kate brushed off Nick's words as anger welled and her focus on ending this nightmare became laser-sharp. She stepped out of the car and drew her weapon. "I'm approaching the home's entrance," she whispered. A quick look back, believing she heard another car approach, but there was nothing behind her.

With her gun pointed ahead, she noticed the door already ajar. Once inside, her eyes continued to adjust until finally bringing into focus the living room.

"FBI. Come out where I can see you." Her pulse elevated, an involuntary response to the adrenaline that pumped fast, but she maintained complete composure. "Zachariah Durham, this is Agent Reid. I'm the one who gave you that parting gift on your shoulder." She stepped with caution farther inside the home.

"I was beginning to wonder when you might show up." Durham held the woman in front of him with a gun pointed at her head. "Your friends outside waiting for me?"

"They're keeping their distance and as long as you don't hurt her, it'll stay that way." She looked at the woman. "Are you all right, ma'am?"

Jenny Sykes nodded through tears that streamed down her face.

Kate looked back to Durham. "Anyone else in here?"

"Not anymore."

"I'm not sure what you've hoped to gain by insisting the two of us meet again, Zach." Of course, she did know. He'd wanted another shot at her and now he had it.

"You know, I lived in this house for a while." Durham looked at the woman. "You didn't know that, did you?" He returned his sights to Kate. "Yep. Moved here after my time with Mrs. Gustafson. I hated that old hag. Then I came here and, for a while, it was good. Until Mr. Sutter thought he could do to me what he'd wanted to do to his own kids. He sure took it out on me, though." Durham shook his head. "I shoulda done to him what I did to my dad." He looked at Jenny again. "Hey, you know that room in the basement? That was Mr. Sutter's special room."

It had been a coincidence that those boys lived here. Durham seemed to have no idea they were the ones who found Sydney Hawthorne. His boastful nature meant he'd have certainly made everyone aware of that fact. Kate couldn't believe it, but it seemed Durham was only here because he planned on, or hoped to seek retribution on Mr. Sutter. That, and have an opportunity to take down the federal agent who defied him.

The idea that Durham believed he could regain power over her galvanized Kate into action. "Why the river?" She attempted to draw his attention from the hostage and place it on herself.

"I spent a lot of time up there at the cove and fishing along the banks of the river when I lived not far from here. My daddy used to take us camping." Durham paused and seemed to stop breathing for a moment, only staring at Kate, motionless. He blinked slowly and eventually continued, "When I moved up to Georgia, I still wanted to be close to the river and the swamp is a favorite place of mine too. Lots of places to hide things up in there."

"Your victims were eventually found, though," Kate replied. "And that was the only way we figured out who you were. So I guess it wasn't such a great hiding place after all."

His eyes flickered again and he swallowed hard. "Well, not all of them, right? You and your people find the ones I kept at the old homestead?" Durham's face began to mask in various emotions; anger, hatred, fear, sorrow. He was unraveling right before her. "Doesn't matter now anyway. I am well aware that this is my last hurrah. I'm not stupid, Agent Reid. But I guess I was just hoping to take a few more pretty girls with me." He turned to Jenny and licked her cheek.

"I'll tell you what, Zach." Kate watched his transformations, knowing this was what she needed to bring him down. Whatever demons he had inside him were waging one hell of a war. "How about we make this a party for two instead? Just you and me? You're not after her. It's me you want, right?"

Durham looked at the woman and back at Kate, waving his gun around. "Maybe you're right. I mean, coming here was just a means to an end, after all." He turned to the woman again. "I'll tell you what, Agent Reid. How about you put your gun down and kick it over in my direction and I'll let this woman go."

A voice that came not from her earpiece, but from within her own mind whispered for her not to trust him. That he could just as easily shoot her down once he had Kate's gun too. It was too risky and everything she'd been taught up to this point submitted this was a bad idea. But how else could she persuade Durham to let Jenny Sykes go? The problem was, she knew he didn't care whether he lived or died. That put her in a very dangerous position—as well as the hostage.

"We've got shooters in position," Nick's voice whispered in the earpiece this time.

Kate examined Durham's present state. It was his empty black eyes that were the most frightening because they made him appear completely bereft of anything that resembled humanity. He had no reason to let Kate live nor did he have any reason to let the woman live.

"What's it going to be, Agent Reid? Her life or yours?"

22

The question hung in the air and threatened to asphyxiate the rookie federal agent if she could not see her way to a suitable answer. Kate was willing to give her life to save this woman whom she knew to have two young boys in her charge. It was only by the grace of God that those boys were not here at this moment.

However, she would not concede so easily. Durham would not hesitate to kill both of them because he expected not to survive this final encounter. She wanted him alive to pay for what he'd done to those girls. Killing him here would be the easy way out and because that was exactly what he wanted, she couldn't let that happen. "Let her go and I'll stay, but I will not put down my weapon until you do."

Durham pressed his gun against Jenny's temple and eyed Kate with an irreverent smile. "And what about your friends outside?"

"I know you're a smart man, Zach. You proved that when you used the girl from the diner to send your message to me. They won't do anything without my order."

"Is that right? You must be some kind of big shot then, huh?" He pushed the barrel of the gun deeper into the hostage's head until she released a painful groan. "Okay. She can go. It was you who I wanted anyway." He pushed the woman to the ground.

With her gun still aimed at Durham, Kate reached out for Jenny. "Come on, take my hand." She grabbed the frightened woman's hand and helped her up. "Hostage is coming out." Once she was steady, Kate repeated the command into her mic. "Go on now. You'll be safe."

She scurried outside where Burgess waited to take her to his vehicle.

"So I guess it's just the two of us now, Agent Reid. Well, unless you count your cohorts outside. But as I told you before, it won't let you kill me without a fight."

"What won't?"

He turned the gun to his chest, pointing to the three-headed beast tattooed upon it. "It gives me the power and the strength to do what needs to be done. I, in turn, provide it with the lives it needs to survive. It's a mutually beneficial relationship. One which I am not willing to sacrifice."

"So you're not the one in control?" Kate glanced at the markings beneath his now-opened shirt. "That thing is?" She returned her eyes to his. "I didn't realize you weren't the one in charge here. I guess it's a little bit like when you were a kid, then, right? You did what your sister told you."

The smirk on his lips disappeared in an instant.

"And what about your dad? What did he do?" Kate wanted to rattle him; it would be the only way she could get past his defenses and recover his weapon. She knew Nick was listening to her every word and began to worry that he might jump the gun. If he did, the two of them might end up dead. But Nick trusted her and would give her every opportunity to do what she believed needed to be done.

"You understand that I don't care what you say about my—family. They're all dead now and every one of them deserved what they got. You think I'm a monster? You should have seen my father. He destroyed her—my sister and she destroyed me. Now, it's my turn. So, are we going to stand here all night?" Durham tossed a glance toward the front window. A grey light was beginning to emerge. "Looks like daylight's coming." He turned back to Kate. "Everything looks better in the light of day, wouldn't you say, Agent Reid?"

"It's not too late to get you the help you need, Zach. Put the gun down and we can end this now and get you that help."

"You know, the swamp is an amazing place. It's a self-contained ecosystem. Did you know that? That's right. It needs nothing. Feeds off its own resources, thrives from the minerals and bacteria in the water." He shook his head. "It's really an amazing place. I've always been drawn to it. The black waters that flow from it. Dark and deadly. We used to go on boat rides up the river to the swamp—my family and me, before, well—before they died tragically in a fire. It was the one place where I truly felt at ease. You see, it understood me. And so after I regained control of my life, I decided to pay it back. I gave it what it needed."

"How did you make those bodies turn up where they did, Zach? They didn't get there on their own, did they?" It was the one question that no one had yet been able to answer. How they'd managed to get so far downstream.

A visible shudder came over him.

Kate looked on with great concern over this reaction. "What's wrong, Zach?"

"Shut up. Shut the fuck up!"

"What's going on in there, Reid?" Nick whispered.

"How did those girls wind up in the river if you gave them to the swamp, like you said?" Something was happening to him and Kate was growing fearful that he was about to lose control. She needed to pull back—reel him in because there was no telling what he would do if this thing—this beast overpowered him. "There are plenty of people out there who can help you, Zach."

Durham began to scratch his head with his gun. "I'll tell you what, Agent Reid. You stop lying to me and I won't lie to you. How's that?" In an instant, his behavior reverted.

"I'm not lying to you. We can get you help, Zach."

"Why don't you just shoot me?" He held her gaze. "You know what I've done. You know what I'm capable of doing again. Can you really tell me that you think I should live?"

No. She couldn't tell him that. Kate wanted him dead, but at the hands of the justice system, not hers, or any of her fellow agents. But she was running out of options. The odds of him putting down his weapon seemed to dwindle with each passing moment. Her inexperience was coming through in spades now. She'd placed too much faith in herself, and so had everyone else. Kate's life was truly in danger and she didn't know how to talk her way out of it. Signaling for backup could mean Durham would try to take a shot at her. He might hit the vest, he might not. The confidence she felt earlier was beginning to fade. Maybe being faced with this outcome, an outcome she hadn't believed would come to pass, was forcing her to realize that she wasn't ready to die. Knowing what today was. Knowing that on this day, Marshall died to ensure she would be safe. He would not want her to disregard her safety or her own life. Kate was not ready to die, not on this day.

"Put your weapon down, Zach." She raised her gun higher, pointing it directly at his head. "Don't make me shoot you."

"Why not, Agent Reid? You were ready to shoot me before? In

fact, you did shoot me." He glanced at the graze on his shoulder. The blood had dried on his arm, creating a thick reddish-black stripe. "I won't go with you. Like I said before, it won't let me walk away without a fight. And I can promise that it won't let you either."

Walk out of there, Kate. Back out slowly and get the hell out of there. It wasn't Nick talking in her ear. In fact, she couldn't be sure due to her present state of mind, but it sounded like Marshall. Now she was beginning to feel as though she might be going crazy. There was no other way, though. This standoff had to end and although she was confident she was a better shot than Zachariah Durham, she knew that escaping without harm would be highly unlikely.

Kate took a small step back, then stopped. His face masked instantly in anger, as though she was taking charge. She took another step back. Kate knew what to do now. He would not let her leave; she could see that in his eyes. Nick had shooters ready to fire, but if they didn't take him with one shot, and in this light, in the positions they were in, she could still be in his crosshairs. A single step in her direction and she would fire in self-defense. It was the only way. Kate continued to step back, waiting for him to make his move.

"I wish you hadn't done that, Agent Reid." Durham cocked the pistol and in an instant, he took a slight step forward and pulled the trigger.

Kate fired in response and both dropped to the ground. He'd struck her vest. Searching the room that was now filled with the grey, hazy light of emerging dawn, she spotted Durham on the ground, back up against a side chair, clutching his chest.

"Shots fired! Shots Fired!" the voice in her ear erupted. "Kate? Talk to me!"

She pushed to her feet, gasping for breath, but remained steadfast to her target. "Suspect down." She moved toward him, hovering over him, holding her gun at his head.

Blood oozed from his chest. He looked up at her and smiled, then pulled open the shirt further to reveal that she'd struck the beast in one of its heads. The one in the middle, missing his heart by a few millimeters, it seemed. "Congratulations. You killed it. I knew you could."

It occurred to her that this was what he'd wanted all along. He'd wanted to put an end to who he'd become.

Durham turned his head slowly to the left where he'd dropped his gun. Kate's eyes followed him. They held firmly each other's gaze, both knowing what he was going to do. She shook her head.

He reached for the weapon and Kate fired on him again. She hit the target this time.

Nick and Dwight burst into the home, weapons drawn. Kate looked at them as she remained standing over Zachariah Durham, the Blackwater Killer.

"Are you okay?" Nick rushed to her side and saw Durham on the ground. His hand still rested on top of the gun he'd intended to use against Kate.

"I'm okay. Durham's dead." She looked at his body. His mouth hung open, blood pooling beneath his shirt. The beast was gone.

"Burgess, we need to cordon off the scene and get the ME down here," Nick said, noting his approach. "You can let Conroy know that Durham's been killed. He can call off the state police." Nick took Kate by the shoulders. "Come on; let's get you out of here. Are you sure you're okay? We can have the medics check you out."

"I'm fine. He got my vest." Kate turned back to look at Durham and returned her attention to Nick. "We got 'em, Nick. We got 'em."

Their arrival back to the sheriff's office was heralded by flashing lights and helicopters. The state police sent their lead officer to speak with Sheriff Conroy and the FBI, ensuring the upcoming media statements coincided with one another.

Kate rode back with her team, the ones who had her back this time as they had every time. She was shaken up, but it was over and she'd put down a killer. It was the first kill—not just an injury this time; she actually murdered someone. Her old Quantico classmate was right—there would be no getting used to it. And especially today. She cast her gaze through the passenger window as they were ready to step out of the car and into the chaos this killer created.

"How you holding up?" Nick asked just as she was about to push open her door.

"I got this. Don't worry about me." Kate stepped outside and inhaled the cool air that now held a lingering dusty odor thanks to the chopper having just landed.

Nick and Dwight followed behind, ensuring Kate was steady on her own feet. She was. Fortunately, the media hadn't descended on the small town yet, but that was only a matter of time. Once word got out that they took down the Blackwater Killer, they would feast upon the town like vultures surrounding roadkill. Kate hoped her team would have been long gone by the time that came to pass, but someone from the FBI would need to make a statement. Nick would be the one to handle that duty. He was the Supervisory Special Agent and Resident Agent for the BAU in the Washington Field Office. He'd done it before—he'd do it again.

Deputy Burgess pulled in moments after the agents' return and Kate stopped to wait for him to emerge.

She approached the humble, small-town cop who'd put his faith in the FBI and in Kate. She hoped she hadn't let him down. Leaving him stranded the way she did—well, maybe he wasn't too happy about that. "Hey." A thin, tired smile appeared on her lips. "Listen, I'm really sorry for leaving you the way I did...I haven't had a chance to..."

"You had to do it, Agent Reid. I understand. I'm just glad it worked out and that you're okay." He moved next to her. "You know, I've never killed anyone. I don't imagine it's easy to get over."

"No. Not easy." She grabbed his arm. "I could use a coffee." Kate led the way inside the building.

The agents were speaking with the state police when Nick noticed Kate walk inside. He returned his attention to the officer. "Let's go on in. We'll need to brief the sheriff—have him prepare a statement for the press."

Once all involved had converged inside Sheriff Conroy's office, discussions on how best to inform the public ensued. The woman who had been taken hostage was moved to the local hospital as a precaution while the coroner's office converged on the property to take away her husband and Zachariah Durham.

"I'd like to get back to the scene and assist with evidence collection to ensure our protocols are followed," Kate said.

"Of course," Conroy began. "Burgess can take you and your team back down there to make sure everything is being handled according to procedure."

"Thank you." Kate glanced into the hallway and then at Nick. "Myers leave already?"

"I imagine she's already made it to the airport and is heading back to the WFO."

Kate knew better than to continue with this line of question, especially in present company. She knew the deal. Georgia was out of Nick's life and that would make things difficult, for a while, at least. But Georgia had been an asset today, as usual. Kate regretted what had happened. It felt like the team was broken.

"Agent Scarborough," the sheriff began. "I'm assuming you'll want to put together a statement for the press?"

"I'd like to make a joint statement if that's all right. I think the people of this community will want to hear from their sheriff and know that their needs will be addressed accordingly."

"Certainly. Why don't we let these fine officers do what they need to do and you and I will draft something? We won't have much time. Anyone who was listening to the police scanners is going to know what happened. Best to nip it in the bud now." Conroy waited for the others to leave his office.

Burgess followed the other agents into the lobby. "Y'all ready to head back out there?"

Dwight looked at Kate. "I'll tell you what, why don't I head out to the house and coordinate with the M.E? You and Burgess should go back out to the Durham property and get them started on exhuming the remains of the three other victims. We'll need to get to work on identifying them."

"Sure. That sounds like a plan. You ready to go, Deputy Burgess?" She turned back to Dwight for a moment. "What about his place in Fayetteville? Someone should get over there and handle that scene as well."

"Lyons and his team are taking care of it," Dwight replied. "Touch base with me once you arrive and keep me posted."

Kate nodded and walked outside with Burgess.

"Seems like the three of you are a pretty close team. Y'all look after each other, don't you?"

"Yes, we do. We've been through a lot together." Kate stepped inside his cruiser and waited for him to enter before continuing. "Have you worked here as a deputy for long?"

"Only my entire fifteen-year career." Burgess smiled before turning the engine. "Started right out of high school and been here ever since. Of course, we don't get these kinds of things happening around here. I can only imagine the types of cases you must see working for the FBI." He pulled out of the parking lot and onto the main road. "I heard Agent Scarborough mention that you were a rookie?"

"That's right. I graduated only a couple of months ago. This was my first case as a full agent."

"Jeez. What a way to break you in."

"I guess so." Kate wouldn't mention her past or what she'd seen up to now. Not much point in it and it only made people feel sorry for her. She was through with that. What had happened, happened and it was a part of her now. That was what made her see a solution with Durham. She'd witnessed that sort of cold calculation in a man's eyes before.

"Looks like we aren't the first ones here." Burgess pulled up the long dirt driveway toward the empty lot. "Who is that? State?"

"I don't know." Kate narrowed her eyes to see through the rising rays of the sun. "Who knew we were coming?" She picked up her cell phone to call Dwight. "It's me. Hey, we already got some people out here. We're just pulling up now, but it doesn't look like state or any other local police. Did someone call the Jacksonville field office or something?"

"Not to my knowledge. Just go ahead and find out what we're dealing with up there and call me back."

"Will do." Kate ended the call and turned to Burgess. "He's not aware of anyone else who should be here. Let's go introduce ourselves."

They reached the top of the drive in front of what used to be the home. Kate stepped outside and began walking to one of the men whose back was turned. He wasn't in uniform, which made her suspect he was one of theirs.

"Excuse me." Kate extended her hand as she approached the man in the suit. "I'm Special Agent Kate Reid and this is Deputy Burgess with Baker County Sheriff's office."

"I'm Special Agent Mitch Sturgeon. Pleasure." The man wore a wide grin.

"What office are you with?"

"Atlanta. I work with Agent Lyons. He asked me to come down here and help y'all out."

"Oh. We weren't expecting anyone from your office down here. We thought you all were handling Durham's residence in Fayetteville."

"We are, but I was asked to hop on a charter and head down here. I think our office is concerned about the press and wants to be sure everyone's on the same page."

"Sure. Okay. Well, I'll show you what we've got. If you don't mind, just give me one minute to make a quick call." Kate stepped away, leaving Burgess to deal with the Atlanta feds. "Yeah, it's Kate. Looks like Lyons requested some of his agents to come down here and help out. You okay with that?"

"I guess," Dwight began. "I'll let Nick know what's going on. In the meantime, just work with those guys and get a team in place to recover the bodies."

"Got it. I'll keep in touch." Kate returned to the men, who seemed to be engaging in small talk. "All good; let's get started."

DWIGHT WAS ALREADY on his way to the Sykes' home when he got the call from Kate. He decided to try Nick and find out what was going on. Inter-agency squabbles were common, especially on a case of this nature. Everyone wanted to take the credit.

He made the call. "You got a minute?"

"Sure, what's up?" Nick replied.

"I just heard from Kate. Looks like Lyons sent some of his people over there to, I don't know, help out."

"Shit. I knew he was angling for information when I spoke to him a while ago after Kate took Durham down. First, he takes my girl and now he wants to take my case?"

"I don't know about that, but it does seem like he's positioning himself for something here. Like maybe taking credit for bringing Durham down?"

"Hell, I can't worry about this right now. Just let them do what they need to do to get those remains back to the families. Is Kate all right?" Nick asked.

"Seems to be. She just gave me the heads up about Lyons, but I told her pretty much what you just said."

"Okay, good. Not that he deserves it, but I'll give Lyons the benefit of the doubt right now. We'll see what happens once the media gets wind of this. I've got to get back with Conroy. He's scheduling a press conference for eight a.m."

"Ten-four. I'll check in with you later." Dwight placed his phone back onto the center console of his borrowed patrol car. He didn't like what Lyons was doing and didn't know the man's intentions. But it was starting to appear as though he'd wanted to take not only Nick's girlfriend but maybe Nick's job too.

23

The saying that things always looked better in the morning didn't ring true on this morning, despite what the now-deceased Blackwater Killer had to say about it. Outside the Baker County Sheriff's office, a bright and cloudless sky contrasted beautifully with the changing leaves on the trees, but the ugliness waited in the form of throngs of reporters. Local, national, and even international. They were all there and Nick would be the one to face them once again—along with the sheriff, and he was a man who knew little about the power of the press. Nothing like this happened in his small county and while they would likely be kind to the sheriff at first, once it was discovered that the killer had slipped through two states unnoticed, killing three other people in the process, their fangs would be exposed and they would go in for the kill.

Certain things about the case could not come to light, however, and it would be up to Nick to make sure they didn't. A killer was dead, that much was true, but until they could identify the three unknown victims buried on the Durham property, that part of the investigation would remain concealed—for now.

"Morning," Nick began. "I'm Agent Nicolas Scarborough with the FBI and I'm here with Sheriff Conroy." He cleared his throat. "As you may have already heard, the suspect in a series of murders associated with the Okefenokee Swamp and the Saint Marys River has been eliminated. We are continuing to work with the Georgia State Police as well as the Florida State Police, who were instrumental in helping us to locate the man who has been identified as twenty-one-year-old Zachariah Durham. He also went by several aliases, which made it difficult for us to track him down. But he is no longer a threat to this or any other community. My team will remain here in Baker County until such time as we have finalized this investigation. This was a multi-agency effort that resulted in a successful outcome. We realize there will be questions, some of which we will not be able to answer here today. There is still a great deal to sort through and I can only hope that you all will allow this community to heal from its losses and respect the families involved. Thank you." Nick stepped away from the podium and let the sheriff say a few words.

Some of the reporters began to shout out questions for Nick, but he returned inside the building.

"Leave 'em wanting more." Nick patted one of the deputies on the back and continued into the conference room that had been set up as a communications center for the FBI and the other agencies. He reached for his cell to get an update from his team, however, the voices coming from the hall indicated the call would not be necessary.

The agents had returned along with Deputy Burgess and caught up with Nick in the conference room.

"We're going to have some problems with Agent Lyons."

Nick had hoped Dwight would deliver better news and

decided to take a seat and wait for the other shoe to drop. "Why do you say that?"

"I think he's going to try to make it look like Agent Reid let Durham get away at the Gustafson residence, resulting in the deaths of two additional victims. The man on the highway and Mr. Sykes."

"That's bullshit," Nick replied. "She was the one who followed him after the state police let him slip through their road-blocks." He turned to Kate. "Who's telling you this? Lyons?"

"No. It was his guy on-site at the Durham property." Kate pulled up a chair next to him. "I don't know what to think right now, but they've got it in their heads that we, *I*, should've been able to take him down after he murdered Mrs. Gustafson. That it was me who let him escape to the river and then our team failed to track him down from there."

Nick was appalled by this latest development. "You know what he's trying to do here, right?" He eyed both of them.

Burgess leaned into the doorway, arms folded and listening to the conversation.

"This whole damn thing started in his backyard. The first two victims may have been found across the border, but Durham was based near Fayetteville. Lyons was the one who called us in to help and now he's shifting the blame that more people died because we screwed up."

"Because *I* screwed up," Kate replied. "A rookie agent."

"The same rookie agent who ended up facing Durham and taking him down," Burgess spoke up. "How the hell can they dispute that fact?"

Kate tossed an appreciative glance to Burgess. She had faced the killer and it scared the hell out of her to have taken his life, but she knew there was no other way. Now she was being called on the carpet for it? Was this what it was going to be like? She'd watched Nick having to defend his actions after the Corbett raids, nearly losing his job as a result. And now this. The job was hard enough, but facing the politics of it seemed beyond what she had been prepared to handle.

"This isn't about you." Nick looked at Kate. "This is about me. I'm going to have to deal with Lyons." He rose from the table and left the room.

"We got the killer." Kate turned her attention to Dwight. "That should be the focus here. Not some personal vendetta against Scarborough."

"I know. Look, you did what needed to be done, Kate. Don't let anyone tell you any different." Not wanting to forget Burgess' contributions, he looked to him. "Both of you did what you had to do. And this community is safe because of it. Let's just get our ducks in a row and worry about the rest later. ASAC Campbell is going to be fielding a lot of calls and he's going to need to have the files in order, including our accounts of what happened. We need to get those other victims identified." On his way out the door, he turned back. "I'll talk to Scarborough—find out when we're heading out of here. We've still got plenty of work to do on this case."

Dwight disappeared from view as Deputy Burgess made his way toward Kate. "I thought small-town politics were a pain in the ass." He pulled a chair up beside her.

"Yeah, well, a lot is going on behind the scenes in this particular incidence." She began to rise. "I'd better get back with my team. Jenny Sykes' boys—do they know about their mother yet?"

Burgess nodded. "Their father is bringing them up this morning. Terrible thing—what's happened to that family, but it could've been a hell of a lot worse if you hadn't known how to handle Durham. He would've killed that woman the same as he did the last three people."

"Thanks, Mike, but you know—I'm pretty sure I had some help in there." A warm smile formed on her lips.

"How's that?"

She considered telling him. He was a good man—kind. Marshall would've gotten along well with him. They were both cops, none of this federal agent bureaucracy she'd gotten herself tangled up in. "I had an angel on my shoulder." Her smile slowly faded as she left the room.

In the end, it wasn't a tale she was prepared to share. The sting of it still burned and it would only result in the same pitying look most people gave her when they discovered what had happened with her fiancé. Maybe the two of them would become friends and maybe one day she would tell him, but not today. Too many people had suffered at the hands of Durham and it was not a day to detract from what that monster had done.

Kate found herself standing in the lobby of the station, searching for Dwight or Nick or whoever might know of their whereabouts. She should have felt good about the fact that they'd gotten their man. Wasn't that the purpose of this job? Instead, she felt a sense of grief. It was probably just the timing or that she feared Nick would meet fresh scrutiny for her rash behavior in going after Durham on her own. Then again, she had just killed a man. Whether or not he deserved to die mattered little. The mark it left on her could never be erased.

"Hey, you ready to head out?" Dwight appeared as if from nowhere to bring Kate back to the moment.

"Are we going back to D.C.?"

"Soon." Dwight studied her face. "You okay?" He glanced uncomfortably at his feet before returning his attention to her. "Jeez, Kate. I'm sorry. I—I almost forgot. What a hell of a day for all of this to come to a head." He reached out for her. "Nick and I can handle things from here. You should go back home. Not the office—I mean, home."

"No. I want to be here, Dwight. It's better that way. I'm not going to lie. I'm still pretty shaken up about Durham and then the whole anniversary thing." She couldn't bring herself to say the words. "But being at home, by myself, probably isn't the best idea. Besides, I'd like to make sure I'm there for Nick. Campbell's going to have some questions and it should be me who's there to answer them."

"How did I know you'd say something like that?" Dwight displayed a half-cocked grin. "Come on; let's get with Nick and wrap things up here." The two began to walk along the corridor. "Oh, have you seen Deputy Burgess?"

"I was just with him actually—back in the conference room."

"Okay. I didn't see him in there, but we'll find him. We might need him to come back with us to the WFO."

"Why?"

"Just to tie up any loose ends. He's been heavily involved in this investigation—and with you too."

By MIDDAY, they were back in Washington and word had reached the field office about Durham. As the team walked out of the elevator and into the bullpen, the staff stood for a round of applause.

It gave Kate a sense that she had done what she needed to do. That it was part of the job and they all knew it. Many had been in her shoes before.

Vasquez was the first to approach. "You did a hell of a job, Reid."

"Thanks to you," she replied, returning the friendly exchange. "I appreciate the support."

"I'll let you get back to it, then. I know there's a lot of cleanup left to do. But you should be proud." She nodded to Nick. "He was right about you." With that, Vasquez returned to her desk.

"Kate, why don't you take Burgess to the kitchen? I'm sure he'd like a coffee. I know I would," Nick said. "Agent Jameson and I need to have a word with ASAC Campbell."

"Shouldn't I be there too?"

"Not yet. I'll let you know if we need you—either of you." Nick and Dwight began walking toward Campbell's office.

"Well, you want some coffee?" she asked Burgess.

"Sounds good to me."

Kate led him to the kitchen and the two sat down at the table, waiting for their number to be called. "Sorry to take you away from your office, but federal murder cases can get pretty involved. I assume you'll be home by tomorrow, if not tonight."

"It's fine. I understand—and I don't mind. Whatever it takes to make sure we've dotted our i's and crossed our t's. I understand the drill." He sipped on his coffee. "Good to know the FBI's coffee is better than ours." A small chuckle escaped him and his cheeks flushed a light pink.

Kate smiled in return. He was a small-town cop trying to deal with a big-time serial killer investigation. She understood what he was feeling better than most. "I suppose we should get whatever information you've got into our reports. We received the coroner's reports from the Atlanta office already. So I'd like to make sure we have your witness statements, including the boys who found Sydney Hawthorne."

"I've got all of that with me." Burgess gently swished his coffee cup for a moment. "You know," his eyes raised to meet hers, "I've noticed that you don't say much about yourself. I mean, I know you're new to the FBI, but what about before that? Why did you become an agent?"

"I wanted to catch the bad guys," Kate replied. "That's all. I thought I might be good at that sort of thing and so here I am."

Burgess grunted and began to nod. He saw through her but didn't press for more information. "Okay."

"Reid?" Vasquez leaned into the doorway of the breakroom. "Scarborough is looking for you."

"Guess that's our cue," Kate replied.

The two stood up and followed Vasquez back out into the bullpen. Nick stood in front of Kate's desk, peering into the corridor as they approached.

"Campbell wants to see Deputy Burgess. Why don't both of you come on in?" Nick waved his hand and the three began their way into the ASAC's office.

"Deputy Burgess." Campbell stood and extended a greeting. "Pleasure to meet you. I'm Assistant Special Agent in Charge Campbell. I hear you were instrumental in helping us solve this investigation."

"I don't know about that, sir, but pleasure to meet you as well."

"Please." Campbell gestured for the deputy to take a seat. "Agent Reid, I'd like to say that, once again, you've proven that you're an asset to this team. You've taken down a very dangerous man. Please, sit down as well."

"Thank you, sir."

Nick and Dwight remained standing, each at opposite ends of the back wall.

"Deputy Burgess," Campbell began. "Might it be possible to get a statement from you regarding your understanding of events leading up to the confrontation between Agent Reid and Zachariah Durham in the early hours of this morning?"

"Of course." He proceeded to explain the course of events that transpired during the night and how the two of them had met with another agent from Lyon's team at the Durham property. "The agent indicated that he was there because it had involved his office and that he would handle it from that point."

"I see. Do you believe that you and Agent Reid were cooperative after that?"

"Absolutely, sir, without a doubt, I called for the coroner and I informed the sheriff what had happened. We did everything by the book, no question."

Campbell folded his hands on his desk. "Thank you, Deputy Burgess. I know there's still some sharing of information that needs to occur to finalize the case, so I'll let you and Agent Reid get back to work. Again, thank you for your assistance. Reid has spoken very highly of you and now I can see why. I'll be sure to let Sheriff Conroy know that he'll have his man back before dawn." Campbell rose to again shake hands. "Thank you for your time."

Upon closing the door to Campbell's office, Burgess began, "He seems a little intense."

"He is. He's a good boss, but intense describes him perfectly. All right, let's get what we need so you can go home."

The two hours that passed went quickly before Kate realized that Nick had returned. He now stood at her desk where she and Burgess were finishing up with the paperwork.

"How's it going over here?" Nick asked.

"Good." Kate turned to him. "I think we're about finished here. We haven't received any word regarding the identities of the remaining victims. Do you know if we'll get that information or will it go to Lyons?"

"We should get it. Campbell talked with Lyons' boss and he's backing down. Both of the offices are keen to ensure outward appearances indicate nothing but cooperation between us." Nick looked to Burgess. "I'm sure you'd like to get back home. Have they booked you a flight yet?"

"I haven't checked, actually. I'm in no rush. If I can still be of use, I'm happy to stay here longer. Maybe leave tomorrow?" An inquisitive look was directed to Kate.

"That won't be necessary." Nick quickly intervened, offering his hand in thanks. "You've got your own situation brewing at home that I'm sure Sheriff Conroy will need your help with. The media will keep you all on your toes for a while. I can't thank you enough for all your help. Really. Agent Reid couldn't have followed through on her lead if you hadn't been there to help."

"Thank you, Agent Scarborough, I appreciate that." Burgess stood. "So, who should I see about that flight home?"

"I'll make the call for you," Kate replied. "If Scarborough can give us just a few minutes to wrap this up, we'll get you on the next plane out of here."

"Of course." Nick bowed his head and left the two alone.

"I'm sure the Bureau doesn't want to foot the bill for a hotel stay," Kate began. "Don't take offense. They're pretty cheap."

"None taken. I'm just glad to have been of service." He sat back down. "Well, I guess I'm not going to get a chance to say this before being unceremoniously shipped off, so I might as well say it." He inhaled a deep breath. "I'd like to see you again sometime, Kate. Outside of work." As if he needed to clarify.

His sincerity was quite clear as she studied his face. "Look, I'm sorry, Mike. I've got more baggage than most men could handle."

"I'm not most men."

"Please. If you knew, you'd think twice, I assure you. And I'm just not ready for anything like that right now."

"Do you think you might be in the near future?" A coy, single brow raised. "I know the distance thing might be a problem, but I'd just like to get to know you better—and see where it goes. Look, it doesn't have to be anything serious. Just, you know, whenever you have a spare weekend or you're in my neck of the woods—that kind of thing."

He was an attractive man; she'd felt that twinge as soon as she saw him and, for a moment, she did consider his request. "Maybe dinner. I don't know. Sometime in the future, I guess. When we're not busy finding serial killers."

"That's all I ask." Burgess smiled wide and bright. "Okay, let's get this finished up so I can get out of your hair."

24

The television screens in the bar periodically rotated pictures of Zachariah Durham, but none of them could hear what the news anchors were saying. It didn't really matter anyway. The press would beat the story to death, giving the killer all the attention he could have ever wanted. Durham was dead, but they continued to glorify him in such a way that it reminded Kate of Edward Shalot. His death seemed to spur on the media. All kinds of psychologists and so-called experts talking about how Shalot's childhood would have been traumatic.

Maybe it was and Durham's childhood certainly was, but where was the attention for the victims? Who would talk about the things they did in their lives, or could have done if they'd been given a chance to live? What about their families? Kate learned long ago that ratings were all that mattered and so the talking heads continued to explore the perverted and twisted life of Zachariah Durham.

Meanwhile, she tossed back the rest of her beer, returning her attention to Nick and Dwight. "Anyone ready for another?" She'd had enough already, but hey, she'd killed a very bad man. Didn't she deserve to get drunk if she wanted?

"I am." Nick raised his index finger at the cocktail waitress passing by and swirled it around, indicating they were ready for another round of drinks.

"Did you get your appointment with the counselor?" Dwight asked Kate.

She nodded. "I'm supposed to see him tomorrow afternoon."

"Good. It's just standard protocol, Kate. It'll be fine."

"I know." She turned her sights on Nick. "What's going on with Georgia? I saw her in your office a while ago."

"She came in to apologize for what Lyons did. I guess she was pretty upset about the way he was trying to shift blame onto our team—making us appear incompetent. She also told me that she was going to request a different assignment—a different field office."

The drinks arrived and Nick picked up his glass and raised it to his lips. "I knew better than to get involved with her. From the very first minute, I realized it was a mistake. But you know, I thought we were good together—for a while." He poured the drink down and firmly placed the glass on the wood-top table.

"It's probably best if she does leave, Nick," Dwight said. "I wouldn't discount her talents for a second, but it'll be best for both of you."

"I didn't ask her to leave. That's on her. I could've handled it just fine. But I guess she can't." Nick looked at Kate. "Sure seemed like that Deputy Burgess had a thing for you, though."

"What makes you say that?" She knew, of course, but didn't think anyone else had overheard their conversations.

"I saw the way he looked at you. Reminded me of..." Nick turned away briefly, focusing on the one football game they were showing on one of the screens. He'd regretted beginning that sentence. "Nothing," he said in a whisper.

It was obvious what he was about to say and Kate was glad he'd stopped himself.

"We should get preliminary autopsy reports from the Jacksonville coroner tomorrow," Dwight said. "Hopefully, it will give us enough information to identify the remaining victims. I assume they'll be girls from the area, so, Kate, you may need to get in touch with Burgess to make sure he gets a copy of the reports as well."

"Of course."

"I'm sorry all of this had to happen this week, Kate." Nick seemed ready to return to the conversation. "It couldn't have been easy for you."

"I'm sure it hasn't fully hit me just yet." Kate pressed her fingers against the necklace she still wore every day, although it remained beneath her clothing so as not to be a constant reminder to her friends sitting with her now. "I don't think I want it to either. I'd just like it to be over, you know?" She cast her gaze down, shielding from view her welling eyes. "It never goes away, though. Not even for a second."

"It will. Trust that it will get better," Dwight began. "To be honest, you haven't given yourself much time to deal with it. I mean, you moved here, you went through the Academy, which is hard enough, let alone dealing with a personal loss. I think that was your intention, but there has to come a time when you will have to deal with it all and that time might be now."

She looked up at him, eyes still reddened, but not spilling with tears. "I have been dealing with it, Dwight. I just don't let you guys see it." She filled her lungs with air to bring calm. "And I'll deal with this too, but maybe you're right about Deputy Burgess. Would it be a bad thing for me to have someone to talk to and go out with every once in a while? I'm not talking anything serious, but I've only got you two in my life. Don't get me wrong. I love having you both around. You're my best friends, but Nick, you had Georgia and Dwight, well, I know your divorce has held you back for a while."

"Don't use me as an example. My relationship just flamed out." Nick swallowed the melted remnants of his drink.

"You know what I mean," Kate replied.

"If that's what you need, Kate, then you should see him every now and again," Dwight said. "He seems to be a good man. And you're right, you should have more friends besides the two of us schleps." Dwight elbowed Nick and laughed.

Kate glanced at the televisions again before returning her attention to the two of them. "None of this matters much anyway. Not when there are people out there like Durham." She took a final swig of her bottle of beer.

"There's always going to be another Zachariah Durham, Kate," Nick replied.

"You're right about that." Dwight pulled out his wallet. "I'd better get out of here. I've got the kiddos this weekend and need to put some food in the fridge before tomorrow night."

Nick slid out of the booth, allowing Dwight to edge his way through. "This case isn't over yet. The sooner we can identify the other three victims, the sooner we can put this to bed and let those families have the closure they need." He dropped a ten on the table. "I'll be in early. Guess I'll see you two tomorrow."

"Goodnight, Dwight," Kate replied.

"Night, buddy." Nick watched Dwight disappear and began, "You took a lot of risks to get Durham, you know."

"Yeah, I did." She studied his face for a moment, waiting for some reprimand, but none came. "Would you have done anything different?"

He pressed his lips together, forming a wry smile. "No. No, I wouldn't have done a damn thing differently. But it wouldn't be a bad idea for you to take a few days. Let things settle in. And I don't just mean with handling the Durham situation."

"I know."

"I'm worried about you, Kate."

She nodded. "I know that too, but you don't need to be. I chose this. And, I don't expect I'll just forget about what I did. I suppose it'll haunt me for a long while. Durham was a son of a bitch and we stopped him."

"*You* stopped him. We had your back, but you pulled the trigger and that's no easy thing to come to terms with, but I know you will—eventually, we all do." Nick raised a hand to get the waitress' attention. "You ready to get out of here? I don't need any more to drink."

Kate was relieved to hear him say that. Maybe she didn't have to worry about him any longer. "I'm ready. Got a busy day ahead of us." She pulled some cash out of her purse.

"Put your money back. I got this. It's the least I can do considering you risked your life and all for the Bureau." Nick grinned.

"Thanks, I appreciate that." Kate returned a smile after placing the money back in her bag. She retrieved her phone to check for messages while Nick paid the bill. A missed call from Deputy Burgess caught her eye. Kate raised the phone to her ear to listen to the message. She noticed Nick's glance for just a moment while it played, but darted her eyes away, feeling the slightest bit awkward by the exchange.

Nick placed the tip on the table and slid out of the booth. Kate soon followed. "Anything important?"

"No. It was just Deputy Burgess checking in to see if I needed anything from him. He's back home and says things are pretty crazy at the station."

"I bet. Let's get out of here." He stood aside while Kate made her way in front of him. He followed closely behind to the bar's exit. Pushing open the door for her, Nick squinted from the bright lamppost only feet from the entrance. The streets were almost empty. It was late fall in D.C. and the weather was verging on cold. The Indian summer had finally abated. "You okay to drive home?"

"I'm good. I've been nursing the one drink for the past two hours." She pressed the remote to unlock her car door, but it didn't work. She tried again, but still nothing. But the third time was a charm and it flashed its lights and clicked open. "I've got to get a new car." Kate chuckled. "I'll see you tomorrow and don't worry about me. I'll be fine. I'm a big girl." She reached around his firm chest and held him tightly for a moment. Her head pressed against his right shoulder and she could feel him tense his muscles as if he objected to her embrace. She pulled back, mildly concerned by his reaction. "What's wrong?"

"Nothing. Just had a chill jump up my spine." He gripped her with one arm. It was a distant response. "Goodnight, Kate. Try to get some sleep."

THE PORCH LIGHT in front of her door had burned out, but fortunately, Kate kept a small flashlight in her purse. Shining the light onto the lock, she inserted her house key and opened the door. In the darkness, she found the hall light and flipped the switch, closing the door behind her and turning the deadbolt.

The first thing Kate always did once she was home was head to her bedroom and stow her weapon. A change of attire immediately followed and tonight it would be cut-off sweatpants and one of her FBI training t-shirts. The time was approaching midnight, but she didn't feel tired. The rush of adrenaline must have still been coursing through her veins. Although she'd hoped the beer might have taken the edge off—it hadn't.

Kate curled up on her couch and turned on the late-night talk show she enjoyed watching if she was home on time, which wasn't often. She turned to the picture on her side table. The one of Marshall and her at her parents' home. The one she still kissed before going to bed. Kate held it in her hands, studying it closely. She already knew every inch of the photo. Every wrinkle in Marshall's smile. The moment sprang to life in her mind again, the memory bringing warmth to her heart.

He had been with her at that moment yesterday. She knew he had. She wasn't ready to join him and he wasn't going to let her. But perhaps the time had come to let go. A year had passed. A painful, difficult year, but she made it through. He'd helped her understand what her past meant. The challenges, the losses. Marshall would always be with her, but Kate believed she was ready to move on. It had been a long time coming—years, actually. She'd already decided to bury the memory of her abductor. Marshall helped her to bury the memory of her dearest friend and now she would have to put his memory in the same place where Sam lived.

Kate placed the picture back on the table. "I know you'll always watch over me." She looked at her phone on the couch and, with firm resolve, pressed the contact button and waited. It was late, but he would answer. "Hey, Mike. It's not too late to call, is it?"

"Not at all. I was just thinking about you."

NICK PLACED his suit jacket over the dining room chair and walked straight into the kitchen. A cabinet above the refrigerator was where he kept the booze. With an old-fashioned in his hand, he poured himself a double over the two ice cubes he'd dropped inside. Carrying the bottle in one hand and his glass in the other, Nick headed to his living room and dropped to the couch. The bottle of Maker's Mark, an expensive whiskey that Georgia bought for him a few weeks ago after learning he was going back to work, was placed on his coffee table. Nick tossed back the drink without hesitation.

A single lamp on the table next to him glowed softly. Nick hunched over and grabbed the bottle, pouring himself another. This time, he rose to his feet and carried the drink to the sliding glass door that led to the balcony outside. He watched the boat he'd purchased bob gently in the water as the waves rolled into the bay. "God damn boat." He threw back his second drink.

Nick began to think about his last conversation—argument— with Georgia at the sheriff's office. He hadn't wanted her to leave. Not then and not now. Her request for a transfer stung almost as badly as her betrayal. But it was the words she said in that final argument.

All this time and he'd had no idea she felt those things. It didn't make any sense. He thought they were doing all right— getting along well. The job took its toll, sure, but they both knew that going in. Nick pushed his hand through his hair, trying to get around the idea that she was gone. And for that asshole, Lyons. They weren't exactly friends, but they'd worked together. It was a pretty shitty thing for her to do. Then the guy tries to point the finger at who screwed up and let Durham go on to kill three more people. Would have been four if it hadn't been for Kate. Nick was her supervisor and Lyons wanted the blame to fall on his shoulders, just to dig the knife in a little deeper.

He pulled open the glass door and stepped outside. The air was crisp and helped to cool his rising temper. He inhaled a deep, calming breath and looked out again over the water. He began to recall how Georgia loved to sit with him out here and just watch the water for hours—when they had the time, of course. Nick closed his eyes to revel in the thought.

But it was her words that he couldn't shake now. He had done things to help Kate, but everyone knew that. Dwight knew it and understood. Nick had persuaded her to move across the country for a job that was difficult for the most stable of people, let alone one who was in a state of grief.

And he'd helped to oversee her training. Even going so far as to get her involved in an investigation she probably shouldn't have been involved in. But it worked, didn't it? It helped her gain the support she needed and she graduated. That part, he would not take credit for. Kate was a smart woman—she graduated for that reason.

Had he crossed a line by going around his supervisor to the director? Yes. He could admit at least that much. But it was only because he wanted to continue to offer his guidance and support. Kate had no one else.

"Dammit, Georgia." Nick hit the railing of the balcony with the palm of his hand. He stared out over the horizon again, trying to clear his head, but the two double whiskeys were starting to hit him. "You're wrong, Georgia. You're wrong about Kate."

He turned his back and looked into the empty space that he called home. All he could see was Georgia smiling at him. Her beautiful red hair that cascaded over her shoulders. Her pale skin that was porcelain-smooth. He had loved her, there was no denying that.

Nick walked back inside and returned to the couch again. He grabbed the bottle, knowing he would regret drinking any more, but right now, it just didn't matter. Because what bothered him the most—what hurt him the most—was that Georgia, in the end, didn't believe he had loved her. She chose to be with another in the face of Nick's darkest days because she didn't feel loved by him.

Georgia believed that it was Kate. That it had been Kate all along. Nick drained the glass of its contents yet again and rolled it between his palms.

What bothered Nick the most was that he was afraid she was right.

THE END

ABOUT THE AUTHOR

Robin Mahle has published more than 30 novels in the mystery/thriller genre. She also writes historical fiction as <u>Christine Chase.</u>

It is Robin's fast-paced style of storytelling combined with tense action and thrilling twists that bring her readers back for more. So be sure sure to subscribe to her newsletter to keep up on all the latest releases, sales, and giveaways. Go to <u>robinmahle.com</u> and sign up today!

Robin lives in Coastal Virginia with her husband and two children.

If you enjoyed Ms. Mahle's work, please share your experience by leaving a review on <u>Amazon</u>

ALSO BY ROBIN MAHLE

The Kate Reid FBI Thriller Series (17 books)

The Chef (stand-alone psych thriller)

The Man in My Attic (stand-alone psych thriller)

The Compound (standalone psych thriller)

The Remy Fontaine Fugitive Hunter Thrillers (4 books)

The Det. Rebecca Ellis Thrillers (5 books)

The Allison Hart PI Thrillers (5 Books)

The Lacy Merrick Thrillers (4 books)

**Visit Robin's website robinmahle.com and sign up for her newsletter to stay up to date on her upcoming releases, events and contests!